To Dwaine,
Best in Your
New Venture
with Blessings,

TWILIGHT IN THE CITY OF ANGELS

Chris Ahrens

LIMITED•FIRST•EDITION

San Diego, CA

Copyright © 2014 Perelandra Publishing Company

Perelandra Publishing Company
Chris Ahrens
P.O. Box 697
Cardiff, CA 92007
Website: Perelandrapublishing.com
Email: Perelandrapub@gmail.com

All rights reserved. No part of this publication may be reproduced, distributed, or transmitted in any form or by any means, including photocopying, recording, or other electronic or mechanical methods, without the prior written permission of the publisher, except in the case of brief quotations embodied in critical reviews and certain other noncommercial uses permitted by copyright law. For permission requests, write to the publisher, addressed "Attention: Permissions Coordinator," at the address below.

This book is a work of fiction. Names, characters, places, and incidents either are products of the author's imagination or are used fictitiously. Any resemblance to actual persons, living or dead, events, or locales is entirely coincidental.

Cover art created by: Michael Cassidy
Editorial and production services provided by: Cara Highsmith, Highsmith Creative Services, www.highsmithcreative.com
Design and formatting services provided by: Mitchell Shea

The ESV® Bible (The Holy Bible, English Standard Version®) copyright © 2001 by Crossway, a publishing ministry of Good News Publishers. ESV® Text Edition: 2011. The ESV® text has been reproduced in cooperation with and by permission of Good News Publishers. Unauthorized reproduction of this publication is prohibited. All rights reserved.

The Holy Bible, English Standard Version (ESV) is adapted from the Revised Standard Version of the Bible, copyright Division of Christian Education of the National Council of the Churches of Christ in the U.S.A. All rights reserved.

Good News Publishers (including Crossway Bibles) is a not-for-profit organization that exists solely for the purpose of publishing the good news of the gospel and the truth of God's Word, the Bible.

ISBN: 978-0-9640858-4-8

Printed in the United States of America
First Edition
10 9 8 7 6 5 4 3 2 1

Dedication

To my wife Tracy,
Thank you for reading this story, re-reading it, and reading again. And, thank you for allowing Jose to occupy our home for the past twenty years. Love Eternal.

To my wonderful family: my parents, Richard and Lupe Ahrens, and my grandparents Jose and Soridtha.

To my sister, Jackie, and my brothers Dave and Rick. To my daughter, Clelia, her husband Craig, and our grandson, Lucas.

To my agent, guide, and editor, Cara Highsmith, who believed in this story from the beginning and always kept me on track.

To everyone struggling to have their story heard above the roar.

PRAISE for
Twilight in the City of Angels

"I have always loved the history of Los Angeles and *Twilight in the City of Angels* nails it."

—Danny Trejo, actor

"I rarely see anything come over my desk like *Twilight in the City of Angels*. I will do whatever I can to see this story gets produced as a motion picture."

—Carlos de los Rios, writer/director/actor

"Chris is one of my favorite storytellers—full of salt and surprise."

—Jon Foreman, Switchfoot

"Chris Ahrens' work is that rare intersection of underground pop culture and masterful storytelling—a place where you know that when you pick up one of his books you are about to experience a window into a world you would never otherwise get to experience."

—Lawrence W. Roeck, movie director

"Chris Ahrens is an amazing writer. Nobody could have done a better job helping me write my book."

—Christian Hosoi

"[*Twilight in the City of Angels*] is very moving. I knew there had been another, different LA ."

—Peter Hitchens, author

"With *Twilight in the City of Angels* Chris Ahrens has emerged as one of the most important writers of modern times."

—Robert Wald, publisher, *The Ocean Magazine*

"Chris Ahrens has crafted a compelling story that invites us into the heart of old Los Angeles. Like the city he describes there is an alluring and inspiring quality to Ahrens' characters that made for a rich, page-turning experience. *Twilight in the City of Angels* is a very rewarding read."

—Roger M. Freet, Executive Editor, HarperCollins Publishers

Where were you... when the morning stars sang together, and all the sons of God shouted for joy?

—Job 38:4-13 [ESV]

Contents

Prologue

1. Jose of the Light	1
2. Magia and Jose	19
3. City of Angels (and Devils)	31
4. Stations of the Cross	53
5. Jose's Kingdom	63
6. The Tower	75
7. Fruits of the Earth	89
8. Sister Mary Bernadette	97
9. The Weight of the Curse	107
10. Kill the Priest	119
11. Henry	135
12. Vaya Con Dios	163
13. Sarah Jane	175
14. Uncle Dexter	195
15. The Broken Heart of the City	205
16. Four Wise Men	223
17. A Kind of Salvation	241
18. Jose of the Light	257
Epilogue	279

PROLOGUE

The doctors have pronounced my death sentence. The parish priest has administered *extreme unction* to prepare my soul for heaven, although hell could be my final destination. I can feel my life pouring out like blood sacrifice until I am left alone with my pain, prayer, and remembrance. My thoughts are my only family now, and just as comforting. Aside from my few pieces of clothing, I own five things—a small, leather-bound worn out Bible, a scapular I have kept around my neck since I was a boy, a broken toy train engine, a deck of playing cards, and an unframed photo of an old man. Kissing the scapular, I look at the toy train, laughing a little to think of a great miracle "The miracle of the train," he always called it. I have heard those words my entire life.

    I pull a card from the deck to see the ace of spades, the luckiest of all cards. This is when I know today is a good day to die. The card has the lingering scent of tequila mixed with tobacco, and I hold it to my face until memories flow like tears. Looking closely at the picture of the old man, my eyes fix on a dent in the right side of his forehead. "Hello Jose," I say aloud, laughing painfully. His hair, as white as snow, and his deeply creased, dark skin gives him the appearance of an ancient warrior. The eyes alone are alive with the light of eternal youth. All other men with such eyes have been dead for a hundred years. Jose is my grandfather, and certainly he is the grandfather of the city of Los Angeles. Sometimes I think he was the very city itself.

Jose has been gone for nearly twenty years, but until the day he died he could remember everything, even things he could not remember. Without being told, he knew all about his own grandfather, Encarnación "del Agua" Santiago, who was born in Mexico City around 1820. Jose clearly recalled seeing his grandfather as a baby of three years old in the company of his parents crossing the Rio Grande to enter the US through Texas—the Mexican territory then called *Tejas*. While fording the river, the family cart was jostled and the baby fell into the cold, rushing water. He was whisked downstream as his mother, who could not swim, looked on, screaming and watching helplessly. Instead of drowning, however, the child swam to shore where he was given the name "Agua".

Since nobody had ever taught the baby to swim, his parents knew this was a miracle and a sign from God that the Santiago family would find fortune in the new land. Instead of fortune, however, the family of farmers found dirt as hard as granite and struggled to eek out a living. Twelve years later, they made the long trip back to Mexico City emptied of the hope that brought them to their personal promised land.

In Mexico, Agua grew into a powerful young man and joined the Mexican Army. But, Agua's battalion did little more than help put down a few small skirmishes where local ranchers and farmers fought for independence. Because he never hesitated in killing his enemies and even some of his friends, he was promoted rapidly. With nobody left to kill, he deserted his post and again crossed the river, this time alone. Unable to find work in the new land, Agua again enlisted, this time with the U.S. Army. He was such a brilliant soldier that he was rewarded by the United States government with citizenship and 165 acres of the most parched ground New Mexico had to offer.

Then came the Mexican-American War in 1846 where Agua was sent to the front. Rather than fight against his own people again, he deserted a second army. For nearly two weeks he wandered through Texas before returning to his land in New Mexico. He was drinking tequila directly from the bottle then put on his uniform and began circling the grounds on his horse, imagining a barn here and a bedroom there with two or three women to keep him company in his old age. He was taking long pulls from the bottle and shooting his pistol into the air when, in the distance through the dusty sunlight, he spotted something that had not been there before. Thinking it to be an Indian about to attack his land, he automatically aimed his service revolver. He had not yet become so sensitive that he would not kill an Indian, but for reasons only providence can explain he delayed shooting for a moment. Closer inspection proved him partially right; it was an Indian, but a girl of about sixteen. She was pretty, Apache, and staggering from thirst after wandering in the desert for two days. The battalion of soldiers Agua had recently deserted had killed many in her family, along with some others in her village. He rode over to the girl, gave her water, and kissed her on the lips. Placing her on his horse, he claimed he would take her back to her original home in Chihuahua, Mexico.

Instead, the drunk and crazy Agua began riding west, hard and fast. As the girl revived she hit, kicked, and bit her way along the canyons, prairies, and mountains. By night he took shelter beneath trees or in desert caves while the girl slept alone in the open, preferring death from exposure to snuggling up with an American soldier. On their journey, Agua shot small game and cooked it over a brush and stick fire. They saw nobody but a small band of Indians. Fearing Agua's uniform, they caused no trouble, but traded ample food and water for one of his long knives. Within a week, Agua had fallen in love with the girl. She, however, did not love him and said nothing to him, not even her name. And so he called her *Quieta*, a name she would carry for the rest of her life.

Some days they traveled on flat, dry ground and made good distance. When facing severe weather or exceptionally rough terrain, however, they only won a few feet at a time. As they rode, the terrain changed from forested mountains to deserts and back to mountains again several times. They waded through flooded streams and wound along slippery, craggy, dangerous trails into deep canyons. They fought storms and heat and wild animals, including a mountain lion Agua shot and turned into a feast after the wicked animal tried to steal a rabbit he had killed. It was more than two months after leaving New Mexico when, nearly dead from thirst and starvation, half blind from one final and great sandstorm in the Great Desert, they broke through the heat and blowing sand and found a paradise filled with fruit trees, fish, and clean water on a winding river kissed by clean air and warm sunshine. They continued walking near the river seeing large encampments of peaceful Indians who freely gave them whatever they needed. Having had little contact with the world to the east, these Indians had no fear of Agua's uniform.

They continued moving west until suddenly Quieta joined her captor in reverent contemplation of the shimmering and endless body of water that stretched out warm and blue to greet them. Never before had they seen anything so large, so terrible, so wonderful. They would soon learn that this was called the Pacific Ocean and that the land at its edge was called Santa Monica after an apparently wonderful but dead woman the Spanish conquers adored. They built a house on the bluff from adobe and pine logs on that very spot overlooking the ocean, and lived in the one-room shack as large ranchos grew up around them.

Quieta never did love Agua, but when she realized it was hopeless to resist his advances any longer she agreed to become his wife. They were married in a ceremony performed by a Franciscan friar who rode thirty miles in two days by wagon from the San Gabriel Mission. After a month-long celebration, the couple settled down into life on the newly discovered California coast, never again returning to the dry, hard land of New Mexico.

Every day for the rest of their lives they observed the great water's changing moods. While little is known about the couple beyond that, it is believed they spent a non-prosperous twenty-five years and died within six months of each other. They had only one child, a daughter they named Matilda who grew up to marry a cruel Mexican man known as Scarface Charlie—a name he acquired after his face was mangled by a broken beer bottle in a bar fight.

At exactly the stroke of midnight on New Year's in 1900 Matilda gave birth to her own child. Dying as she brought her son into this world, the last thing she uttered was the name Jose. They all believed she was proclaiming the name she wanted the boy to carry. And that is what he was named without anyone knowing she was actually calling out for her secret lover.

    Jose would tell the story of his mother's death without sorrow, as if he remembered it perfectly. "My head was too big to pass through such a small woman," he would say. "And so I remember her crying as I laughed, not knowing she was dying, feeling happy to be free from inside of the belly."

    With Matilda dead, Jose's father, Scarface Charlie, returned to Mexico to lose his grief. He abandoned the baby near the lagoon on a vast stretch of beach called Malibu, or *Maliwa* (where the surf sounds loudly) as the local Chumash Indians called it. Pinned to the child's diaper was a paper stating nothing but his first name: *Jose*. Because he was found near the water, the baby was called "Little Moses" in his youth. Soon he was common property of the ranch, much like a wild dog.

    On the ranch, Little Moses, barely into his teens, had miles of wide-open beaches to run wild and hunt deer with the bow and arrows he made. On other days he would paddle the Chumash-style canoe he had built from planks coated with pine pitch and sealed with the tar that bubbled up from the ground. He would paddle alone, far out to sea, taking the Chumash trade routes all the way to the Santa Barbara Channel Islands where a few Indians still lived and traded precious golden cowrie shells for knives and pottery from the mainland. It would sometimes be days before Jose returned home, his boat low in the water from golden cowrie, abalone, lobster, huge sea bass, and sharks he killed with the spear he had carved from an oak branch before forging a deadly iron tip onto it. Back in Malibu, he often slept outside with the few remaining Chumash who still occupied the canyons and mesas there. When he wasn't with the Indians, he lived with the wolves and coyotes as family, giving names to each of them, speaking to them kindly, praying with them, sharing food with them, and chasing off any bears that tried to raid the camp.

By an early age, Little Moses had proven himself on the ranch and was given back his original name, Jose, and lived mostly in the bunkhouse with the other ranch hands. From them he learned ironwork and carpentry; he learned to ride, break, and shoe horses, to operate and fix machinery, and to fight with his fists. The cowboys often arranged impromptu bare-fisted boxing matches on Friday nights; and, by the age of fourteen, Jose could beat anyone on the ranch. More important even than boxing, however, he learned to play poker from a wandering Bronc rider and famed card shark called Black Jack Murphy. This trade would give him a living his entire life.

The entire story of the ranch is long and sad, and best left for another time. In short, it begins with a preacher named Fredrick Hastings Rindge who bought the former Spanish land grant known as Rancho Topanga Malibu in 1892 for ten dollars an acre (up from ten cents an acre thirty-five years prior.) When Fredrick died in 1905, his widow, Rhoda May Rindge took control of the 17,000 acre estate, with the desire to live in peace and tranquility. Instead, the Southern Pacific Railroad illegally built a rail line, followed by a highway through the ranch. May Rindge was forced to sell most of the property to pay for the lawyers she had hired in an effort to stop the invasion. In spite of her heartbreaking efforts, the road opened up this secluded paradise to the masses that apparently hated it enough to suffocate it beneath concrete and asphalt. In time Rindge was unable to pay anyone, including Jose.

Jose was sixteen when he moved from the ranch to the Eastern section of Los Angeles and commuted into the growing downtown where he found work on the city's railroad lines, doubling his wages each Friday night through cards.

Jose's wife, my grandmother Soridtha could trace her roots to the Gabrielino Tongva Tribe that had once lived in what is now the Los Angeles Civic Center near the Los Angeles River, in a settlement they called *Yangna*. The moderate climate, long growing season, quiet loveliness, and sparse population there would soon attract farmers, ranchers, priests, prostitutes, hustlers, gamblers, and land speculators among others.

One of my grandmother's ancestors married (or more likely raped and abandoned) a Gabrielino woman. She bore a son whose Gabrielino name is lost in history, but whom everyone called Hank. To the great shame of his mother, Hank hid his Indian heritage and defiled the land by becoming a developer. All this ambitious young man knew was he was building a massive store—a place future generations would call a supermarket, where you could get everything under one roof! He did not realize he was digging in the sacred Gabrielino burial ground where his ancestors had been resting for a thousand years.

Each time his shovel hit something hard, he cursed, pulled the thing from the ground and took it to the rubbish pile amassed with broken baskets, pottery and fragments of bones, which in his blindness he mistook for the skeletons of animals. Anything not burned was plowed under and eventually sealed beneath the concrete slab poured for the structure. Soon he developed a mysterious illness that killed him before he could realize the futuristic dream of entering the promised land of air-conditioned isles and automatic doors.

Before dying, Hank requested a woman be brought to him to share his deathbed. A strange Gabrielino Indian woman who toiled weaving baskets in the Plaza downtown was summoned. She was known for bearing strong children and working magic. He held on longer than expected, however, and she stayed with him through his final year. Only days before Hank died, the woman gave birth to their daughter. Because she did not cry when she was born her mother named her *She Who Does Not Cry*. He, however, insisted the girl be named Guadalupe after the Virgin of Guadalupe, the patron whom he believed had kept him alive that year, and ordered her raised at the San Gabriel Mission. With the man dead the girl's mother raised her on own near the downtown plaza in the ways of Indian sorcery and continued calling her *She Who Does Not Cry*. Of course that was not her name in her native language. I never did know that name, but most everyone called her Soridtha, the Mexican name her mother gave her. From her mother, she learned to live off the land, weave baskets from reeds gathered in the river and practiced Indian medicine and magic. All over the city people spoke of the raven-haired beauty with the shiny black eyes. By the time she was in her teens her quiet power and angelic appearance were legendary and attracted many suitors. My grandfather Jose prevailed among them.

And, this begins the story of a great man and the boy who spent his life trying to imitate him. It is also the story of Los Angles and modern pilgrims seeking a shrine that may or may not exist. We are nothing like the first pilgrims who came to this country, and we only faintly resemble other people driven from their land. They were not able to go home, but at least there was a home left to go to. These same hills, trees, and clear-water pools mark the areas where their parents were shot and killed by the soldiers. They dreamed of killing the soldiers and taking back their land one day. It was a good dream, but one we cannot share. That dream lies dead beneath freeway abutments, shoe circuses, and seven-story parking lots.

Some pray for "the big one" to hit and smash the concrete blocks into sand, or to make cracks wide enough to reveal the broken heart of the earth below. Others move away, drink themselves numb, or wait for Jesus to return. We would love nothing more than to be an army of earthworms, to break up the soil and become part of it again, as our people used to be. Unable to find anything so good as before, we wander the earth for a home, eventually turning inward. The world laughs at us, but sometimes we stumble upon the answer. When we do, nobody listens. We are always finding answers, but on certain days we laugh harder than the world.

As a boy I laughed as hard as anyone, but my laughter turned to sadness, tears, prayer, and repentance as I grew to be a man. Now I am a Catholic priest called Father John. Friends from my childhood call me Jack or Jesse. The church in East Los Angeles where I serve my parishioners is known as Saint Veronica's. I have lived there in the rectory with four other priests for more than forty years. Three days a week I say the mass. On other days I listen to the people and their problems, of which they have many. I baptize their children and bury their dead. I hear their confessions and absolve their sins if there is a good act of contrition. If there is no confession I absolve the sins anyway. I would love these people no matter what they did.

But I wonder, would they love me if I confessed my sins to them? Sometimes I catch one of them staring at the faded green tattoo of the cross on my left hand or the impression above my left jawbone that exactly matches the imprint of a woman's high heel. They never ask, but I hear them whisper about it. Would they love me if they knew how that got there? Would they love me if they knew my other sins, some committed right here in their church? Would they love me if they knew the dark thoughts that plague me, even in times of prayer? They might not understand that I, a priest, once suffered the growing pains of a frightened and unholy boy. Although my deepest sins occurred long ago, time has not dulled the pleasure and pain of their memory. I was different then. This was a different city. A different paradise.

It is fashionable in these days of cynicism and bumper sticker poetry to refer to the city of LA as "Hell-A." Fair enough. Even I sometimes think the angels have fled in anticipation of the place burning long and hot like Gomorrah. The signs—earthquakes, riots, droughts, floods, fires, and power failures—have been coming for years. Still, I see much light here, light made brighter because it stands against the blackness of the sins of this city. There were not many shadows then and it truly was a city lit by holy angels. In those days if you believed strongly enough, anything would be possible. Where else on this earth could a man be run over by a train and live to tell about it? That man was my grandfather, Jose de La luz Santiago.

CHAPTER ONE
JOSE OF THE LIGHT

In 1952, I was Javier Alfanso Santiago Flanagan. I was eight years old and living with my Irish-American father, James Patrick Flanagan, and my Gabrielino Indian, Mexican-American mother, Juanita Maria Santiago Flanagan. While my birth certificate carried my formal name, I was sometimes called *Jesus* by my mother. For several years I was not called any of these names; I was called Jack or, in polite company, John. The name changes started when my father decided we were no longer going to be half-Mexican because Mexicans were forbidden to buy property in the City of Bell, the Los Angeles suburb where he purchased our tract home on his GI loan for one dollar down and the promise to pay the remaining $5,999 over the course of his lifetime.

I moved to Bell along with my mother (renamed Judy), my sister Janice, and my brother Richard who did just fine with their already Anglo-sanitized names. Even then, Dad worried that the name of my youngest brother, Benjamin, sounded Jewish, and they ended up calling him by his middle name: Carl. Not that it mattered to me. By the time I was old enough to care, I no longer lived with the rest of the family, but with my grandfather Jose and my grandmother Soridtha. They called me Jesse.

For eight years I lived like most of my friends, with a mother and father. My father was a courageous man made nervous from the hazards of serving in World War II. While in the Navy he attempted rescuing seven men whose boat had been torpedoed. He saved six of them, but the seventh man died in his arms. He was decorated with several medals for his effort, but threw them overboard in memory of the man he lost.

While he hated war, he never did get over the structure of the military. In my early years he behaved like he was still in the service and we were his recruits, making sure we were up every morning at 6:00 a.m., even on the weekends. We were ordered to clean our quarters and make our bunks before he bounced a quarter off the sheets to be sure things were "ship shape." We had chow together at exactly 6:20, and then the galley was swabbed. We were ready for school and out the door at precisely 7:30, Monday through Friday. We were home from school by 3:30 in the afternoon when the strict schedule resumed with homework until 5:30, dinner at 6:00, and chores until 7:30 p.m. We were allowed half an hour of TV before we prayed one decade of the rosary together, brushed teeth, put on pajamas, and said we loved each other. It was lights out by 9:00. On Saturdays we did yard work until noon, then did whatever we wanted until dark. On Sundays, after church, we played tag and then hide-and-seek until after dark when we were called inside to prepare for Monday morning.

  I was sent away from my parents' home two days after my ninth birthday because the new place was too small, or I was too big, or because I was caught wearing my mother's lipstick, fake pearl necklace, Christmas dress, and high-heeled shoes. Or maybe it was because I painted my six-month-old naked brother along with the crib in the color of the morning sky. When my father saw my hands and clothes perfectly matched his baby son's ass, I was forced to wash the baby down with turpentine before dad beat me sensible with a belt. Just a few days later I was caught trying to light the baby's wooden cradle on fire.

  To this day I am unsure of the real reason, but I clearly recall being driven from the Bell house in shame and silence by my father, several miles across town to East Los Angeles, to the sprawling wood and stone house belonging to the large piece of land now buried beneath a mass of concrete and steel supporting 350,000 cars a day on a blink of the freeway known to millions as Interstate Five.

Before the freeway, this now-famous slab was home to several communities and all of the accompanying sights, sounds, and smells of life. In the mornings, barking dogs alerted you that the food trucks had arrived, selling fresh fruits, eggs, and vegetables. In the evenings, the same trucks carried meat, tortillas, tamales, tacos, and hot sauce. Neighbors sat on their porches talking or shouting, playing cards, checkers, dominoes, or guitars and accordions. On occasion, some of the men would rise at daybreak to sing what everyone called the morning song.

From the moment my father pulled to the curb of my grandparents' house, and then watched as I carried my cardboard suitcase up the wooden steps, he hoped, I think, I would return to his car in tears and repentance for whatever it was I had done wrong. Instead, I moved out of the car and toward my grandfather, Jose. I will forever see Jose standing on the wooden porch like a pillar holding up the entire house . . . the entire block . . . the entire city . . . and ready to hold me up for eternity. He was smoking and laughing, his eyes like fire, and fixed on mine. Believe it or not, I had seen the light from his eyes all the way across town, and it was that light that led me up the stairs and would always lead me home. I knew from those eyes and my pounding heart that I had become Jose's boy that day, and that I would be his forever. While he had once visited his other twenty-seven grandchildren, he no longer cared about them and, to my knowledge, never spoke to them again.

My punishment was supposed to last a week at most, but my parents' house was never my home again. At first my parents phoned me every day and dropped by a few times a week with food, sometimes with extra socks and underwear, to see if I was okay. Seeing I was adjusting well to my new surroundings, they eventually quit coming.

Jose stood five feet, eight inches tall with a barrel chest and thick arms he claimed had been forged of iron by an angel—something you too might believe if you ever saw him. Attached to those arms were hands so large they could have belonged to a man twice his size. His head was large and the closest thing to a perfect square I have ever seen in nature. His eyes were grey, but flashed blue when he was happy or angry. He had a full head of white hair, combed straight back, and a thin white moustache. Nearly every time he left the house he wore pressed cuffed pants, a black belt with a solid silver belt buckle molded in the likeness of a lion, a pressed white shirt, a black silk tie, and a black or grey felt hat. On special occasions he also wore a dress coat. While otherwise immaculate in appearance, his broad chest would often cause one of his buttons to pop loose. His shirtsleeves were also too short and narrow for his long, thick arms, so he was unable to use cufflinks and had to leave his cuffs unbuttoned. Jose was not handsome, but women looked at him longingly. Most men who did not know him, however, did not want to look at him at all, preferring to step into the gutter rather than pass him on the sidewalk.

He spoke decent Apache and perfect Spanish; but, being raised in the US, he preferred the broken English of poor immigrants. While his words were easily understood and highly descriptive, educated people often enjoyed correcting his many grammatical mistakes. But he rarely talked with such fools, so that didn't bother him.

My grandmother Soridtha was an American Indian sorceress of great power and fading beauty. She was fourteen years old when her last living relative, her mother, died. She spoke decent Spanish and a little English, but mostly the Takic dialect of her people who had been dispersed and assimilated to the point there was nobody to speak to any more.

She sometimes tried to fit into modern culture, but more often she rebelled against it, even to the point of building her own *wikiup*, a traditional Tongvan hut made from willow branches and reeds. She often lived for weeks out there in our backyard.

Because she was skilled in reading the signs of heaven, Soridtha, or *She Who Did Not Cry*, was also called *Magia*. While most others prayed kneeling, she would stand praying, making a circle, facing what she called the four directions: north for fire, south for earth, east for air, and west for water. The only times she entered a church were for her wedding and for her funeral. She kept to the old Indian ways, staying close to the earth and the spirits that inhabited it. While others were learning math and science from books, she was reading something far deeper. I never knew how she did it, but looking into a cloudless sky, she could predict to the hour when the rain would come and when it would end. She could tell you even before the doctor or the mother herself knew if a woman was pregnant and if she was going to have a boy or a girl. Although still in her teens, even the older Indian women in the Plaza came to her for advice on everything from growing corn to making love.

The houses in our neighborhood on First Street in East Los Angeles were all different, many of them built by their owners. Some were ornate and beautiful while others were crude shelters, good for nothing but keeping out the weather. They were not crammed together as the houses were in Bell, and there was a lot of land between them. The open spaces were filled with tall grass and fruit trees, chickens, and a cow or two. Each morning the smell of the rich earth mixed with ripe tomatoes, melons, and the sage that grew wild on the hills combined with the chirping of sparrows as a sensory alarm clock to wake you to new life. Each fall and spring, a million ducks would fly overhead, sometimes stopping to visit a puddle in the yard if it had rained. The poor ducks were usually shot and eaten by Jose or one of our neighbors before they could finish their southern migration to spend their vacations in Mexico.

The house was surrounded by a rusty wire fence overgrown with blackberry vines that, beyond the thorns, carried delicious fruit in the summer months. Behind the house were two large pomegranate trees, a fig tree, an orange tree, an avocado tree, and a garden that produced tomatoes the size of baseballs and corn stalks taller than a grown man. There was also a garage for fixing cars, a pen for the chickens, and three wooden stalls—one containing a goat, one a milking cow, and one for Sofia, the once beautiful race horse originally named Razor's Edge that Jose won in a card game. Old, blind, and half-crippled now, Sofia had only recently been retired as Jose's main source of transportation to town.

In the backyard was a little fishpond where Gilberto the giant goldfish lived with Hilberto, the wooden angel who stood guard over Gilberto and the property. Everything in the house and the yard, including Hilberto, had been built by the sturdy hands of Jose.

    Unlike my parents who never let me do anything, my grandparents only had two rules. I was not allowed to enter the cellar and was forbidden to ever enter their bedroom. Of course I tried breaking both rules immediately, first going to the cellar and attempting unsuccessfully to pry the lock from the door. When that didn't work, I found easy access to the bedroom when my grandparents were gone.

    The door was never locked, and I looked inside to see the small room with the uneven wooden floors. It seemed as holy as a church, and I genuflected before entering. Lingering within was the scent of burnt sage, fresh herbs, tequila, cigarettes, and what I later would learn was sex. Set in the middle of the room was a beautifully carved wooden framed bed Jose had built for his wedding night long ago. Carved on one bedpost was the face of the devil. On the opposite post, looking directly at the devil was an angel. And on the headboard Jose had carved a train engine.

    To the right of the bed he set up a simple card table covered with the skin of a deer he had shot with an arrow in the Los Angeles River a few years earlier. His fully loaded, pearl-handled pistol, rested in one corner along with three extra bullets standing up straight in a row and pointing north, an opened pack of Lucky Strike cigarettes, a cigarette lighter, and several packs of firecrackers. In the center of the table, Jose had neatly arranged a toy train engine (in honor of the train that had spared his life), a large bottle of tequila (in recognition of the spirits intoxicating him when the train hit him), and a statue of Our Lady of Guadalupe (in tribute to the Holy Mother) whose medal he had around his neck at the time of the miracle. He called this assembly of items his altar and he prayed loudly before it several times a day. He was a religious man who had been excommunicated from the Catholic Church for committing, and not repenting of, mortal sins. Many mortal sins, I am told.

To the left of the bed Soridtha kept her medicine on another card table. This was not regular medicine, however, like pills and powders, but plants and herbs she had gathered in the wild. The display also included the feathers of eagles, hawks, and crows along with many arrowheads and colorful beads that Soridtha had made from baked clay. A tower of baskets of all sizes rose nearly to the ceiling, some to be sold and others used by her for carrying groceries or laundry. Some of these were so well made they could even hold water. From the time she was a young girl she had woven these baskets from the cedar bark and swamp grass that grew in the Los Angeles Riverbed.

Jose had only recently quit carrying his pistol into town, complaining there was nobody worth the price of a bullet anymore. Still, like most everyone else in our neighborhood, he fired a few rounds into the air on holy days, or just for the fun of it. Sometimes he let me shoot the pistol being sure I aimed straight up, and not at anyone's house. In those days everyone had a gun, but there was never any thought we would shoot a neighbor for no reason.

    One thing that gave Jose his great power was his belief in the miracle of the train. He was lying in the pouring rain, his head between the railroad ties. It seems he had passed out in the mud after staggering toward home from a card game held in the back room of one of his favorite bars. When the train ran over him, it pushed him deeper into the mud caving in the right side of his forehead. He said an angel of mercy had taken him to a hospital where he faded in and out of consciousness for a week. While he was not expected to live, he had a miraculous and complete recovery. Nobody in the neighborhood saw or heard from Jose the entire time he was gone. Believing him dead, his friends and neighbors had a funeral for him and, lacking a body, built and buried a child's coffin in Jose's own backyard. The coffin contained an unopened pack of cigarettes, a deck of cards, and a good bottle of tequila.

    Only Soridtha was certain he was still alive and so she laughed, sang happy Tongvan songs, and danced on the grave at her husband's funeral. When he arrived at his house a week later, everyone in the neighborhood was gathered near the grave to console Soridtha, whom they figured had gone insane with grief since she camped out on the grave, laughing, drinking, and eating the entire time. When Jose walked up to them, they all thought it was his ghost they were seeing. Proving he was no ghost, however, Jose kissed his wife endlessly.

While everyone loved him, they had hoped he would remain dead since most of the men were wearing Jose's clothes when he returned from the grave. But he was so happy to be alive, he let them keep whatever they wanted and dug up the coffin with his bare hands for the tequila. Once the tiny coffin had been exhumed, Jose lay on top of it, folding his arms as if he were dead while Soridtha rested her hands on his head and wept for joy. He was soon up, laughing, singing, eating, and drinking as no ghost can do. Even the doctors, who usually forgot about the works of God, called Jose's recovery a miracle.

Jose *knew* it was a miracle and at least once a day he stopped whatever he was doing, crossed himself, and took a shot of tequila from the bottle he usually kept in his back pocket. He looked fondly at the bottle, before speaking to it. "I was taking just a little nap after drinking from you, sleeping on the iron tracks when the great wheels came down and hoped to kill me. It was the miracle of the train," he would say, laughing and touching the deep dent the train had left in his forehead with his fingers before retiring to his bedroom with Soridtha.

Soridtha and Jose loved each other deeply and, at home, were inseparable, rocking the house daily with their lovemaking and laughter, their tears and sometimes nearly violent arguing. At other times, however, they lived separate lives—him with his gambling and carousing, her making medicine, weaving baskets, and casting spells on various neighbors, such as the man she prayed would be turned into a dog who was found howling at the moon and defecating in his own yard.

    I was no older than ten when Jose began driving me to town in his black Chevy. More often, however, we took the East LA trolley, riding the red cars to the Sixth Street Station downtown. From there we walked through the city streets. But walking with him through the city was like having a lion on a leash made of kite string. He usually acted tame, but if he wanted to break away there was nothing I or anybody else could do about it. Mostly things were peaceful and we would run into friends and he might flip a coin for a prize of one hundred dollars on a single toss. But a hundred dollars was nothing compared to the thousands he often won at poker. Sometimes he would be paid in bullets, tequila, or other things, and he had many promissory notes he either burned up or forgot about.

    Win or loose he would laugh and receive or pay whatever was owed. But losing didn't happen often. Usually he won stacks of money. Those few times when he was unlucky, he lost every dollar in his fat wallet after playing cards all night. Since the trolleys quit running early each evening, a bad night meant there was nothing left for a taxi. Everyone knew Jose, and usually someone offered us a ride home, but sometimes we would walk forever it seemed, moving between the lights of the city and the darkness of night.

On the way home, we encountered hobos, wealthy men, and pretty women. Jose greeted everyone as they crowded in to ask his advice on everything from love to gambling. Along the way we passed closed department stores, all-night restaurants, and greasy bars. He would slip in and out of each bar with me in hand. There, Jose bought everyone drinks or, if he was broke, found a friend glad to buy him a drink. He would give me a sip before I was given a soft drink that I always lifted in a toast to Jose as everyone laughed. I drank in anticipation of having more liquor when I was old enough.

On some Saturday mornings Father Thomas, the parish priest from Saint Veronica's visited the house and tried tempting Jose back into the fold, saying, "I will not give you the sacraments until you have confessed your sins and done your penance, Jose." At first the priest was friendly, but eventually he became angry and raised his voice against Jose. Then Jose too became angry and told the priest he could not be like him, "a half-man, alive only from above the belt." These words so infuriated Father Thomas he stormed out of the house, banging the door shut, shouting, "You will certainly burn in hell Jose if you do not repent of your sins and do the penance." This was very troubling to Jose; but, no matter how he tried, he could not find a way to repent honestly, since he did not consider sex or gambling or drunkenness to be sins. Still, he had no intention of suffering the eternal fires. He was a devout man with his own religion—a complicated spirituality loosely based upon Catholicism, Apache magic, the Union Pacific Railroad, and *Jose Cuervo* Tequila.

One night, Jose knelt for hours at the altar in his bedroom, drinking, praying to the statue of Our Lady of Guadalupe, and burning white sage in order to ward off evil spirits. You could hear him weeping, laughing, and pounding the wooden floor with his iron fists until you thought the house would fall down. I sat frozen on the couch in the front room while Soridtha clutched an old photo in her hands, rocking increasingly quickly in the ornate rocking chair Jose had carved for her. When the pounding stopped he shouted for all the world to hear, "Seven daughters and not even one son. Why have you cursed me *Madre Mia*? I am a good man."

While his legacy troubled him, he was equally concerned with the death of Los Angeles. He began shouting again, "How can this good city now go to hell and have no more trolley cars to ride on? Why am I alone left to fight against the people who want to bring a freeway and destroy even the red trolley cars?" The louder Jose shouted, the faster Soridtha rocked. The pounding resumed, and we listened to him beat his big square head against the floor with such force you might swear there was a big California earthquake. Finally, it went quiet and then he laughed loudly, pulled himself from the floor, took one final shot of tequila, and strolled into the front room with an unlit cigarette in his lips and dripping sweat to embrace first me, then Soridtha, whom he held and kissed deeply for a long time.

While he loved other women, he loved Soridtha more, calling her "the other half of my heart." As Jose kissed her she relaxed her grip on the blurry photo she had been clutching prayerfully in her hand and it fell to the floor. I picked it up to return it to the shelf in the front room, recalling what I had heard from Jose that some of those in the photo were warriors from his grandmother Quieta's family, standing tall in the dirt, proud and tired as wild horses after running all day, holding rifles they were surely not afraid to use. There were no women in the image and I can only assume they had already been imprisoned by their American captors.

History does not record what happened after that photo was taken, but there was apparently a skirmish when some of the men attempted escaping the soldiers who were herding the tribe onto the San Carlos Reservation in Arizona. Four of those in that photo, including Quieta's father and her youngest brother, were shot and killed only days after it was taken. In return, the warriors killed four soldiers. After a brief gun battle, the remaining warriors surrendered and, along with the other survivors in the band, were quietly marched to the reservation. Quieta alone escaped the iron grip of captivity, only to be abducted by Jose's grandfather, Agua.

Jose rarely spoke of Agua, but he spoke of Quieta often, sometimes telling stories of her boldness after looking at the photo. And I always wondered, would he be like her father and brother and die in a fight he could not win?

CHAPTER TWO
MAGIA AND JOSE

As a young woman Soridtha once made a good living as the best weaver of Native American baskets in the LA Plaza. People quit buying her crafts, however, after a competitor spread the rumor she was a witch. Even though she was beautiful and filled with laugher and had once entertained many suitors, most everyone was afraid to get near her then. Even the Indian women who had once treated her like a daughter abandoned and even scorned her. She may have been a witch, but she was also a brilliant woman simply trying to live the way her people had always lived, in close harmony with the natural elements.

After the world deserted her, she continued practicing Indian ceremonies and magic, something that only increased the speculation of her witchcraft and led to her complete abandonment and near starvation. But even starving, she was more beautiful than all other women in the Plaza, and I think that is the real reason some of them hated her. Only those men who did not know her violent reputation would get close enough to talk with her. After being spat upon or bitten, they never approached her again. When tourist men offered her money for sex, she would throw the money back and spit directly in their faces, shouting in her native tongue that she would die of starvation before being touched by one of them. When a man hit her in the face for spitting on him, she did not cry or fall down as you might think. No, she hit him back, hard, before biting and scratching and tearing his clothes until he ran into the street, bloody and naked. Finally, everyone left her alone to die in the big oak tree that still stands in the Plaza today.

Each night she slept beneath the shelter of the tree and most days would find her alone, sitting high in the branches. Her hair was matted, her one dress old and worn, and on full moon nights she barked like a coyote. The merchants in the Plaza complained about her to the police, but not even they dared to make her leave. After everyone left the Plaza each night, she came down from the tree, built a little stick fire to cook cakes made from the acorns she had harvested and processed. She would also eat whatever food she fished out of the trashcans, sometimes supplementing her meals with a squirrel she killed with a rock, barbecued, and ate rolled up in the tortilla-thin cakes. By her late teens, she had all the refinement of a ravenous dog.

Jose was celebrating his twenty-first-birthday in the Plaza in 1921. He was with some friends when he told them he would marry the "Indian girl," as he called her. By then she no longer looked pretty, and everyone warned him to stay away from her. But he saw something nobody else did and had eyes for her alone. That evening Jose climbed the tree. Once at the top, he spoke softly and petted the girl's hair, which had gone from black silk to charcoal colored straw. When she bit him on the hand and he began bleeding, Jose simply licked the wound, petted her hair again, and softly called her *El Lobo*. Soon she was screaming and hitting him. He would never hit a woman, so he did not strike her back, run away, force himself on her, or hurt her in any way. Instead, he let her hit him, never flinching as the fine bones of her fists struck his face until he was bruised and bleeding. Like a man breaking a wild stallion, he allowed her to run a little and then reined her in. He gently touched her from time to time to gain her trust before wrapping her up like a doll in his big coat and lifting her into his arms.

After only a few hours she gave up trying to hurt him.

He kissed her softly on the cheek, whispered in her ear, and carried her to his car. He drove her home and nursed her back to health. She slept alone for four months straight in Jose's bed while he slept under the stars in the backyard. The entire time, she woke only long enough to eat the food he made for her.

It took six months before she spoke a word to him and a full year before she spoke regularly and ate with him at the same table. By the time that year had passed they had fallen deeply in love with each other. Everyone knows what love can do to a woman who has lost her looks, and Soridtha now grew more beautiful each day, her hair again flowing silky black. Soon she was more beautiful than ever before and many said she was the most beautiful woman in all of Los Angeles. Certainly Jose thought so.

I once saw a photo of the wedding of Jose and Soridtha, he in a too-small tuxedo and silk top hat resembling a raisin on a watermelon. She was wearing a silk long, white gown that he spent over a thousand dollars to have made. Her black hair and her eyes shined like polished obsidian.

The photo proved what everyone said, that she was the most beautiful of all brides—perfect in every detail. But if you were to look closely at that picture, you would see a big spot on the otherwise immaculate dress. According to Jose, *Magia*, as he sometimes called her, had overheard a man whispering that she was a witch and that Jose would catch fire when he took her to his bed. Jumping on the man, she beat him bloody with her fists, getting some of his blood on the white dress. Others tried unsuccessfully to pull her away, but only Jose was powerful enough to do so. Again she had reverted to the ways of a wild dog, clenching her teeth, howling, spitting, and snarling at the man who stood frozen on the spot. When Jose knocked the man out with a single punch everyone cheered. The man was still lying at the entrance of the church when the bride made her way inside to the sounds of the wedding march, stepping right onto him, grinding her high heel into his chest as he moaned and she strolled daintily to the altar. And with that, the young couple was married without further incident.

While we lived hundreds of miles from the Apache lands in Arizona and Mexico, Soridtha forever felt a kinship to the warring Apache tribes and loved stories of the brave men and women who fought the American soldiers. In the Plaza she learned the ways of many tribes including her own, and their sometimes enemies like the Chumash, Luiseno, Cahuilla, Sioux, Cherokee, and others. What she didn't learn in the Plaza about the Apaches, she was taught by Jose. But soon Soridtha knew so much about the Apaches that Jose was learning about his own ancestors from her.

By the time I knew, her she had nearly quit speaking and mostly listened. Jose said that is why she heard things others could not. She would tell him that the wind whispered to her about the secrets it saw as it looked in windows. This frightened Jose, since the wind might have seen him with one of the many other women he had been with.

Soridtha and Jose were not like the many Native Americans who were quick to abandon their culture after moving to Los Angeles. Instead, they worked to maintain the ways of their ancestors. Especially Soridtha, who lived freely, wandering the hills near her home foraging for food and seeking visions. Jose never did wander the hills with Soridtha and not many outside our family knew of his connection with his Indian ancestry. He always dressed like an American gentleman whenever he left the house, but at home he would sometimes dress like an Apache warrior in war paint and deerskins, camping in the backyard with Soridtha in her wikiup, shooting arrows with deadly accuracy at a squirrel or rabbit that always fell with one shot and became our dinner.

One of Jose's goals was to become invisible to his enemies like the great Chiricahua Apache leader Geronimo had done. Jose forgave Geronimo for his killing so many Mexicans since it was they who had killed Geronimo's family. And while Jose never did become invisible, he persisted in learning the ways of the great Geronimo. On certain full moon nights, Soridtha would dress in the old style Apache deerskins and beaded moccasins she made from a deer she had killed near the river with a bow and arrow. On such nights she would howl like a coyote and perform ancient dances in the backyard while Jose beat the calfskin drum and burned piles of white sage.

    Most nights, however, the couple was all-American and the neighbors could hear the sounds of their jazz records playing loudly. Soridtha would then dress in a gown of long, black silk that matched her hair, and Jose would wear a tuxedo. They sang and laughed and danced through the house with the music so loud everyone on the block came to the curb to see what was happening. Eventually the neighbors joined the dancing couple in the house, and then followed them out into the streets where they too danced or lined the sidewalks to clap and cheer for Jose and Soridtha. The dance could easily become a fiesta, lasting three days or more.

    At such times the entire community would gather on our front lawn where Jose had dug a pit and roasted half a cow or a pig. Then there would be drinking and kissing and fighting and firecrackers and guns fired into the air for days. This was years before my birth, but I can somehow recall the fiesta right down to the smell of burnt gunpowder, as if I were sitting right there.

    Jose always had to be careful not to anger Soridtha and invite one of her curses, though she rarely used her knowledge for evil. Mostly it was for good things like healing, mixing powerful medicine from roots and herbs that grew wild in the hills and canyons surrounding Los Angeles in those days. Some mornings I would wake and she would be gone. Jose would tell me she had hitchhiked to the desert to seek a vision. Once she went out to the desert for forty days, sleeping in a cave and speaking only with coyotes, hawks, and crows while eating nothing but a few nuts and berries and drinking the clear water from the streams. Then she saw many angels and demons coming into the city of Los Angeles. They spoke to her about a great cloud that would blanket the city. When she returned from the desert looking as thin as a ghost, she tried to warn others about the great cloud. To her face, they listened politely, but behind her back they laughed at her. When the cloud finally came and was named smog, those who remembered the vision believed her. They no longer laughed, but began calling her witch again, and feared being near her. She cried a little when they called her witch, but mostly she laughed as shouts of joy and ecstasy echoed from the house.

As the years passed, the laughing of young lovers turned to the crying of babies, and Soridtha gave Jose first one daughter, then six more in succession. Year after year, the seven daughters arrived like winter rain: Mena, Maggie, my mother Juanita, Baby Sarah, Matilda, Celia, and Sofia (who had originally been named Alphonsina until Jose changed her name when she grew big, buck teeth like Sofia his old horse that still lived in the backyard).

Following the birth of his seventh daughter, Jose carved a special chair from a single block of wood for the arrival of his son, Raphael, the boy he was convinced he would have someday. The chair rested at the head of the dinner table. Nobody was ever allowed to sit there, and when Jose finally realized Raphael was never coming he burned the chair in the front yard yelling, "Damn you, Raphael, why didn't you not never come to my house to live?" Then he stormed into his bedroom where he could be heard all over the block, shouting, "Seven daughters and not no sons is a bad curse, *Madre Mia;* why have done this to me?" He pounded his fists and even struck his head with the palms of his hands until he was bruised and bleeding, this time by his own hand. But he returned to the front room drenched in sweat, smiling and happy to be with his daughters and to give them sticks of peppermint candy, but especially to be with Soridtha. He held her closely in his powerful arms as she smiled a little and remained silent, something she did when she was happy.

I never knew my grandmother in the days when she was the prettiest woman in Los Angeles and filled with life and laughter. In my memory she is a dark, veiled ghost holding onto the rosary beads she always kept around her neck while chanting words that were not Hail Marys, but had sounds unknown to everyone, including me, and even Jose.

When I was sick, the ghost would appear and finger the beads, chanting the strange words over my bed before bringing me whiskey mixed with warm water with some of the wild herbs she had harvested floating on top. It tasted terrible, but I drank it all knowing it would make me well the next day, which it always did. In time she rarely left the house and she never cut her hair, which for years remained as black as a raven, falling perfectly straight, down below her forever thin waist.

Jose and Soridtha were married for thirty-seven years. Every year on their anniversary she would make a small incision with one of her knives on her right forearm and one on Jose's right forearm, before pressing their arms together in order to mix their blood. In the end, they each had thirty-seven little scars. "Wounds for love" Jose called them, to commemorate thirty-seven anniversaries.

The visitation of the Virgin had occurred well before I knew her. Nobody knew if the words she spoke were, as many said, nonsense or the speaking of other tongues, as described in the Bible. Where she had once laughed often, she never did again.

Jose recalls that the rooster had crowed seven times in the morning with the full moon still lingering in the sky before he heard Soridtha laughing and screaming, then falling to the floor. For three consecutive days she neither ate nor drank. She was blind for all three days and never spoke a word to anyone. He refused to take her to a doctor and did not eat the entire time, but burned white sage and either rocked her in his arms or beat her drum loudly over her, day and night. After the three days, she was able to see again but spoke slowly, and only a few strange words into the air—talking and softly patting the hand in a place where nobody stood. Jose said she was speaking to an angel or the Virgin herself. Others said she was speaking to the devil. Still others said she had suffered a stroke. Jose was happy Soridtha had seen the Virgin, and he would often ask what she had said. But Soridtha was speaking almost exclusively to the Virgin and only she heard the reply.

Other than foraging for food, the only times Soridtha left the house were to look for Jose. On those occasions she would pull me along by her rough hands until she pushed me through the door of some bar or made me stoop to look below the half doors to try and spot Jose's brown leather shoes. They looked exactly like every other pair of brown leather shoes except for the tiny red dot on the edge of the right heel Soridtha had painted there for identification purposes.

It was like we were playing a little game. But the game would end abruptly when she boldly burst into the all-male, non-Indian bar to drag the cursing and protesting Jose out by the ear. While he shouted in protest he never tried to break away from her. She never said a word, and the men in the bar did not laugh as you might think. Nobody dared to look into those black magical eyes or to make a sound until after she had left.

CHAPTER THREE
CITY OF ANGELS (AND DEVILS)

Jose often used Soridtha's medicine to heal his wounds, or to try and break the curse of the seven daughters. It was the curse, he said, that made him lose at poker even when he had three kings. The curse too had caused his chickens to lay eggs so small they were good for nothing but target practice with his pistol. Even though he thought of himself as the luckiest of men, he believed things would be much better if the curse were broken.

Year after year he labored alone at his altar daily, sometimes drinking animal blood mixed with the various herbs Soridtha had concocted, trying to break his curse.

While he considered his children a curse, he thought of the train running him over as the greatest event of his life and considered the dent in his forehead a holy mark God had put on him. My mother saw it differently. Once, before I lived with him, I asked her about the dent. She shook her head saying, "Your grandfather was drunk when he fell down between the railroad ties. He thought this was his own bed, and when the train came it hit him and caved in his forehead. Ever since then he has been crazy."

While the basic facts about the train remained the same, Jose's story was far different from my mother's version. He often varied some details, but basically his story went like this: "I had been working all day, pounding the spikes for the railroad tracks. At the end of the day my hands were bleeding and I was tired and thirsty. Then I drank beer with my friends at the bar for a long time, but beer can do nothing against this kind of working, and so I drank tequila. It had been raining even all day, and I was happy. As I walked home, I saw the light of the train, and in the light, the Virgin Mother was coming to me. I prayed to her, and she told me that my first son should become a priest. With seven daughters, I promised her my first son. Then, there was nothing but ugly doctors and pretty nurses and a big headache and this dent you now see in my head." At that point in the story, he would cross himself, rub the dent in his forehead and laugh loudly before continuing.

"You see, Jesse, a little child's drink like beer or wine," he would say, holding both of his hands apart. "A little child's drink would not have shown me the Virgin, or it would have taken me too close to the train and my poor head would have been crushed like a grape." At the word grape, he clapped his hands together loudly, dusted them off, and laughed again while running his fingers gently along the crevice in his forehead, caressing it like a holy relic. "The Virgin made the train to run over my head as just a little reminder of her. But even after a long time there were still not no sons for me. But I was wrong to think this because you are now my son, and you will soon become a priest, and you and me will be happy and I will not have no more curse." After I promised to become a priest we laughed and he crossed himself before hugging me closely. At that time I thought like a child, and so did not consider the sacred promise I had made to be important.

    Magic and cards, food and friends, women and tequila, God and the devil, the trolleys and Sunday fiestas were the consistent things in our lives. Otherwise every day was different a new adventure that could take us anywhere in our beautiful city.

One morning Jose said, "It is true that the angels have

blessed his city, Jesse, my son. Anyone can see that nothing bad can ever happen here except only some bad things and the death of the beautiful Los Angeles. And so I must cry, but only one time every day. If you had seen this city when it was a young virgin, my son, you also would cry, knowing that only nothing could never be so young and beautiful. But the city is growing old and dying now, and I will someday fight with the men who are killing it. Come now and help me to fight them."

    Jose was ready for a good fight and since it was Sunday and the city offices were closed, he took me to my parent's house for a visit. My father and my younger brother and sister had gone to visit relatives, the baby was napping in his crib, and my mother was home, cleaning the house and preparing the evening meal for the family. When she heard the doorbell ring, she ran to the door, hugged and kissed me repeatedly, but only shook hands softly with her father. In old photos I had seen, my mother was a dark, beautiful woman with black hair, dark eyes and bright red lipstick, like those ladies you see in advertisements for Mexican beer. She still looked the same, only without lipstick, and her hair was streaked with grey.

    Mother understood that Jose could not help how he lived any more than her husband, my father, could help the way he lived. She was proud to have a good man for a husband, and a great man for a father, but over time she forgot the goodness and greatness of Jose and only recalled the little things he had done to hurt her. Soon she also forgot much of the goodness in herself. That's when she quit speaking Spanish, making Mexican food, and even being Mexican.

    She made us both peanut butter and jelly sandwiches and cherry Kool-Aid. I inhaled my sandwich and downed my Kool-Aid, but Jose used his food as an ashtray for the cigarette he was smoking, snuffing it out on the white bread. Mother removed his plate, threw the sandwich in the trash and slammed the plate down into the sink. Jose then took a new bottle of tequila from his back pocket, unscrewed it and attempted to pour a little shot into my Kool-Aid glass. "He's just a child," said my mother, halting his arm. "Okay, maybe just a little drink only for you," he said, passing her the bottle, laughing. She pushed the bottle away and busied herself washing dishes. Jose poured her a drink and left it by her side, on the kitchen counter. She did not take it, but continued washing dishes. Then Jose turned to me, saying, "Your mother is not no longer a Mexican woman, only drinking milk and soda." At that, Mother lifted the glass in a fury, turned to us, and downed the shot. I had never seen her drink any alcohol before, and nothing much changed in her, even after a second shot. Soon after a third, however, this usually quiet, refined woman began laughing, crying, shouting, and pounding the table.

Years earlier, my mother had sent herself to a finishing school where she learned perfect manners and the grammar of a *Gringo*. Under the influence of tequila, her years of training were instantly forgotten as she drank, and she began speaking like Jose. "Don't not stay out after dark, or *los hombres* there will throw bullets at you," she said to me, messing up my hair with her hands, while Jose nodded in agreement. She was seated now, and I was on her lap as she held me tightly, saying, "If you are wanting to fight a man, hit them in the *huevos* with a stick as hard as you can."

"Yes, this is the best way, my daughter, Juanita," shouted Jose, standing, laughing, and moving his big arms like he was swinging a stick at someone's huevos.

Kicking off her shoes and letting down her long, wavy hair, Juanita told the stories about Jose forbidden by my father. Putting an arm around him, kissing him on the cheek and turning to look at me, she began. "He was even a good father to each of his seven daughters, but as we grew old, he was very protective. Remember how you chased my boyfriend, Juan, away with your rifle?" she said, laughing. "No, I only took one little shot to miss one time and not with the rifle, only with *mi pistola*," he said, moving his finger like a pistol.

Juanita began again. "Your grandfather is not scared of nothing but only the stupid 'curse of the seven daughters' as he calls it." You see, everybody in those days thinks having seven daughters and not no sons was an evil sign. He loved us, but he sent us from home on our eighteenth birthdays, saying that nobody would want us after that because we would now be only too old and ugly to get married. He would have a little party with food and beer and a cake, but no tequila for each of us on that day." Jose laughed and my mother took another swig and continued. "After the celebration, he would hand the birthday girl a small golden coin along with a blessing and a curse as she was forced to leave the house forever. I can still remember the blessing and the curse to me and *mis hermanas*, "Matilda, you will have much money, and a mean husband to steal it all. Celia, you will find your fame in your great beauty, but not find no happiness. Mena, you will have much love, but not no marriage and no children. Baby Sarah, you will be popular, and when you are old you will only clean the homes of others, but never have no home of your own. Maggie, you will have a good family, with seven daughters of your own, but not no sons. Sophia, you will have two fine looking girls, and your only boy will have the face of a mouse." To me, he said, "Juanita, you will have a good life, but your oldest son will go away."

    Many of the things Jose prophesied came true, like Sofia's son whom everybody would call *Ratón* because he was born looking exactly like a rat, even with small, hairy ears. When *Ratón* grew into a handsome man and no longer looked like a mouse, Jose would laugh and say he had become a big rat, with a big rat heart. *Ratón* was hated in the neighborhood because he had become a land developer, taking all the old homes away from the old people for little money, then destroying them and building endless rows of ugly houses where the old ones had been.

Jose was laughing at the memory, but Juanita, who was not laughing, looked at me softly, touching my hair while repeating Jose's prophecy about her son being taken. "For many years I thought this meant my son would die young, but when you didn't die, I realized Jose himself would take you from me."

Crying briefly then wiping her tears, Juanita was laughing again and shouting when the woman next-door neighbor yelled out the window for her to keep quiet. Then Juanita put her head out the window and called back, "*Quieta*, or I will get *mi pistola*." Jose clapped and laughed his approval. The three of us were having a great time, but Jose wanted to leave the house before my father returned and blamed him for making Juanita drunk. We all hugged each other and I kissed my mother goodbye. As we entered the car, we could hear Juanita's new Perez Prado record coming from the house. "She will now be dancing crazy and then she will fall asleep for a little while," said Jose, laughing. He started the car and drove out into the street, taking a final shot from the bottle before throwing it from the car window where it shattered on the pavement.

    Back at home with Jose, life was much different from how it had been with my parents. While they had certain rules, Jose never cared about things like bad words, drinking or throwing a little food. In fact, he himself would often hit me with a slice of tomato or avocado when we were seated at the dinner table and I was not looking. Then he would laugh deeply, ducking quickly as I threw something back at him. This led to food fights between us that spread out all over the house until the walls were splattered with food. It was a game. If I hit him with more food than he hit me with, he would clean everything. If he won, however, I had to clean up. I didn't mind the cleaning and I laughed the entire time as Jose sat on the couch watching a TV show, yelling for me to bring him a soda or maybe a beer. Then I might stay up late watching TV until I fell asleep on the couch and awoke in the morning beneath a blanket or his thick, tequila and tobacco scented overcoat.

    Weekdays were not much different from weekends with Jose, since I only went to school when I wanted. Jose said the teachers were stupid and I could learn all I needed from him. It was true. Jose had never attended school, yet he knew everything worth knowing. He had seen everything there was to see and done everything there was to do within the city limits of Los Angeles, which, in his time, had grown from a large ranch into an enormous city. He had seen

Gabrielino Indian villages on the banks of the Los Angels River. He had hunted deer with bow and arrow in the river and on the beaches of Santa Monica. He had seen gun duels in streets and in saloons. He had seen three-hundred-pound tunas schooled together so thick you could walk on them for miles in Santa Monica Bay. He had been driven by horse and buggy to Redondo Beach in 1905 to watch George Freeth ride a surfboard. He knew a man who had been killed during the Chinese Massacre when eighteen men were murdered and lynched right there on *Calle de los Negros*, which some fools called a racial name that Jose forbade me to say. He had swung his fists in the Zoot Suit Riots, narrowly escaping arrest after beating up two sailors.

He was one of the only people who knew who murdered Jose Gallardo Diaz in the Sleepy Lagoon Murder. He had lived through earthquakes, floods, and fires. He watched the opening of the California Aqueduct where he spat into what he called "Mulholland's stolen river." He saw the first motion pictures when they played in Hollywood and was an extra in one of Darryl Zanuck's movies. Like nearly everyone of importance in Los Angeles in the late 1930s, Zanuck knew Jose by name and had offered to make him a movie star. But Jose had no interest in pretending to be someone else; his own life was more interesting than any movie you ever saw.

While every day with Jose was an adventure, I really

didn't care much for the card games we attended in Beverly Hills where he took stacks of money from rich people. I would rather visit the other extreme—the poor little community of Chavez Ravine. He never played cards there, but distributed much of the money had taken from the rich to some of the 300 families living there, which consisted mostly of Mexicans who played, worshiped, and worked together almost as a single family. Chavez Ravine was not one place, but was divided into three communities: La Loma, Palo Verde, and Bishop. As a young teenager, I spent a great deal of time in La Loma.

There was a great fight to save Chavez Ravine, but in the end, the families there would give up everything for a team few of them cared anything about. Jose loved baseball—especially the Dodgers—but he also wanted to help save Chavez Ravine; yet, when the bulldozers flattened everything and the sheriffs removed his friends from the homes they had built, he did nothing. I think he was saving his energy for a still bigger fight—the one to save his own home—as rumors of a coming freeway began to circulate. I was just a kid who loved baseball, but years later when I asked him to attend a Dodgers game, he simply said, "No, that place is now a graveyard."

As a child of ten, I most often went with Jose downtown, and we usually rode in the red streetcars to get there. Jose loved the red cars and had worked to lay down their tracks. Once when we drove his car to town, he parked right in the middle of the street and rested his head on the rail as a streetcar rolled toward him. He was lying down, listening, laughing, and nodding his head as though the track was telling him something funny. As the streetcar came closer I jumped from our car and screamed for him to get up. But he simply continued speaking back to the track as the streetcar moved still closer, and I wondered if he would be run over again and not be so lucky this time. Cars whizzed by, barely missing our car and coming within inches of hitting him. Amid the sounds of angry horns and drivers I could hear him saying, "We were young then and we had a good fight, you and me, but I won and now I ride on you. But we are still friends and you are doing a good job for everybody and will maybe go to heaven someday." Turning to the red car that was speeding ever closer, he said, "You are now a good singer, car number eleven, but when we were young you had the voice only of a frog." Then, listening for a moment, he laughed, and said, "Okay, you are right and I am not such a good singer myself. Maybe we will sing a song together and it will be nice. Okay, we will talk again soon." He lifted his head, jumped into the car, started the engine, and sped off just before the red car came roaring through the section of track where his head had been.

    The red cars were always filled with proud men, even the poorest of them in felt hats with starched white shirts, fake silk clip-on ties and, in cold weather, overcoats. The women wore pretty dresses and high-heeled shoes, smelling of flowers and perfume and paradise in the way women used to smell. If we left the First Street Station in East Los Angeles, we might get a transfer to Ocean Park to ride the roller coaster again and again, and I would close my eyes and scream in terror while Jose laughed like a child, standing up in the little roller coaster car with his hands overhead as we rocketed down right over the ocean on the vertical grade.

In the fall, the Santa Ana winds blew and covered the entire city in dust from the desert. I can recall the day a great wind rocked the streetcar as Jose and I rode out into the country where all the streets were lined with palm trees, going all the way to Hollywood Park to watch the horses run. Jose, who knew every horse by name and most of the jockeys personally, shouted loudly when he won and even louder when he lost money on a horse. But wining was the most fun, and it always meant a new silver dollar or some kind of gift for me. That day he won so much money on a single horse we took a taxi into town and he bought a brand new car right off the lot, leaving his old car parked with the window down and the keys still in it on the side of the road. I sat on his lap and steered the new car all the way home and into the driveway.

Only a month later, however, he lost everything, right down to the new car that he sold in the parking lot of the racetrack to bet on a horse he was sure of. Then we had to hitchhike home. But it never mattered to Jose if he had all the money in the world or none at all. He was always happy and he acted as if he were the king of the city and treated everyone else like kings and queens although they were his subjects.

When we rode the red cars, we were shoved up next to all kinds of different people—Russians, Armenians, Indians, Japanese, Chinese, Italians, and Irish and others—most trying to forget what they were, but not quite able to be Americans yet. You could hear them all laughing and eating and talking in Spanish or English or other languages I didn't recognize. They conversed as the red car creaked through town, the electric wires overhead sparking. "Listen," said Jose turning attentively to the sparks. "The very wires are now talking to me and even singing an old song that only we now remember." He hummed a few notes from a tune I had never heard.

As we turned slowly onto Broadway, past the May Company and the other department stores, the world changed and we saw the storefront windows filled with brightly painted bicycles, pogo sticks, toy trains, stilts, shiny musical horns, guitars, and many other wonderful things all displayed perfectly in the big windows. One time, he walked in and paid cash for the best bicycle at Macy's. He rode it through the store and around in circles on the sidewalk for a while, pretending he was going to keep it for himself. But I knew him better than that and I was soon seated on my new bike, riding happily and slowly, ringing the bell as he walked along beside me.

During Christmas time, the store windows were decorated with gigantic mechanical toys and waving Santas, and the streets were hung with bright, colorful lights. Best of all was Barker Brothers with the Christmas tree nearly as tall as the building itself, all decorated and beautiful. It was then Jose first implanted a longing in me for heaven, leaning out of the red car while he pointed to the top of the tree, rubbing the dent in his forehead saying, "When I was in heaven after the train, I saw many trees, my son, all of them much bigger and brighter even than this one, even though it too is a wonderful tree and I love it and pray that it too will go to heaven and grow still taller. 'Be a good tree and you will go to heaven,' " he shouted to the tree, nodding as if the tree had said something in return. Then he turned to me and said, "And be a good boy and you too will see heaven yourself. I myself have been to heaven many times and it is more beautifuler than anything you see, even here in this city, Jesse." He pulled himself back down to his seat, smiling and putting his arm around me.

We stepped off the streetcar and strolled the sidewalks, peering into the little shops that suffocated beneath the tall buildings. The smells of the city changed as quickly as the street names themselves as we wandered—handmade tamales, fresh roasted meat, and chilies on Olvera Street; the steamed vegetables and hot spice of Chinatown, mixed with the smells of melting tar, cigarettes, cigars, sweat, and perfume. Chickens, rabbits, and ducks were hung up by the feet and sold everywhere as crowds pushed in to get whatever they wanted. In Chinatown you could buy bowls of live frogs to take home, kill with a knife, and eat the legs. "I have better chickens at home and the ducks fall from the sky. Frogs, I can catch anytime from the river. But if I catch all the frogs who then will sing me to sleep at night?" Jose said, splashing the water in the frog tank, saying, "You are lucky little frogs that you are only too tiny for me to eat." The frogs all scattered as he pointed and laughed at them.

On the street, Jose reached into his pocket and pulled out a string of firecrackers, lighting them all at once, laughing hard and stomping his feet as a withered old man with a straw hat and narrow gray beard looked on in hollow-eyed silence from the shadows, smoking a pipe filled with what Jose said was opium.

We turned into an alley and I followed Jose down some damp concrete stairs where we stood, huddled with a hundred Chinese men all smoking cigarettes and sweating and swearing as their prized roosters tore each other to pieces with sharp silver spurs attached to their talons. Then one was the proud victor and the other limped off defeated to die in disgrace. A lot of money changed hands, and Jose took his share of it.

Although, he was hungover, Jose was up early burning sage in Soridtha's wikiup. After that, she wandered away into the hills for some sort of secret ceremony. Back in the kitchen, Jose took a shot of tequila and poured two huge bowls of the menudo he had made the night before using the stomach lining of the cow he had recently butchered. After breakfast, he put on his best black suit. I had no idea where we were going, but I hurried to get ready in my best suit and we raced through the city, running stop signs and lights and enjoying the morning.

It had rained for twenty-one days straight; most everything had flooded and the Los Angeles River was threatening to burst its banks. As we drove over the Sixth Street Bridge that spans the river, Jose closed his eyes and threw a silver dollar into the water for luck.

About a mile from Mulholland Drive, Jose began saying that Mr. Mulholland had stolen water from the farmers in the San Fernando Valley and destroyed the Owens River Valley to fill the swimming pools of the rich in Los Angeles. It was still raining hard; the windshield wipers were moving fast and you could barely see the road ahead. Still, when we arrived at Mulholland, he closed his eyes and even though the light was red, crossed the road as he stepped on the gas, laid on the horn and shouted, "Thief, thief, thief," in disrespect for Mr. Mulholland. There were many cars on the road and he nearly crashed once and nearly hit an old man and a woman as they crossed the street before breaking into a run to get out of his way. "Slow down, idiot," yelled one man as Jose peeked to see who had yelled at him. Then he closed his eyes again and more than one driver waved his fist at us, some swearing, all panicking and honking and swerving to miss our car. I crossed myself in thanksgiving as he somehow made it across the street, opened his eyes, crossed himself, and continued driving happily.

As the rain subsided, we had lunch at Clifton's Cafeteria, and later, dinner on Olvera Street. It was nearly dark as Jose parked his car in the worst part of town, a place everyone called Skid Row. "Sit here for only a short time, my son, and then we will go to the pictures," he said. He walked away and I looked up to read the hand-painted sign that read: "Bed, fifty cents." Then I watched him walk up a flight of old broken wooden stairs into a dark house, arm-in-arm with a pretty woman. People on the street walked up to me, curious to see a young boy in a car alone at night. "Jose's boy," they would say brightly if they recognized me. One man leaned into the car and gave me a stick of peppermint candy he took from his thick coat.

    I didn't recognize him, or he me. He was a tall, thin man with a flat nose, pale white skin and a black suit like an undertaker. He was drinking beer from a bottle and smoking a cigarette as he got into the seat next to me. Jose had taught me how to tell if a man was carrying a gun by the bulge in the coat pocket, and both his coat pockets were bulging. "Happy New Year," he said, lifting his beer. I lifted my peppermint stick and said "Happy New Year" back to him. He put his hand into his pocket, no doubt holding on to his pistol. "This is a bad place and you shouldn't end up here, like me," he said.

    When I told him Jose Santiago was my father, he took his hand from his coat and I thought, *Nothing bad can happen in this place to a son of Jose*. A pretty woman leaned in through the car window, and said "Happy New Year," first to me, then to the man. We both said "Happy New Year" to her, and I sat up a little to see down her blouse. She got into the car, sat down with us, and after kissing him she kissed me, smearing thick red lipstick on my cheeks and mouth. Like every other woman in that area, she smelled of beer and cigarettes and perfume. "Ruby, this is Jose's boy," said the man to the woman. The woman looked frightened and the man and the woman excused themselves and left me alone.

    I was asleep in the back seat beneath Jose's

overcoat when he returned and woke me. Later that day we walked to the pictures together to see a movie called *Mogambo* with Clark Gable and Ava Gardner. Together we drank sodas, ate hot dogs and popcorn, and he stood up, shaking his fists and yelling, "Clark Gable, I am a much better lover than you." Later, he stood to shout, "Kiss her you stupid Clark Gable." When the kiss finally came, Jose slinked low in his seat, crossed himself, and moaned with satisfaction.

After the movie, he quickly found a card game with some friends. I was again sent to the car where I curled up in the back seat beneath the great coat. He woke me just as the sun was rising, laughing to show me the big stack of hundreds and twenties he had won playing cards and gave me a twenty-dollar bill.

As I slumped down beside him in the front seat, he put a hand on my shoulders and said, "Sit up tall. Be bold, as bold as a lion, my son." I sat up and puffed out my little chest and let out a roar you could hear all over the city. Then he laughed so loudly I thought the doors would fall off the car.

While Jose lived life out in the open, Soridtha was sly like a coyote and lived without being noticed. When she was noticed it was not always good. Once she was featured in the *Los Angeles Times* holding a loaded shotgun to keep someone's little home from being flattened by a bulldozer. The photo did not show her being hauled off to jail after nearly beating one officer to death with the butt of the rifle. Jose bragged that his wife was tougher than all the men in the city. Except for politicians, cops, and her enemies, everyone who knew her loved her. How could you not? She was mysterious and still beautiful with smooth, dark skin and those deadly, black eyes; her hair alone betraying that she was growing older having gone from black like a raven to having pretty silver streaks in it. If you were smart, however, you did not love her; you feared her, or you too might end up living like a dog. Jose feared the curses of Soridtha, but his love for her was stronger than his fear.

Life changed little until the day Jose had a message from heaven at his altar. I was seated near Soridtha in the front room, watching television while she sat weaving pine needles into baskets to sell. I turned up the sound on the TV so I could hear it over the voice of Jose who was arguing with the Virgin. But on that evening he screamed extra loud and no matter how much I turned up the volume, I heard every word he said. "Why is nothing not no good to see at the picture shows no more, and why is gasoline now twenty cents for only one gallon? Why do I only have seven daughters and not no sons? Why am I losing at cards and where are my three kings?"

    As usual Soridtha was silent, awaiting his return. He, however was loud, pounding the floor beneath his altar, reasoning with the good and evil spirits there when he shouted something I had only heard him whisper before, "Jesse, my son, you must break the curse that is upon me. Yes, you must lead a holy life and a good life always. Then, maybe you must become a priest. Yes, a priest, a good and holy man who is near to God always." He finished as he always did, saying, "Thank you, Holy Mother, for showing me these many good things." Then he came into the front room, lifted Soridtha from her rocker and took her to the bedroom where the sounds of their lovemaking again made the TV useless.

    A few days later, I found that Jose had enrolled me in Saint Veronica's Catholic Grammar School. There I would try to be holy, to become a priest, and to be Jack Flanagan again. It was there also I found a love even Jose would not approve of.

CHAPTER FOUR
STATIONS OF THE CROSS

The next Monday I began seventh grade at Saint Veronica's, or Vernie's as everybody called it. There, you stood when you spoke to a teacher, called the teachers "Sister," and prayed before class started. The girls wore dark blue loose-fitting skirts and white boluses while the boys wore tan pants and white shirts. Everyone wore navy blue sweaters. The old red brick school buildings with the thick wire-reinforced glass windows were surrounded by an endless field of blacktop. This was all bad, true enough, but the church sitting on the edge of the schoolyard, like a window to heaven, rising from the black flatness, was the most beautiful thing I had ever seen. I loved every panel of stained glass, the towering crucifix, and the tall stone walls.

If the church was filled with magic, the priests were the magicians watching the Word of God come down like a dove, filtered by colored glass until it touched lightly upon silk vestments embroidered with silver and gold. The sacred bird of faith fluttered upon the altar before ascending to be received into holy hands and holy hearts. Only Jose and Soridtha (who were their own type of priests and, I believe, saints in their own way) knew as much about God as the priests of Saint Veronica's. I had such great reverence for the priests of Saint Veronica's, I would lower my head and cross myself each time I saw one of them walking through the schoolyard.

The ringing of the big church bells in the tower, which could be heard from any part of the city, always filled my heart with sacred joy. At those moments, I stopped whatever I was doing, and bowed my head in reverence, even if it was schoolwork or standing up to bat in baseball—stared silently in the direction of the bells, ignoring the Sisters who yelled for me to pay attention or my teammates who cussed at me while I prayed silently without ever lifting the bat from my shoulder. The bells stirred piety in me, something that pleased Jose greatly since, as he always said, "A priest must have great piety."

I was doing my homework on the kitchen table after

school as Soridtha stood in the backyard chanting and pouring animal blood into a jar when I heard the sound of breaking glass and Jose shouting loudly from his altar. "What if my son now becomes a priest and there is nobody to carry on the name of De la Luz? What then, *Mi Madre*?" Listening closely, I wondered if the blessed Virgin would respond to Jose. Then fear gripped me and I left my books, dashed from the kitchen to the front room and turned up the TV as loud as possible to drown out the words of Jose and not hear the Virgin's pronouncement against me. I was shaking, waiting for Jose to stop screaming, waiting for life to begin, waiting for nothing, terrified at the new life the Virgin would have for me.

According to Jose, the Virgin's voice came softly and sweetly, so that nobody except him, and sometimes Soridtha, could hear. There was no trouble hearing Jose, however, who prayed loudly. That evening he wrestled with the Virgin for over an hour, and then entered the front room with messy clothes, sweating, smiling, laughing, and holding the toy train engine, which had been cracked and chipped after he threw it from his altar during the devotions. He stood in the front room, holding the broken train in his hand, looking at me as if I should know what this meant.

When I said nothing, he shook his head, then shook me by the shirtsleeve and said, "*Estupido*, pay attention." Cuffing me playfully on the head, he laughed and let the train engine fall from his hand to the floor where it hit and nearly broke in two. He looked to me again, smiling, believing I would understand the sign.

But I had not yet learned to read "the messages of heaven," as Jose called them. I understood nothing. He shook his head and laughed at my ignorance and began pumping his arms like a train, making little *choo-choo* noises, looking at me to see if I finally understood. When he realized I did not know what any of this meant, he sat down and put his arm tenderly around me. "No, the train is only your life, *mijo*," he said to me, gently, "and you should now carry a long line of little De la Luz boxcars behind you. A virgin priest can not pull many little boxcars, but a very pious altar boy, one without no mortal sins, he can do even everything a priest can do." He laughed hard, clapped a hand against his knee, and leaned back next to me on the couch with his arm still around me. Then he lit a cigarette, took a deep drag and passed it to me while I took a drag and passed it back.

"And what of the crashing of the train? It has been ruined," I said to him. He merely laughed saying, "Oh, the broken choo-choo means nothing; it is just a broken little toy choo-choo. Can you not see that, my son?" motioning with his head to the toy train that lay on the floor. "And you will now become an altar boy and not a priest, and you will become married and have one son and maybe more, as many more as you like," he said to me, with a big laugh, kicking the broken plastic train beneath the couch, then sitting nearly silently to watch TV with me until dinnertime.

It was a cold morning made colder since Jose had the windows of the car down as he drove me to the church, singing loudly with the radio. Between songs he talked to the Virgin, somehow communicating with her even though he was not at his altar. "Yes, yes, that is good;" and, "Yes, of course the boy will now become an altar boy and not a half man, like the Father Thomas. But maybe it is better, *Madre Mia*, if he is a half man for a little while longer. Okay, okay, yes, yes. Okay, I said yes and I meant it. No, I am not shouting at you, *Madre Mia*," he said gently before letting go the steering wheel, clapping his hands together, making the sign of the cross, and kissing his open palms. With his eyes closed and his hands off the wheel, he nearly hit a parked car. When I grabbed the wheel and swerved to miss the car, he opened his eyes, firmly taking back the wheel, saying, "You must not take the wheel when the Virgin is driving for me. Now be good *mijo* and do what the Father Thomas is telling you." He stopped at the church, hugged me, and kissed me on the forehead before I got out of the car. Jose drove away, praying, eyes shut, swerving down the road;

and, I could hear a car honking at him, and him singing loudly until his car was out of sight.

As I approached the church, I heard nothing but the rough voice of Father Thomas. He was holding the chalice steadily in his hairy hands, teaching two other boys to be altar boys as I walked in. Setting the chalice on the altar, he turned around, lifted his black sleeve to check his watch, and scowled at me. Then, without a word, he poured the wine from the cruet into the chalice and drank it. He continued to practice pouring and drinking the wine as we altar boys practiced with tin cups and water until we could pour the pretend wine to the top without spilling a single drop.

From the church it was a short walk to my classroom where nothing much happened until Jose picked me up in front of the school later that afternoon. As he drove me home, he asked if I had ever had sex before. When I told him no, he frowned a little and asked, "And so my son, you are maybe *joto*?"

"No, Jose; I am only twelve years old. I am nothing," I said. Then I remembered the boys calling me queer and I wondered if it was true. I thought about some of the boys in my class, but I had no feelings for them. "No Jose, I am not *joto*," I said. Jose smiled and told me what to do in sex to assure the baby would be a boy, pumping one arm back and forth, driving a little too fast and laughing as he spoke.

The night ended with me watching TV and him praying at his altar, thanking God that I was not *joto* and glad I was going to become the best of all the altar boys.

Whenever I served mass, he sat in the first pew, even though he had been officially excommunicated from the church for his unforgiven sins. The excommunication had been a long process with Father Thomas coming to the house many times, warning Jose to go to confession and repent of his sins. When Jose refused, Father Thomas told him he was no longer in "the good graces of Mother Church." According to Father Thomas this meant Jose could not take communion. Even Jose would not defy Father Thomas by walking forward to take communion, but he never did quit attending church.

As an altar boy, when the priest raised the sacred chalice, I rang the cluster of bells with heartfelt devotion, putting all of my strength into the ringing. At such moments everyone could hear Jose gasping loudly, watching him as he rose to his feet, shouting and beating his chest hard and probably painfully. Father Thomas turned around and motioned for Jose to sit, which he did. Even seated, however, you could hear the thumping sound of him beating his chest and groaning reverently throughout the church. I am glad he prayed fairly quietly at church, however. If he prayed loudly, like he did at home screaming about sex and using many swear words Father Thomas would stop the mass and insist Jose keep quiet. Maybe the priest would even try to kick him out of the church. Because of this Jose might become angry and then maybe there would be terrible words from him against the priest. Or, maybe Jose would hit the priest and be condemned to hell forever. I did my duty as an altar boy, pouring the wine for Father Thomas, which he took gladly, demanding I fill the chalice to the top.

With church finished, I watched Father Thomas still in his holy robe unscrew the top of the bottle of communion wine. "Drinking this wine from the bottle is not a sin because the wine has not yet been consecrated to become the blood of Christ, altar boy," he said without looking at me, cleaning the neck of the bottle with his robe before tilting it to his mouth in search of the final drops. Father Thomas finished the entire bottle, sealed the left over consecrated hosts from the chalice in wax paper and put them into a little refrigerator. As I removed my robe, he spoke to himself, "Everyone thinks it is easy to be a priest, but it is difficult with a congregation as stupid as this one." I think I even heard him cuss, but that is impossible since no priest could do such a thing in a church. He turned toward me, grabbed my ears and said, "You tell your grandfather to be quiet in church, altar boy." Then he held me tightly, but not in the way Jose ever held me. He was breathing hard before I pushed him away. "Damn you to hell, altar boy," he said, "Get out of here." At home that evening, Jose asked me, "Why is only the Father Thomas and me now the only ones to speak to God in the church?" I told him I didn't know, but I didn't dare tell him what the priest had said and done.

 I continued being as pious as Jose had hoped, telling my little venial sins quietly to Father Thomas once a week in the confessional. I was glad to go to confession, proud to be absolved from my sins such as smoking, drinking tequila, looking at pictures of naked women, talking in class, punching a boy in the face, cussing, and copying an arithmetic test. When I ran out of venial sins, I retold my one mortal sin of trying to kill my baby brother by lighting his crib on fire. After I told this sin and all of my other sins, the priest told me to say two decades of the rosary as my penance. I lived an entire year without committing any more mortal sins; and, because of my piety, the curse of Jose weakened and he began winning big at cards.

 Still, he continued to be troubled over the curse. One day I heard Jose at his altar, yelling, "My son can not be an altar boy only; he must become a priest and have a boy for a child." I had no idea how such a thing could happen. I asked Soridtha and even she did not know. I dared not ask Jose or Father Thomas. Maybe Sister Mary Bernadette would know. But I could not approach Sister Bernadette easily. I was falling in love with her.

CHAPTER FIVE
JOSE'S KINGDOM

A year passed and all the eighth graders at Vernie's were headed straight for puberty. It was Sister Mary Bernadette's duty to prevent us from getting there. Sister Mary Bernadette, "Nadie," as we called her, was the Sister Superior. At first she seemed more like a normal nun, but I quickly learned she was only this way when visiting the classroom. Looking deeper into her soul as Soridtha had taught me to do, I saw a beautiful woman floating above the earth like an angel. Her skin was snow white and would be like velvet to touch. The voice—mechanical in the classroom—was more like singing than speaking when we were alone, each note so beautiful I can still recall single words as they were given birth in the air around me. When she said my name I was weak and strong all at the same time. It must have been the way Jesus called to Miriam at the gravesite when his whisper awoke new hope of life within her. Sister Bernadette's sternness in the classroom probably came from a job that was impossible, trying to use mere words to halt our devotion to Maria Ortiz who sat directly across from me, filling out her blouse, her bra showing between the buttons, as her good Catholic breasts cast shadows over all the boys halting the best intentions of the Sister. Maria was a good girl who always had good grades, and most of the nuns loved her. But they hated the boys and the punishment for Maria's beauty fell to the boys who wanted her. While I was unafraid to speak to some girls, I could not say a word to Maria Ortiz. Instead I watched her when she was not looking, dreaming that we would someday come together.

    I usually rode my bike to school, but occasionally Jose drove me in his car. After school, he would sit waiting for me with the engine running, singing and taking shots from the bottle. Most everyone was used to seeing him, and they didn't pay him any mind. Jose and I waited in his car as the school kids, Maria Ortiz among them, walked by. I pretended not to notice her, but Jose did notice and honked his horn, saying, "Look at this beautiful girl, like a grown woman, my son. Maybe you will want to marry her, or maybe you will just want to have a baby with her, and then you can name him Raphael and go to confession and have the one sin forgiven and become a priest. God will forgive you and you will go to heaven. I will go to heaven with you because I will then have not no more curse." Maria glanced over but did not react to seeing me or to Jose, who smiled and waved at her. When he attempted to honk the horn again, I grabbed his hand. He placed his hand on my head and messed up my hair, laughing. I did not laugh, but continued watching Maria from the corner of my eye as she walked down the street.

As we drove home, Jose told me all about sex again, this time revealing how to touch a girl and gently remove her clothes. "You must always have the girl's permission and you must be strong but nice, my son, going slowly into love and never hurting the woman, as some men will do," he said. He took his hands from the wheel and thrust one finger in and out of his loosely closed fist, laughing the entire time.

I thought of Maria constantly, even (Father, forgive me) in church. In class, I stared at her for hours, picturing the warm flesh stacked beneath the white blouse that failed to keep me from noticing she was becoming a woman.

At the last bell, most of the boys ran to the schoolyard to play marbles on the cracked asphalt. I too played marbles, but didn't care if I won or lost any longer, instead looking toward the basketball team practicing hard for last place, led on by the strenuous rooting of the cheerleaders, which included Maria Ortiz. The moment she left, I filled my leather pouch with the marbles I won and rode hard for the bushes that lined the sidewalk on the way to Maria's house. After ditching my bike in the bushes, I waited quietly for her to walk by.

    Crouched in the dirt behind the hedge, I waited to jump from the bushes when I saw her—to tell her that I wanted to take off her clothes and be with her and to have a baby we would name Raphael, just as Jose had instructed me. I loved and hated my feelings for Maria that hid behind thoughts of love like a boy hiding in the bushes. As I waited, I hoped and believed, even against salvation, that she would want me in the way I wanted her and that she would join me in the bushes, or, better, in the back seat of Jose's car. I was bold then and ready to jump out and tell her everything as soon as she approached. But when I heard the click of the taps on her black and white saddle shoes against the sidewalk, my heart melted like wax and I ducked low like a frightened bird among the dirt and the leaves and the bugs. Every day for more than a month, I did the same thing, once lying for two hours in a hard rainstorm before realizing that someone had given Maria Ortiz a ride home.

    Once, instead of seeing Maria, I was jerked from my dreaming by the honking of a car horn. Peering through the thick hedge I saw Jose sitting in the old black Chevy, laughing and waving for me to come out. I stood, retrieved my bike and walked it to the car. Jose got out and brushed the leaves from my sweater without laughing at me. Then he opened the trunk of the car, lifted my bike into it with one hand and tied the trunk shut with twine. He drove home, laughing hard while repeating lines from *The Cisco Kid* TV show, taking the parts of both Cisco and his sidekick Poncho, all the while patting me on the head.

Then, in a serious voice he said, "Jesse my son, of course you must be bold, but you must also remain pure until after the curse of me has been forever broken. And, of course, you will want to be with the girl, Maria. And, when the time is good, you must want to marry her. And then, maybe this Maria will die of a bad sickness, but without no pain and she can go straight to heaven, just as I have prayed." He made the sign of the cross and handed me a silver dollar as I nodded in agreement. Still, I was confused.

First he wanted me to be a priest, then an altar boy, then to get married, then to have a baby, then not to be a priest, then not to be married, and then to be a priest again. I turned over the dollar in my hand and sat quietly in the car, distracted by thoughts of Maria Ortiz while Jose drove home, singing loudly.

One night Jose cooked carne asada and nopales— the cactus pads Soridtha gathered from the hills in the neighborhood, along with prickly pears from the cactus and the green chilies and tomatoes he grew in his garden. He rolled tortillas by hand and cooked everything in the adobe oven he had built in the backyard many years earlier. I could smell the food for blocks, and when I got home it tasted good, even for a boy in love.

We ate together on the front porch to the sounds of crickets and frogs as neighbors laughed or fought while some of their kids shouted over games of kickball, and others raced their bikes down the big hill. As we sat there, Jose told me how he had once caught twenty giant steelhead in one day with a pitchfork as they attempted to migrate up the Los Angeles River. That, he said, was before the entire river was covered in cement and the fish and other wild animals like deer and coyotes quit coming. After dinner, he went to his altar to pray and seek a sign from heaven while I joined in the kickball game on the street where we ran in the last flickers of sunlight. Then our shouting turned to silence, and the crickets and frogs alone could be heard. It grew so dark you could not see your hand in front of your face and the frogs and crickets sang us to sleep.

Sometimes Jose went out alone for the night. Then Soridtha knew he would not stay alone, but would be with some other woman. On one occasion, when her suspicions got the better of her, she took me by the hand and went looking for Jose, quickly finding him with a woman in a hotel room.

After beating both of them senseless, she walked home, packed a few things and, without a word, hitchhiked to the San Carlos Apache Reservation in Arizona.

Neither Jose nor Soridtha could read or write, but he wanted to send her letters and convince her to come home. Instead of using his own words, he cut out scraps of stories from the *Times*, including ads and his favorite cartoon of "Li'l Abner," who was always in love with some girl or other. Then I would mail the pages to Soridtha care of the San Carlos Reservation. Looking back, this went on for years, but he never did receive a response.

With Soridtha gone, Jose concentrated on his other love: the city of Los Angeles. We often went to the Plaza to eat dinner. One Friday night in the Plaza, he stopped and bowed his head to pray silently in front of the old oak tree. Once he finished praying, he looked high into the branches and said, "This is the spot where I met the beautiful Soridtha, sitting in this very tree." He laughed a little, made the sign of the cross and we strolled deep into Olvera Street.

Since it was Friday night, all of the little shops on the street were open, selling religious articles and paintings along with goods made of leather, clay, and tin. Jose gave me money to buy whatever I wanted and I bought a black purse and had the strap stamped with the name *Maria Ortiz*, even though I knew I would never give her that purse. After sitting with Jose and ordering food, we listened as his mariachi friends played beautiful Mexican music, along with jazz and blues. I never did know the real name of the band, but Jose called them "The Four Friends." These were some of Jose's best friends and they often came to the house for card games, spending the night when they became too drunk to drive. The Four Friends consisted of Giermo, the trumpet player; Ignacio, who played guitar; Joaquin, who played accordion; and, Jose's negro friend, Blind Willie, who was not blind, but wore dark sunglasses even at night and sang and played every instrument.

The smell of hot chilies, entire pigs, and huge sides of beef, the fat crackling while rotating over open flames permeated Olvera Street. Old women hand rolled tortillas that were even better than Jose's. "Real Mexican food, almost as good as mine," Jose said, after taking his first bite. Jose ate slowly and had a beer, offering sips to me that I usually refused, instead preferring Nehi Orange Soda. He paid with a hundred dollar bill and left the waitress a ten-dollar tip.

I bought a large bag of Mexican candy and we walked along eating as we approached Angel's Flight, the little train that traveled the one block from Olvera Street to Hill Street, winding up near the Victorian houses of Bunker Hill. Jose handed the train conductor two nickels, one for each of us to ride the little train. Once in Bunker Hill, we walked around the once fancy and now dilapidated houses, and he talked to friends sitting outside on their porches in the warm evening. Bunker Hill had once been an exclusive area but was now falling apart and many poor people now lived in the once fancy Victorian houses, some of them Indians from reservations who roomed together in hopes of saving money for some American dream. Most of the Indians were trying to assimilate by looking and acting like everyone else while secretly practicing some of the old ceremonies behind closed doors. Jose asked one of them if they knew where to find a card game, but they did not.

    With no card game, we continue riding the little train up and down, again and again "This is only a tiny choo-choo we are now riding on," he said. "But the train that tried to kill me was very big and very black, perhaps the biggest and the blackest of all the trains. Still, I love that train that tried to kill me even much more than this little one that cannot kill nobody. Once a year I visit the big train and I pray that God will not punish it for running over my head. The train is not to blame. It is not evil, but only being a train," he said, laughing and making *choo-choo* noises and the whistling sounds of a train, standing up and stomping his feet. While I never grew tired of hearing the story, I was quickly bored going up and down Angel's Flight.

    After riding the train at least twenty times, he put me on his big shoulders and strolled the few blocks to Chinatown. There, in a dusty shop, he looked through rows of broken clocks, nice paintings and jars with strange contents in them. When he found a jar with a dead newborn cat inside, he crossed himself and bought the jar for a few pennies. He examined the piles of dusty books, silk fans, paintings of cowboys, Indians, kings, queens, lakes, mountains, and many other wonderful things. Jose touched each item gently, sometimes holding it up to the light, sighing deeply and praying quietly. He bought a lamp of a king and a small painting of a lake. We lugged his three treasures back to Olvera Street where I had another soda and ate three or four churros for desert, and he drank a beer while listening to the Friends play, throwing money into their guitar cases and requesting his favorite songs, mostly songs about the Mexican Revolution and the great Poncho Villa. He had written a song about Poncho Villa that he had taught the mariachis to play. Taking Ignacio's guitar, Jose began playing the guitar and singing. It was a good song and everybody liked it. But, it was not a good song and nobody liked it. Still they clapped hard because everyone loved Jose.

    The crowd cheered as Jose finished the music and took a deep bow. He paid the Friends to play the slow and beautiful, *Guadalajara*. Then he took a fat woman with brightly painted lips from her seat and the two of them danced cheek to cheek, moving fluidly over the uneven sidewalk. The dance ended in a kiss from Jose and everyone clapped and threw money when it was over. Jose didn't care about the money, but I scrambled to pick it up. He let me keep some of it, but insisted I also share some with the fat woman and the mariachis.

That night, he took the newborn kitten home, named it Raphael, and placed it on his altar where he prayed for all the unborn kitties in the world and for the living baby he wanted me to have. He hung the painting in the front room, but ended up giving it to a neighbor who admired it. The lamp, he polished and set up in the front room, but the next evening he snuck back into the junk store and returned it. It was a little game he played from time to time, and the owner knew all about it. But I had more problems than old lamps to think about.

CHAPTER SIX
THE TOWER

At school my days were long and hot and there were problems of God, and math, and girls I didn't like who liked me, and girls I liked who didn't like me. At recess, we played kickball or baseball and sometimes watched a good fight between two boys who hated each other. Sometimes I got into a good fight with somebody I hated and used all the tricks Jose had taught me, so I always won.

On the first Friday of each month, the entire class was marched, single-file, as if to an execution, through the schoolyard to the church where we were to reveal all of our sins to Father Thomas in the darkness of the confessional. The confessional was a set of two closet-sized, dark rooms, set into one wall of the church. In one room the poor sinner knelt while the priest sat in the adjoining room as the judge who heard and absolved the sinner. I stood in a line of sinners, waiting behind the greatest sinner of all, Darryl Donnelly, who walked in to occupy the sinner's confessional room and have his sins absolved. He started the way everyone always started, "Bless me, father, for I have sinned." He spoke loudly and I could easily hear him and expected he would tell the priest about the bike he had stolen and that he tried to kill somebody with his knife, as was the rumor. Instead of confessing his sins, however, he said he had no sins and had never committed even one sin. Father Thomas asked Donnelly if he had ever lied or stolen or even been angry and Donnelly answered, "No, I never did no sins, Father." Only the day before, I, myself, had seen Donnelly commit the sin of beating a boy with a belt and taking all his money. The priest asked Donnelly to search his heart again for sins. Donnelly was quiet, and then yelled, "Shut up, stupid Father; you got sins, too." After slamming the confessional door, Donnelly stomped out. Father Thomas must have been scared of Donnelly because he did not leave the safety of the confessional box to pursue him. Donnelly sat amid a group of other boys from my class, kneeling at the communion rail, pretending to pray.

When it was my turn in the confessional, I told

everything, even confessing sins I had never committed to make up for Darryl Donnelly. Confession never took me long before, but now my little sins had piled up and some of them had become big sins, maybe even mortal sins, the ones you go directly to hell for if you die with them on your soul. I tried to hide behind words, saying only that I was taking pleasure in thinking about one of the girls I saw in class each day. This felt like a sin when I thought about it, but not when I said it. But Father Thomas was an expert in sin, and he knew what I could not say.

I thought of buying a scapular, the holy pieces of cloth fastened by a string and blessed by the bishop or maybe even the pope himself. A scapular would take you straight to heaven even with mortal sins on your soul if you died wearing one. But the Sisters had told of murderers dying in hospitals, asking the nuns to place the scapular on their chests only to have their skin burn like fire when the holy cloth touched them. Maybe a scapular was not such a good idea. And maybe there would be a story about me, a boy who had died, unable to bear the pain of the scapular. For years the people would tell their children that fire had come from his chest and he had burned up and died in the confessional when he was unable to bear the scapular's judgment.

Father Thomas pronounced a hard penance on me. "For the sin of cheating on a test, say one decade of the rosary. For the sin of lying to a nun, say two decades of the rosary. For the sin of disobeying your grandfather, say five "Hail Marys." For the sin of lust, say three complete rosaries." He told me to make a good act of contrition and to go in peace. I said my act of contrition, left the confessional, and walked without peace to the communion rail, ready to offer my long penance to God.

    As I walked to the communion rail, I rolled the new three-rosary word *lust* off my tongue again and again until I could taste the sweet darkness in it. Lust was a knife with two edges. One edge of the knife could kill, and the other edge could slice open a world filled with forbidden and delicious fruit. Lust was a knife you did not want to give away, even if you could. I knelt at the rail and began the rosaries, saying them as quickly as I could, *Hail Mary, full of grace. The Lord is with thee . . .* over and over again. But an entire rosary is filled with sixty "Hail Marys" and six "Our Fathers" and I had a long way to go to drive out lust.

    As I prayed, I spied Maria Ortiz from the corner of my eye, kneeling near me. I continued praying until I realized I was staring at her again. Then I saw my prayers bending away from heaven and moving into her fingers and down her blouse, to be taken into her heart. She received the prayers, half-smiling, as she knelt with her hands folded to heaven and her rosary beads twisted around her fingers. It was blasphemy and I was going to hell, but I didn't care.

Those who had single-Hail Mary-sins such as talking in class or lying to nuns came and left the rail quickly. I clutched the rosary, saying it twice, squeezing off the beads in rapid succession. Maria and I were left alone at the communion rail. I had less than one full rosary to go when I realized she too could be saying rosaries for lust, and this lust could be for me. I stared at her, prying into her mind as Soridtha had taught me to do. If she stared back, she had lust for me. I felt she was about to turn and face me when Darryl Donnelly knelt beside me with folded hands, pretending to say his penance. Once his dark spirit broke into my prayers I could no longer contact the spirit of Maria.

I closed my eyes tightly as he yanked the rosary from my fingers and threw it down where it bounced and slid over the marble floor. He said no prayers, but knelt quietly, his hands folded mockingly. He tapped me on the shoulder and I turned to see him holding his hands out beyond his chest as he motioned with his head in the direction of Maria Ortiz. I got up and walked forward to light a candle to the Virgin, pouring my last dime into the hope of forgiveness.

Finding my way back to the communion rail, Donnelly and I were again wedged in together. Cupping his hand to my ear, he whispered, "She's Dibella's girl." Dibella! The very name Dibella was blasphemy when spoken in a church. Mario Dibella was sixteen years old and had spent a year in juvenile hall for his many crimes. "Do you know what will happen to you if he finds out? You'll be a goner," said Donnelly, running a knifed hand over his throat. Donnelly's voice cracked with restrained laughter as he whispered again in my ear, "Be in front of the church at lunchtime." Then he left me to finish my rosary while the rest of the class whispered about my sins. When I looked to see Maria again, she was gone.

Donnelly and his friend Ronald Clancy, whom everyone called "Clank" because he sometimes used a length of bicycle chain for fighting, were waiting for me near the big wooden doors of the church when I arrive at noon. They looked around, nervously giggling as I followed them into the darkness of the empty vestibule. Clank dipped his hand into the holy water basin, made the sign of the cross, and genuflected reverently before the altar. Donnelly pushed him aside, stuck his mouth into the basin, sucked in a mouthful of holy water and spat it out at both of us, laughing like a demon. I reverently dipped my hand into the holy water, genuflected before the altar and crossed myself, fearful that I could receive some of the eternal punishment for what Donnelly had done against God.

Donnelly ordered me to follow him down the hall. The high pitch of our hard shoes on marble echoed against the stone walls as we walked to a damp and slippery wooden ladder that led to a room forty feet above us.

You had to jump high to grab the first slick rung of the

ladder and it was hard to hang on. Donnelly, who was first, made it to the top quickly. Clank, moving shakily, was next. I stuffed my lunch sack beneath my sweater and jumped for the ladder, missing the first rung twice. On the third try, I barley hung on and then began a long, hard climb. Halfway up, my arms burned and I nearly fell. My knees shook as I looked at the floor far below, frozen, unable to move up or down. "Be bold," I said aloud repeating the words Jose had taught me whenever I was afraid. I continued climbing and made the top where Clank waited, hunched over with his hand extended to pull me into the dusty light of a small, empty brick room. We were in the bell tower.

Once there, Clank took hold of the thick rope attached to the bells. He was ready to ring the bells when Donnelly knocked him to the floor and told him to sit down and shut up. I stood and moved toward the ladder hoping to escape, but Donnelly yanked me by my sweater and said, "Sit down, Jack." As I sat, he said, "Listen, Jack, we watched you today at the communion rail. I know you got big sins," he said, grabbing his crotch, laughing. "I thought you might be in the new gang." When I looked away, he punched me in the arm. Speaking louder, he said, "You know . . . a gang that makes trouble and makes money on things and does things, and a gang for people like you and me and even Clank."

"We don't want no Mexicans," said Clank, before

Donnelly slapped him across the face, and told him to shut up again. "No Mexicans, and no Indians," said Donnelly. "We don't want no queers," said Clank. Clank and Donnelly laughed as Donnelly examined my dark skin and said, "You aint no Mexican, are ya, Jack?"

He would kill me if he knew I was not only Mexican, but also part Indian. "My name is Jack Flanagan," I said, looking first at Donnelly, then at Clank. "Flanagan is Irish, pure Irish," I said, using the words my father had taught me to say whenever anyone questioned my nationality. "From the north of Ireland where the people have dark skin," I added, when he said nothing.

Donnelly stared silently at me for a long time, finally saying, "I guess Jack Flanagan ain't Mexican."

"Jack Flanagan," I repeated, nodding.

"Death to Mexicans." Donnelly spat the words into my face.

"Death to Mexicans," I repeated in fear and shame for betraying Jose and Soridtha. Giving me a playful shove toward the hole, Donnelly said, "Okay, don't fall off, Jack."

"Jack off," said Clank, and we all laughed hard. Donnelly turned to the wall and pissed on the bricks as Clank laughed and I laughed nervously. Donnelly turned around, still partially unzipped and loosened a brick in the wall. From it he took a pack of Marlboro cigarettes, a cigarette lighter, and a bottle of wine with something that looked like crackers taped to it.

He lit a cigarette and threw one to Clank and one to me. After lighting our smokes, he peeled the packet from the bottle and loosened a stack of thin white wafers that floated to the floor. "The sacred hosts," I shouted, reaching down and gathering the hosts with all that remained of my altar boy piety. To Donnelly this was nothing but dry bread and he laughed and yanked the hosts from my hand, laid one on top of another and made a little unholy sandwich that he ate in one mean bite. The hosts were just plain bread until the priest consecrated them and they became the body of Christ.

"Did you steal these from the priest's refrigerator?" I asked.

"Yeah," said Donnelly.

"These are consecrated hosts, the body of Christ. Don't eat them, or you'll be damned to hell, Donnelly."

Donnelly laughed, placed a host on his tongue and swallowed. Clank chewed a stack of hosts like potato chips. As they ate, an evil yellow light came from their eyes and into the room. Donnelly moved in close to me, his face almost touching mine. "Jack, you need to eat some of the hosts or you ain't in the gang." He held a single host out to me and I turned away from him and took a deep drag of my cigarette. "Eat one," Donnelly said, facing me and holding out a host again, daintily, in the way Father Thomas offered it at the communion rail on Sunday mornings. "You eat one or we're going to throw you down that hole," said Donnelly, pushing me toward the hole, smiling through his crooked teeth. He was crazy enough to do it. I looked away and took another drag of the cigarette.

"Jack, do you want to be in the gang, or not?" shouted Donnelly, kicking me toward the hole. He offered me a host again, and again I turned away from him without responding.

Closing my eyes I could see Jose, warning me to be bold. After another drag from the cigarette, he was gone. Then I took the wafer from Donnelly's fingers and choked it down, trembling as the Holy Eucharist entered my dark heart. I prayed for forgiveness, but could pretend nothing.

Donnelly slapped me on the back, smiled happily, and nodded his head. Clank passed the bottle, and I took a long drink, washing down my sins. Fear and joy ran through me like naked electrical wires.

A tree of knowledge grew around me, and many new things came to life on it. I saw that I was no longer under the protection of God or Jose, but something new and fierce had taken their places as my protector. I tried to pray, but could not say the words. And how could I think of God now? I had killed God and sent my grandparents to hell. I lit another cigarette and inhaled before blowing smoke into the dusty air and saying the name *Jack*. Donnelly and Clank sat in a far corner, smoking, drinking, and writing something onto a piece of binder paper. "Kill Mexicans, kill the priest," shouted Donnelly. "Kill everyone," said Clank.

Donnelly staggered from the corner and stood before me. The yellow light was strong as he held out the paper containing the gang's commandments, to me. "Listen," he said. "You have to do all the things written on this paper." He read slowly and loudly, stumbling over many of the words. "One, you must always defend the gang. Two, you must not never talk with no Mexicans, Jews, or queers. Three, you must not never tell nobody about this secret hideout. Four . . ." He quit looking at the paper and looked at me, the yellow light was almost blinding now. "You must help to kill the priest." He lowered the paper into my hand and said there were other rules, but he didn't have time to write them down. "Now, do you know the rules, Jack? The rules . . . you got to know the rules," shouted Donnelly when I didn't reply.

"Kill the priest," shouted Clank. It was quiet when I took a pen from my pocket and signed my name to the paper. Then guilt was lost in the sickness and the smoke, and Donnelly threw me yet another smoke and I lit it from the one already burning in my hand. Donnelly made the sign of the cross backward, genuflected, inhaled, and coughed, laughing hard, pretending to be a priest. He burned his commandments with his lighter, and we watched the flames like a priest watches a crucifix. Chewing the remaining hosts, he spat them onto the wall, shouting "Death to Jews. Death to Mexicans. Kill the priest. Kill the priest. Kill Mexicans. Kill the priest." Clank shouted the word death over and over as he smoked and drank without cleaning the spit from his chin. The yellow light now came also from my own eyes, illuminating a new world to me. I stamped out the fire from the burning commandments with my shoe.

When the first bell rang, signaling two minutes to class, Donnelly broke the empty wine bottle against the brick wall, stuffed the remaining hosts into the hole in the wall and covered it all with the loose brick. "Clean up this mess," demanded Donnelly, motioning to Clank. I kicked the biggest chunks of glass toward Clank with my shoe and followed Donnelly down the hole. Clank followed behind me. Guided by the yellow light in my eyes it was an easy climb, and I made the floor without any trouble.

From that day on, I climbed into the bell tower alone to smoke and drink and think about my new life. One evening, I passed out after drinking an entire bottle of the communion wine I had stolen from the church. The church was dark when I staggered down the ladder smoking a cigarette, feeling unafraid of God, Donnelly, and even Jose. I threw the empty bottle toward the altar, but it fell far short and shattered on the floor.

If I found Donnelly I would fight him. More than that, however, I wanted to find Maria Ortiz. Locating my bike, I pedaled down Whittier Boulevard as the yellow light in my eyes lit the way to the bushes, and I was barely missed by a car that honked its horn. In response, I gave the driver the finger, his frightened eyes making me glad to have attained such power. When I arrived at the bushes, I lay down and waited for Maria to walk by.

    I would jump out and take her in my arms the moment I saw her. But I was drunk, so didn't realize it was nearly midnight and I fell asleep dreaming of her. Later that night, after many good dreams, I woke in the bushes and rode home slowly through the empty streets in the light of dawn. When I arrived home, Jose was waiting for me at the table. He was not angry with me for being out all night, since he always let me do what I wanted, except in the ways of piety and boldness, where he ruled me completely. Removing my sweater gently, he brushed the dried leaves from it, saying, "Now my son is learning the ways of the devil. That is good. Everyone must learn his ways, but it is not good to stay with the devil for very long. You must fight the devil, my son, but know that he is only a cheater and will not fight fair, and maybe he will destroy you when you think you are beating him." Jose made me hot chocolate with hot pepper and a little tequila in it. After drinking it, I went to bed and dreamt of winning fights with strong men and kissing pretty women on the lips. I dreamt of more than just kissing and woke to realize no altar boy can dream such dreams.

CHAPTER SEVEN
FRUITS OF THE EARTH

The next morning, Jose drove me to school, speaking the entire time of boldness, piety, being a father and, of course, the miracle of the train. "The train came from the clouds and was shining like the sun before it hit me, and I broke into a thousand little pieces. After that, it took many beautiful women to glue me together again," he said, changing the story once again. He also talked to me about sex—not as a bad thing as most adults do, but as a gift from God and he also told me how to give pleasure to the mother of my son, which I was now ordered to name Baby Jose rather than Raphael.

As the puberty of our eighth-grade class gained power, it became a stench and an abomination to Sister Mary Bernadette. The Sister Superior stood before us like an iron door blocking the entrance to joy. While in the past we only saw her on the first Friday of each month, now she showed up in our classroom every Monday morning. One time she left the girls in the classroom and marched us boys, single-file, across the playground and down to the school hall. There, she told us to sit on the floor in three even rows of seven. She spoke sternly, trying to beat lust out of us with nothing but words, like a Dutch boy hoping to stop the ocean with only one finger.

She was angry, she said, that some of us had been in the company of girls. She warned us not to follow the girls down "the wide path," as she called it. She also warned that the evil committed in life would ruin the girl's beauty forever, and that we would be with an ugly girl for eternity. It was a good argument, but the nodding of our heads was nothing more than what a puppet does when the string is pulled. She warned that the end of the world was near, when everyone would see everything we ever did or even thought, and all our actions and our thoughts would play before all people who had ever lived, as if on television. This truly scared some of us, but not enough. When she told us to think about our sins, I tried to think and not to think of Nadie or of Maria Ortiz —a power even the Sister could not override.

I walked with Donnelly and Clank as we laughed our way back to class. Anyone who saw the rest of those fools walking slowly with their heads lowered would have thought they had been defeated by the logic of Sister Mary Bernadette that day. But her words did nothing but fuel a fire already burning in their hearts; and, while nobody had done anything with a girl, except for maybe Darryl Donnelly who claimed he had gone all the way, we had all gone crazy with lust. When the last bell finally rang, I ran to the church and climbed into the bell tower alone to smoke the two cigarettes I had taken from Jose's pack. I didn't drink any wine that night and arrived home just in time to see Jose turn over a card from the deck he always kept on the kitchen table, with one hand while eating with the other. "King of diamonds," he shouted. "A good card . . . and a king, much like I am the king of cards. I must go tomorrow night to the city and play cards for money, then we will again be rich."

Of course he told of the miracle of the train, this time saying it was talking before hitting him. "And how was your day at school today, my son?" he asked. I shrugged my shoulders silently and continued looking down, eating. Following his usual big laugh, he asked, "Are there not no pretty girls in your class that you now think only of the girls in the magazines, Jesse?" He was talking about the magazine with pictures of naked women I had taken from his room. Without looking up, I said, "My name is Jack, grandpa, not

Jesse."

I didn't even see it coming, but I felt it—the big open hand falling down on the side of my head with such force I flew from my chair and landed, hard, on the floor. Then the same big hand gently helped me back up to the table as he softly said, "A boy with a silly name like Jack can not do what you must do, my son. Now you must be Jesse and please to finish your food, *mijo*." Instead of eating, I rose from the table and stomped to the front room to sit on the couch, covering myself in a blanket and watch TV.

Jose continued eating at the table, shuffling cards and shouting, even breaking into song once in a while. After that he retired to the front room where he offered to show me a card trick he invented called the *Magic Aces*. Instead of looking I got up and turned to walk to my room as he said, "Jesse, my son, it is the cards that have brought to us all you now see." I looked around at the useless trinkets and paintings and holy and unholy statues in our home.

For the first time since living with him, I went to bed without kissing him or even saying goodnight. It was also the first time I had called him "grandpa" instead of Jose. As I lay awake, I sensed his pain as I pulled away from him and the old ways he had taught me. I didn't want to abandon Jose, but a stronger force even than him was pulling me deeper into the modern world of treachery and sin. Still, I kept my bedroom door ajar, wanting his protection as I slept. From bed, I could faintly see him beneath the light bulb in the kitchen speaking to the cards, kissing the queens and cursing the deuces and shuffling all of them together before dealing them out onto the table with joy or anger. He spoke to each card as if it were an old friend, saying, "Oh silly three of clubs, you are nearly worthless; please to stay in the deck." And, "Beautiful ace of spades, please call your three sisters to join me in my hand; I have not seen all of you together for a long time." I fell asleep to the rhythm of the cards against the hard wood of the table.

That night I dreamt I was again in the school hall with the rest of the boys in my class. Sister Bernadette spoke about girls, just as she had that day. It had come to her attention, she said, that some of the boys had been visiting girls after school, going to their houses, maybe even sneaking into their bedrooms.

In my dream, Maria Ortiz walked into the hall and sat down at the edge of the group of boys who were seated in rows, close together on the wooden floor. She raised her hand to ask, "Is it okay for a boy and a girl to have sex if they are going to be married someday?" Everyone turned to look at her and I could see up her sleeve, to the bra, as I often had the pleasure of doing in real life. When she stood up to speak, her blouse popped open along with her bra, and all of the boys quit looking at Nadie, turning to Maria Ortiz who now danced at the head of the class. Without shame, wearing a sinful smile, looking directly at me, the word sex came from her full, red lips, again and again.

Maria swayed slowly as she looked at me, and the nun moved forward and shoved her onto the floor where she stayed with her head in her hands, sobbing. Suddenly, Sister Bernadette too was topless, dancing in thin, white panties. Her breasts were smaller than Maria's but firm and as round as oranges. They did not bounce freely either, but in tight little hops as she danced for us.

Walking up to me, waving her index finger in my face, the nun sternly said, "Do not let me catch you with any girls after school or I'll give you a living doll to play with!" She brushed her breasts against my open hands, before reaching to hold my face in her long, pretty fingers. Her fingernails cut slightly into my skin in a somehow pleasant way, and she kissed me deeply on the mouth. Then she pulled away, throwing back her head, laughing, spinning, and dancing while the boys of my class rose from the floor, clapping and laughing. They balled up test papers and made paper airplanes and spitballs of homework, throwing them all around the hall. Then Jose appeared and began dancing with both Maria and Sister Bernadette. Jose then became Donnelly and he danced with Maria slowly, cheek to cheek. Donnelly held her tightly to keep her from everyone else as he looked over her shoulder at me while laughing meanly. Maria scowled at me as she danced with

Donnelly before kissing him on the mouth right in front of me. Then Donnelly became Mario Dibella who held onto Maria with one hand while the other hand flashed a bloody knife at me. When I turned to look again, I could see Jose looking small and old as he peered into the window from the outside. Most of the boys had taken off their shoes and some had taken off their shirts and pants and were dancing with each other in their underpants and socks on the wooden floor. I alone watched Sister Bernadette, who danced only for me now.

    I tried to convince myself that I was only dreaming, so I could force my dream-self to kiss her. But my legs were as heavy as lead, and I could not move from the floor. She never took her martyr's eyes off of me. Then, for the first time I saw her, really saw her. She was the most beautiful woman I had ever seen, perfect in body and face and mind. I loved Nadie more than any other woman and would watch her dance forever if I could.

    There was a sound at the hall door. When I opened the door, there, hanging by a rope, was the dead body of Father Thomas with Dibella holding the rope while Maria hung onto Dibella's neck. I awoke feeling more love and fear than I ever had before. How could I make Nadie love me?

CHAPTER EIGHT
SISTER MARY BERNADETTE

That day I volunteered to be a teacher's aid in order to work with Sister Bernadette in her office after school. There, I quietly dusted erasers, emptied wastepaper baskets, and put papers in order. I was not really there to help out, however, but to be close to her. Hoping to hide my newborn love for her, I excused myself early and biked home, glad to have been in her presence for even a few moments.

On my desk the next morning was a note saying, "For helping a teacher, you ain't in my gang no more." On the back of the paper was a drawing of a boy hanging from a rope. The name "Jack" was written above the dead boy as red ink poured from his face into a red pool as a nun stood beside him, crying. But even such a warning could not stop my love for Sister Bernadette. I would fight Donnelly, Dibella, and even Jose for her if need be. I had lost all interest in the bell tower, however, and had quit the stupid plan of waiting for Maria in the bushes. I was in love with a nun who could not love me back. With nowhere else to go, I went home directly after school.

    The evening was warm and I sat on the porch swing, rocking alongside Jose. We talked as the sun fell on the street filtered by the smoke of the cigarette he passed to me, which I inhaled before giving it back to him. We spoke of many things as the sun set, and I apologetically said, "I have decided to be Jesse again, not Jack."

    "Jose is best, and then Jesse; truly, these are the best names," he said, laughing loudly, nodding his head.

    As we moved through the warm evening air he talked about life in the city, his recent turn of good luck at cards and the many good things the Virgin had showed him at his altar. Behind his words were the sounds of crickets, frogs, doves, and the coyotes that lived on the hill, above us. Everything was good, but something was troubling Jose. "We now have a crazy man to run the town," he said, referring to Mayor Paulson, who had been elected mayor of Los Angeles several years earlier, in 1953. "Why does he now want to destroy the homes of everyone in Chavez Ravine?

Why does he want to rip out the beautiful red cars, the streetcars I put my very life into—building them and fixing them and many times riding them, even all my life? The red cars are little veins all carrying blood to the heart of the city. Even a child can see this, but not the crazy Mayor Paulson. Once this city was as good as heaven itself, but now maybe this one man will want to send everything to hell. Perhaps he is the devil, this Mayor Paulson. I will speak of him to the Virgin and to see for certain if he is the devil or not." Jose shook his head violently. It was only May and he caught an early June bug in his hand. But it was too nice a night to hurt even a bug and he let it fly back into the night.

For a while, there were no sounds but those of the little night creatures and the rusty chain of the porch swing as we continued swaying. Then Jose calmed down and asked me as he often did, "And so, Jesse, do you now have any girls that you like at the school?"

Hoping this was not yet another sex talk, I was, nonetheless, polite to him and happy, even proud, to tell him of the girl in my life. "Yes, Jose, there is a girl," I said, shyly.

"Please to tell of her," he said with a big laugh, pounding the wooden swing with the palm of his hand, straightening up as he leaned forward a little to hear about the new girl.

Then I told him her name was Nadie and all about the pretty face, the long fingers, the musical voice, and even her naked breasts I had seen in the dream when she had danced for me. He smiled and listened as I talked, clapping his hands, shouting, "Please to tell more." I told him that she was much older than me and had never been married and that I was praying for her to be my wife. "And did she take off all of her clothes, even the panties, my son?" he asked, leaning forward a little further. "No, only the top," I replied, as he sat back on the porch swing, and his big smile became a smaller smile. Then he laughed lightly and said, "It is okay, Jesse with just the top. And, who is this Nadie who dances for you and all of the boys at the school in your dreams?"

"She is Sister Mary Bernadette, the principal of the school," I said to him. For a moment, he continued laughing. When he quit laughing his mouth moved, but no sound came from it and he formed the words, "a Sister." Then came a peep from him, "A Sister." And then, a little louder, "And not just a Sister, but the highest of all of the Sisters." He dug his heels into the wooden porch to stop the swing from moving and I fell down, hard. This was not like other times when he became angry quickly and calmed down just as quickly. No, this time he became angry slowly, and I knew he would also be slow to lose the anger. "Why would you now go to find a Sister? There are very many pretty girls in the school for you, even Maria Ortiz, and still the highest Sister, the very Sister Superior is now the one you want to be in love with! It is better for you when you are in love only with the pictures!"

he said, his voice rising to the level of a train. "You must be bold, you idiot son of mine, but not with the Sisters. Never with the Sisters!" He stood and kicked the porch railing so hard it cracked one of the wooden boards. Then, turning toward me he began swearing loudly while throwing punches that landed near my head.

He began pacing the full length of the porch, stomping, swearing, and shaking as the boards vibrated beneath us. He turned his head and then rubbed his hands together, shouting to heaven, then to me, "You have cut the heart from me, and I will now not never be free of the curse." I covered my ears and lowered my head before he pulled my head up into his hands and looked at me without a word. When he let me go and took another swing with his fist, I felt the strong wind of the punch.

He stormed off to his room, shouting curses while I lay down alone on the porch swing, huddled up and crying with my head in my hands. Even from there, I could hear Jose at his altar, praying I would not be in love with Sister Mary Bernadette. He stayed at the altar long into the night, shouting, drinking, slamming his fists and breaking things on the floor, but his prayers were useless this time.

The next day at school a messenger girl delivered a note to our teacher, Sister Mary Victorine, who was an old woman nobody could be in love with. The nun called me forward, handed me the note, and told me to report to

Sister Mary Bernadette's office. As I approached the office, I heard the loud and happy voice of Jose explaining the meaning of the jack and the queen—the playing cards that lay, face up, on Sister Bernadette's desk, between her and Jose. It looked as if they were playing Black Jack, but they were not.

Jose stood up and smiled at me as I walked in. "Here, my son, you must sit next to me. I have been talking about something very important for you and your girlfriend, the Sister. She is pretty as you have said, and now I understand everything." I sat down in the chair next to him, but was too embarrassed to look up at Nadie after Jose had called her my girlfriend. Jose held up the two cards so we could see them clearly. "I was telling to the Sister what I have found in a new deck of cards today. It is a miracle, but not like the miracle of the train. Nothing is as good as that." Then he told Sister Mary Bernadette the details of the miracle of the train, this time saying that the train was the entire city that had tried to kill him. Returning to his conversation about the cards, he said, "All of the cards were in order until after the ten of hearts. Where the jack should be, there was now only a queen. And the jack, believe it or not, followed the very queen. A queen before the jack! I told many of my friends—good card players all—and nobody had ever seen such a thing before. This is a very strange miracle for me, Sister Mary Bernadette. The Sister does not know what the cards mean, but certainly you do know, my son," he said to me. I nodded my head even though I had no idea what Jose was talking about.

He continued, "An angel of God has changed the order of the cards, Sister Mary Bernadette. The jack is a lonely card and the heart is the card of passion. The queen is of course for the Holy Mother or maybe a good virgin, like you, Sister Mary Bernadette. When the Virgin first spoke to me, I thought my son had been called by God to be a lonely man and a priest, like the jack, which was his very name before it was changed back to the good name, Jesse." Jose laughed loudly and held the jack up for us to see. "Now I see what God is saying to us. Is it not clear to you also, Sister Mary Bernadette?" The nun shrugged her shoulders and Jose continued. "You, Sister Mary Bernadette, are the queen of hearts and God wants you to be married and to lie close with my son, the jack, like the jack and queen in the cards!" Jose laughed, pounded his fist on the desk and rubbed the dent on his head with his fingers. "And so I am here to convince you to be in love with this good boy who is not no more the jack, but Jesse and very kind and handsome, as you can see. I give my blessing for you to take him. The Virgin herself has given this blessing. Look, see the cards for yourself, Sister Mary Bernadette," he said, pointing to the jack and the queen lying side by side on the desk.

Jose smiled sentimentally at Nadie before he quit speaking. She sat quietly, looking first at him and then at me, as I sat, shyly. She was not shy, but said she was married to God as she touched Jose's hand softly and he moaned lowly.

"That is no problem," answered Jose. "If you are married, you can become soon unmarried. I am married every night and I become unmarried every morning." Jose was exaggerating a lot about all of his women, but the nun could see he was not going to change his mind and so she quit trying to convince him. Jose, who took her silence as her consent of marriage stood, shook her hand, and then mine. He thanked her and walked from the room humming a wedding march. She was nearly laughing before excusing me to return to class.

After class I went directly to Sister Bernadette's office and helped her clean her office as we both tried to say what we could not say. When she finally spoke to me, I discovered her more completely still. Her voice was clear and her words were music. She placed a record of Handel on her little record player, shutting her eyes in parts, breathing hard and telling me of Handel writing *Messiah* in only three weeks in a fit of passion. Passion—she knew it, and I could hear it in her voice and feel it on my skin that tingled at the thrill of the touch of her fingers when she placed them on me gently. The music played and she held my hand, eyes closed, breathing hard.

Fearful of trying more than simply holding hands, I was content until the music quit and she let go of me. As she did, she again turned into an angel of stone. I excused myself and returned to class, head down and sobbing. That night she visited my dreams where I married her at the church and Jose was the priest performing the ceremony.

School dragged by the next day until after class when I returned to her office. After we did a little work, she took the scapular from her neck and put it around mine. "Jack, please wear this scapular always. It has the blessing of Pope Pious himself and is filled with my prayers and many blessings from the saints and of God. As you know, anyone who dies wearing the scapular will go straight to heaven," she said with a sad smile.

"I'm not going to die, Sister," I said, wondering if she had actually seen something about me in the spirit world. Trembling, I removed the medal of Saint Christopher from my neck that I had worn since third grade and put it around her neck to complete the ceremony. To me, we were married before God. I kissed her on the cheek and she closed her eyes, half-smiling and sighing a little. I touched the cloth of the scapular, kissed it, put it beneath my shirt and looked up into the eyes of the Sister, hoping to see she loved me as I loved her. When the eyes told nothing, I prayed silently for a sign of her love, but still nothing appeared. I left her office feeling married but unsatisfied.

I had forgotten all other women, even Maria Ortiz. For weeks, I went to her office each day and we laughed and played little word games while inventing a language that was part English, part Latin, part nonsense and love—the love coming mostly from me. I kissed her on the cheek often and she always breathed hard, shutting her eyes and smiling gladly. When I finally had the nerve to kiss her on the mouth, she closed her eyes, still smiling. When she did not try to stop me, I threw myself on her, to kiss her again, hoping to kiss her in the way a man kisses a woman he loves. She was still for a time and then finally pushed me away tenderly.

"Jack, please stop," she said as she stood and brushed the wrinkles from her habit. "I am married to God and can have no man on earth." She said the words kindly, letting her fingers fall slowly through my hair before resting them gently on my face, looking at me. Before pulling away, she kissed my cheek and rested her hand softly on my shoulder. I looked up to see that her eyes were sadly true as mine filled with tears. I was now jealous of God, that she belonged only to Him. I would fight even the devil for her, but I could not win her from God. I was merely one of His creatures, something she stopped to touch like a flower surrounding the convent wall. I touched the scapular and prayed for my heart to stop beating so I could die.

CHAPTER NINE
THE WEIGHT OF THE CURSE

It was dark as I ran straight from Sister Bernadette's office to the empty church. In the daytime or when the church was filled with people good spirits were everywhere. At night, when the people had all gone, however, the dark spirits moved freely.

The only light in the church came from the rows of small white candles burning to a statue of the Virgin on my side of the altar and a statue of The Holy Family on the other side. At first I was quiet and scared, but soon I was angry and bold, screaming out to God. But these prayers never did go to heaven. Instead, they were blocked by the evil spirits crowding the church just as Jose said they would be after dark. Fear shot through me like the arrows that pierced the flesh of Saint Sebastian. Repenting of my cursing, I walked forward, put a dime into the offering box, lit a candle and returned to the rail, where I cried into my hands. "Please, I will show her the love of heaven all the days of my life," I said, lifting my eyes to the Virgin's statue.

"Sin of lust, sin of lying, sin of fear, sin of drunkenness, sin of smoking—all sin, be no more," I shouted again and again, praying and fighting the evil spirits. A dark and evil spirit, twice the size of a man rose from the floor behind the altar and floated forward and pressed my face onto the hard marble floor. I fought him by promising God, my God, the spirit's God and master that I would be holy; I would be good; I would be Jesse; I would be bold. When I prayed in the name of Jesus, the spirit let me up and retreated to the corner behind the Virgin's statue.

I knelt before the Virgin until my knees hurt, leaning down, beating the floor with my fists and then with my head. A little sliver of light illuminated the white marble body of Christ hanging on the large cross, dead white, above the church altar. The light was coming from heaven as a miracle and an answer to my prayers. I was saved. She would be mine forever. Then, slowly, the cross fell again into darkness and I heard the shoes of a girl of earth walking quickly, sadly to the rail. I cursed the darkness by name and continued praying, not looking to see her approach.

Forgiveness and joy had fallen from heaven and then were replaced by another type of joy in seeing the silhouette of Maria Ortiz. Then, I thought perhaps this was not really Maria Ortiz, but the very daughter of the devil himself appearing in the form of a woman the way the nuns had told us the devil would sometimes do to trick and to tempt us. The voices of many demons screamed in the church now. They flew fast as lightning, swooping down near me, in the dark. The voice of Jose could also be heard, shouting against the demons, saying that I must remain pure and bold. There was also a small still voice I knew to be true, telling me not to move, but to continue praying.

The large devil that had been peeking out from behind the statue now flew to Maria Ortiz where it shrunk down small and entered between her folded hands. I barely had the strength to fight against the power of the evil sprit or see beyond it into the spirits of goodness and light. I knelt and watched, waiting to see if my prayers would make the evil spirit disappear or catch fire. Perhaps this was not really Maria Ortiz I was looking at. The knife of lust was cutting deep now, attempting to break free from the ropes of faith and goodness.

The devil pretending to be Maria Ortiz continued crying and praying out loud, saying, "Our Father, which art in heaven, hallowed be thy name . . . " After the Lord's Prayer, the devil said other prayers, using the name of God and Jesus and Mary. Then I realized no devil could call upon these names and live. When I knew Maria Ortiz had not been possessed by the devil, my thoughts turned to compassion, enough compassion to please even God Himself. My heart was good then and my hope was only to lift her from her deep sadness. With the purest of intentions, I continued watching her and praying for her. At first, the gates in the dark part of my heart were opened just a crack. But this was enough for lust to squeeze in, open the gate wide, and pour in like a flood. The knife of lust struck quickly, nearly killing faith, shoving it into the same dark corner where lust itself had been, not at all dead as I had thought, but gaining quiet strength, waiting to break free and pounce upon me. Soon lust was as big as faith had been moments earlier, and faith had become as small as lust had been while it was hiding undetected in a corner of my soul. All I wanted now was to go to Maria as she knelt, unaware of me, crying at the communion rail before the Virgin.

Maria prayed for a long time, then took a few coins and a pen and paper from her purse. She wrote something on the paper that she dropped into the offering box along with the coins before Our Lady's statue. Then she walked forward, lit two tall candles, and walked back to the rail to cry and pray a little longer. When I ceased praying, the spirit of lust rose up so fast it blew out the holy candles and swooped down upon me, smothering all remaining goodness.

Again one of the big front doors to the church swung open, this time wide and without effort, announcing with a broad shaft of light on the crucifix that a man or a nun had arrived. Maria turned to face the source of the light and I followed her gaze to see it was indeed a man her dark eyes fell upon. He was tall and he stood, slumped against the doorpost with the door slightly ajar. Then he flicked a lighter to light a cigarette and I could see him clearly. Dibella! He was smoking, right in church! Maria rose from her knees, running to him and hanging herself by her arms around his neck like a golden crucifix dangling from a chain. He kissed her on the mouth. They put their arms around each other and left the church. The door closed and everything went as dark as death while the spirits attacked me with full force.

I was bold then but (may the Virgin forgive me) I needed to know what Maria had written on the paper. I tried pulling against the lock on the offering box, but that was no use. Next, I attempted putting my fingers into the box to retrieve the paper, but the slot was too narrow. I tried prying the box open with my fingers, scraping them against the wood until they bled. The box was well made and didn't budge, no matter how I pushed against it. Removing one of my shoes, I hit the box with the hard leather heel. Again and again I hit the box until there was a crack large enough to force my fingers into.

Sifting through the sanctified mountain of nickels, dimes, and quarters until I touched the paper note, which I pulled from the box. Some of the coins bounced on the floor as I unfolded the note and, by the light of the candles that magically relit themselves, read, "Dear Mary, Mother of God, please protect me." It was signed Maria Ortiz.

I stuffed the note into my pocket and I ran from the church to see Maria and Mario together, now small in the distance, moving slowly down the maple-lined street, visible beneath the street lights.

Mario was balanced, pedaling easily on the bike, while Maria walked beside him like an obedient dog. I ran to the bike rack, mounted my bike, and pedaled fast until I was close enough to see them clearly, but not so close I would be caught spying. When they stopped at the curb, I too stopped and hid behind one of the trees lining the block. Thinking nobody was watching, he put his hands up under her blouse, pulling up her bra and kissing her on the breast. She dropped her schoolbooks onto the sidewalk, and I watched in pleasure and horror. The twin demons of fear and lust had followed me from the church, and so I tried to lose them by frantically pedaling home, sweating and shaking, but too bold to cry.

The next day was Friday and I sat at my school desk like a dead man. I ate nothing and played no games at recess. Only when I was summoned to Sister Bernadette's office did I feel better. As I entered, sweaty and panting from running there, she was seated behind her desk, looking more beautiful even than the statue of Our Lady from the night before. I sat down and lowered my eyes, ashamed that I had run from her, crying the day before. Silently, she stood, reached out and raised my head with her hands until I was forced to look up into her pretty, grey eyes. I wished I could be held in those hands forever, but she soon let go and said, "Jack, I am sorry. I did not want to hurt you. You know that, don't you, Jack?" I didn't correct her for calling me Jack because it no longer mattered who I was. She tried to meet my eyes as she spoke, but I turned away. The angel's voice was sweet as honey, and I nodded before dropping my head again, hoping she would touch my face once more, which she did not do. Instead she reached out and held my bandaged fingers tenderly in a way I loved. "Did you do it, Jack?" she asked.

"Yes, Sister," I replied softly, knowing she meant my breaking into the collection box. I lowered my head, hoping to obtain her pity and her touch. I looked at her closely, and I think I saw love in her eyes this time. Soon, however, she turned from an angel of flesh into a cold school principal, a nun, strict and hard. "Are you feeling okay, Jack," she asked, touching my forehead with the back of her hand in the cold way a nurse feels for a fever. "Jack, we can be friends," she said. Tears again filled my eyes and I ran from the office and down the hall, trying to hide from everybody.

The school day passed like a black mass. After school, Donnelly and Clank were waiting for me at the bicycle rack. I mounted my bike and Donnelly blocked my way, straddling his bike, poking me with his finger and trying to knock the books from under my arm. "You're dead, Jack," he said. "Dead," repeated Clank. Donnelly tried to push me down. Instead, I pushed back at him and he wobbled then hit the ground hard, giving me a head start on him and Clank. I rode fast, but Donnelly was soon on my back wheel, followed by Clank.

Donnelly's front wheel rubbed against my back wheel as I rode. I knew if I slowed down he would catch me. I pedaled harder; but, no matter how I tried, I remained only inches ahead of him. When I arrived at the fence in front of our house, I hit the brakes and Donnelly flew past before falling from his bike a few feet beyond me. Clank, who was right behind him, nearly ran him over. I pulled my bike behind the fence as Donnelly got up and he and Clank circled back and faced me from the sidewalk. Donnelly was yelling out that he would kill me, and Clank repeated every word.

I ran up the steps of the wooden porch just as Jose opened the screen door. They were about to enter the yard when they were halted by the anger burning in Jose's eyes.

He flicked the cigarette he was smoking at Donnelly and it stuck in a crease of his white school uniform shirt for a moment, burning a little hole there before rolling down onto the ground. Jose said nothing, and they were wise to stay where they were. Slowly, they backed away, keeping their eyes on Jose, the way you would from a wild animal. They mounted their bikes and pedaled back down the street, riding hard and screaming the words "Mexican" and "dead man." When they were out of sight, Jose put an arm around me and we walked silently into the house. He didn't speak, but slumped low on the couch and said nothing for a long time. Even though it was Friday evening and we usually went to the Plaza to eat and have fun and find a card game, he fell asleep on the couch without saying a word or making dinner.

    I went to bed and didn't wake again until noon, finding Jose sitting at the kitchen table, looking sorrowfully at the cartoon he had cut out of L'il Abner and at the playing cards spread before him. He had been seated in the same place, for once praying quietly, drinking, smoking, and cutting cards. He shuffled and reshuffled, playing solitaire before dealing out two hands of poker to himself. He flipped a card from the deck, but did not smile or laugh, even if that card was an ace, though it never was. I was not hungry, but he silently made chorizo and eggs, and ate a few small bites at the table while he turned cards with one hand. The eggs had no salt in them and I was reminded of what he always said, "Too much salt means you are happy. Too little salt means you are sad. No salt means you will soon die." He continued staring into the cards, wondering where their magic had gone.

Jose grew more and more sad, drifting about the house, smoking long into the evening, never eating, talking, and only occasionally taking a shot of tequila or going to his altar to seek a sign. I stayed indoors all that weekend, even missing church. I needed to let my heart mend, to take care of Jose, and to keep clear of Donnelly. One night after dinner, when he had eaten only enough for a small bird, Jose told me his troubles. "I have now lost the house to Julio," was all he said. Julio was a known cheater that everybody called "the Shark."

Julio had often come to the house for Sunday dinner, sometimes staying over night on the couch, eating all of the hot chilies from the jar, drinking Jose's tequila from the bottle, and playing cards, sometimes winning, but mostly losing and laughing with Jose and the Friends. Julio often owed us more than he could pay, and Jose always burned Julio's notes where he had promised to pay as much as five hundred dollars to us. Jose did not want Julio's money; he was our friend. But now it was Jose who owed Julio, and Julio would collect.

It happened on a hand where Jose had a full house

of aces over jacks and thought he could not lose, but Julio cheated and pulled up four fives. Jose had foolishly put up the house and a thousand dollars against only a few hundred dollars by Julio. Jose was sad about the loss, but what could he do? He was a man of honor and a man of his word, and we would have to leave the house he had built with his own hands. Bad luck had come to us because of my sins.

CHAPTER TEN
KILL THE PRIEST

For three weeks in a row, Jose didn't even get out of bed until after noon. Then he just hung around the house in his long underwear, without shaving, his hair a tangled mess. All he did was sit and stare for long hours, occasionally holding a picture of Soridtha, crying while looking at it, once saying, "Please come to me now, *mi Magia;* only you can save me." He avoided me completely, and when I asked him a question once, he simply looked straight ahead, saying, "I think a cockroach is now speaking to me." Then he ground his heel into the floor like he was smashing a cockroach.

After three weeks, I could no longer stand the

deadness of our lives and I decided to approach Father Thomas. Maybe he could be persuaded to help save us and our house by praying for us and, maybe saying an entire mass. Prior to this day I had only spoken a few words to Father Thomas in the confessional where there was a dark curtain between him and my sins.

He was a Catholic priest and a holy man, at least when he was being a priest. When he was at our home with Jose, however, he was not so holy. Once I saw him play cards with Jose, losing ten dollars in just one minute. He had crossed himself, hoping to win; but, he still lost, and then he cursed and took a shot of the tequila Jose offered him. Of course Jose gave the priest his money back along with another shot of tequila, which the priest gladly drank. Recently, I had seen him walking with his head down, mumbling to himself as he passed slowly through the schoolyard, sometimes shouting to nobody and swatting hard at the air as if he were hitting at the devil himself.

It was a clear and warm Saturday morning when I awoke and told Jose I was going to see the priest. Jose had recovered some of his joy by then, but not all of it. He simply nodded his head and watched as I walked outside and rode the mile to Saint Veronica's.

When I knocked at the door of the rectory, he answered instantly. He was scowling and wearing his black priest clothes—the small square of white gleaming in his otherwise perfectly black shirt and black socks without shoes. His hands hung straight at his sides and the scowl never left his gray face.

I had stood near Father Thomas before when I served mass for him or when he was at our house, but I had never really looked at him. Now I could clearly see the thin red lines covering his cheeks and nose, rivulets of blue running all through his forehead even into his eyelids, and the watery whites of half-closed eyes. Now, too, I noticed much gray hair growing from the black dyed hair that covered his wide head.

When he opened his mouth in wonder, he smelled of cigars and communion wine. He was maybe a little drunk and we both knew it was a sin for me to see a priest like this. I looked into his lifeless eyes then looked away, down to the red brick steps. Speaking softly and shyly about saving the house, he let me mumble for a while before interrupting.

"What? Speak up, boy; I can't hear you." He grabbed my head and lifted it with his puffy hands, forcing me to endure the venial sin of the raw, red eyes. He was like a man waking from sleep. "Jose's boy, the altar boy," he said with a little anger, as if he had not been holding my face or listening to me, or even seeing me standing there at his door, until now. There was a little smile of respect for Jose, I thought—but soon the cold scowl returned. "What do you want, Jose's boy?"

I told the priest everything as he listened quietly, leaning forward and then against the doorpost with a joyful expression on his face. He knew Jose had helped build the church, given much money and had helped out in many other ways. I was sure he would say at least one rosary for us, maybe even an entire mass. If he said the mass, everything would be good again, for I knew that when even when a bad priest prayed, God must listen to him. When I finished the story, he said nothing. Then he smiled so brightly I thought he was going to laugh. But he did not laugh. He only spoke hard words that did not fit with the smile.

"For many years now I have told Jose that he must repent of his sins. Now those sins will take him down to . . . ," and the priest, growing loud, looked away from me. He was scowling again and he looked directly into my eyes. "You want prayers for your grandfather, boy?" he asked, saying the words with the little smile that had returned.

"Yes, Father," I replied shyly, my hands and knees shaking a little, nodding my head.

"Should I pray for a man who has called a priest half of a man? Should I pray for a man who lives the life of the devil on earth each day, so he might go to heaven forever and live with the angels and the saints of God? What do you think? Would God honor such a prayer, even from a priest, altar boy? Jose's boy, answer me." He was shouting.

When he stopped accusing Jose, I replied to him

boldly. "Father," I said, unable to look at him again, "maybe you can pray that Jose will turn away from the little devil he has, and then later, when he does this, you can pray we will keep our house. Jose is a good man, carrying some sins, true. I know this, but . . ."

"I will pray for your grandfather," said the priest loudly, and my hopes of keeping the house rose. "I will pray for him, but only if he comes to me himself and kneels here on my steps and tells me himself he has quit living the life of a devil and that I am not a half man." He laughed a little. Then I heard a dull clicking sound and I turned to see a lead pellet bounce off the rectory's brick wall and land a few feet away from us. Two more shots were fired and I ducked low.

Kneeling at his feet, my hands covering my head, I looked up and yelled, "Duck down, Father, they are trying to kill you." I knew that a pellet could not really kill a man and especially not a priest, but only cause bleeding and pain. Still, because of the house, I did not want to take any chances. Another shot hit the brick porch close to his foot, but the priest continued speaking before bending down to pick up the pellet, examining it. He threw the pellet onto the ground as another pellet bounced off the brick, near his head. He didn't realize what was happening. He looked at me crouched near his feet with my hands over my head as protection against the pellets. Thinking I was begging his blessing, he made the sign of the cross and prayed some

Latin words. Then, as quickly as he had opened the door for me, it was slammed shut and I was left alone at the rectory door while somebody continued shooting at me from the roof of the church. I looked up to see the tip of the rifle and Darryl Donnelly's blond hair, before he peeked out from behind the peak of the church roof with his pellet gun. Donnelly pulled the gun to himself, and I heard him pumping it so he could fire at me again. The pumping gave me just enough time to mount my bike and begin racing home. Once Donnelly had the rifle pumped and reloaded, the pellets flew again, falling near me at first, and then farther and farther behind me, until they quit coming altogether.

When I arrived home, Jose was at the dining table dealing hands of poker to himself with half a bottle of beer in front of him. He had changed out of his underclothes and was dressed in khakis and a white undershirt, wearing socks without shoes. He pulled a card from the deck: the ten of clubs. Holding up the ten to me, he nodded, "Only last week, I could hardly get nothing bigger than a five. Soon now I will be pulling up aces again and then things will be good for us, my son."

"Jose, I saw Father Thomas today," I said. He slapped the cards onto the table, saying, "That is good, my son. And what did the Father Thomas tell to you when you told him that you yourself were going to be a priest like him, only better than him, because he is not such a good priest all the time? Of course when you told him, he prayed for us and the cards went from fives to tens. He is a good friend to us, the priest Father Thomas and soon he will be praying more and we will get the house back." Jose laughed and held me close to him, but I didn't tell him what the priest had said. I knew he would not kneel before him or any other man. And I didn't tell him about Darryl Donnelly shooting at us.

On the following Sunday, I went to the church and acted as if nothing had happened as I prepared to serve High Mass with Father Thomas. I changed into my white satin robe while he laid out his beautiful gold and purple vestments, kissing the polished pieces of cloth one at a time as he placed them on the table before him. He never looked at me; but, he mumbled some angry words I could not understand, only once speaking clearly as if I were not there, saying to nobody, "I hope the boy does not drop a host and that he will fill the chalice to the top with wine." He returned to mumbling as he kissed the vestments and put them on one at a time. Then, I thought (Father forgive me) that he was a stupid priest and I wished Darryl Donnelly had shot him and wounded him, but not killed him. Maybe Donnelly would poison the wine so the priest would die at the altar. But this was too good for a bad priest to die in a place where all priests hope to die.

Father Thomas did not look at me as I served the mass, but he would bump the chalice against the cut glass cruet to indicate that I should fill the chalice to the top with wine if I quit pouring before the cup was full. After drinking the wine, I watched the priest closely to see if Donnelly had poisoned the wine, but Father Thomas remained alive.

A week later, our class was out playing kickball at recess when the game stopped in response to the sounds of a siren on school property. We watched as the ambulance parked in front of the rectory door, the lights flashing and the siren still blaring. Moving in closer, we could see three other priests from the rectory watching while the men from the ambulance took the lifeless body of Father Thomas away on a stretcher. If he were dead, the hope of keeping the house would also die. I tried to pray for him to live, but was unable to say even one Hail Mary for Father Thomas.

Donnelly and Clank shouted evil prayers, making their typical sign of the cross in reverse, trying to damn Father Thomas to hell as he was rolled away. Not everyone in the class had been afraid of them before, but now fear fell on everybody in the schoolyard and we gazed at the devils that had caused the priest to die. When I looked to Donnelly he formed an upside down cross with his fingers mouthing the word, "Die."

Hours later, back in class we heard the crackling electric voice of Sister Mary Bernadette come through the wooden speaker that hung over the chalkboard. Her voice was stern, calling the entire school together for an assembly in the schoolyard.

We were marched back onto the playground where Sister Mary Bernadette seemed to disappear against the black asphalt as she paced the yard and tried to be heard through her little megaphone. She ordered us to march into the church to pray for Father Thomas who had suffered a stroke, which she explained was like a heart attack. We filed into the church, the younger students first in the back, all the way up to the eighth grade class in the front, closest to the altar. Hundreds of us were packed in tightly, and Sister Bernadette stood before us, telling us to say at least one decade of the rosary each for the recovery of Father Thomas.

I knelt in the pew but was still unable to pray for the priest. Donnelly and Clank sat behind me, praying to Satan for the priest to die. I held my rosary tightly and tried to pray again, but no matter how I tried, the words would not come out. Some of the girls made up for this by praying hard and crying. Rows of students went forward to light candles to the Virgin and to the Holy Family until all of the candles on both sides of the church were ablaze. A lot of money was dropped into the slot of the new, solid metal offering box that day.

The many rows of candles and the prayers of students, of priests, of the Sisters, and of all the people in the parish would certainly help Father Thomas to live. For this, I was glad, since maybe the priest's heart would be softened and he would say prayers and maybe an entire mass for us to keep the house when he recovered from the stroke. I stared across the aisle at Maria Ortiz, again trying to pry into her mind, hoping she would turn to see me, but she never did.

In a few days, the entire school was again called to assemble on the playground. Then Sister Bernadette spoke through the megaphone to say that God had heard our prayers and Father Thomas did not die and would be back at the rectory within a few weeks. Her loveless eyes accused me before she said the priest had lost the use of his right arm. Then I knew that she knew I had not prayed. Everything in the priest's body, except the arm, which I alone was meant to pray for, had been healed.

I lowered my head, reached into my sweater pocket for my rosary and silently started a decade of the rosary for Father Thomas as I stood on the playground. Even an entire rosary said in the heat of the day was not enough now, however, and I soon believed the arm of Father Thomas would never rise again. Many in our class believed Donnelly's curse had caused the crippling stroke, and he gained control over them because of this. Back in the classroom, Donnelly drew pictures of Sister Mary Bernadette and Sister Mary Ignatius, both naked and dead. When nothing else happened to anyone, some realize that Donnelly had no special powers. Still, many continued to fear him.

At home, Jose carved a tiny wooden arm, drilled a little hole in it, put a string through it, and placed it around the neck of the Virgin. The arm joined numerous other tiny arms, legs and heads made by Jose, which he hung from the Virgin's neck. Jose cut himself on the forearm with his pocketknife and covered the little wooden arm for Father Thomas with the sacrifice of his own blood.

I didn't want to beg Father Thomas to pray for us, but what else could I do? He had returned from the hospital and was our final hope for a miracle. I again rode my bike to the rectory to speak with him about the house and to tell him about Donnelly's plan to kill him. Leaning my bike against the church wall, I walked up to the rectory window, and through an open door could see right into his bedroom. I was close enough to see the grey and black bristles of hair standing up on the back of the father's neck as he stood up tall and proud.

I pulled up one of the loose bricks that bordered the flowerbeds around the rectory and stood on it. Then I could clearly see Father Thomas looking into a mirror, holding a large wineglass in the one good hand, raising it up over his head in the same way he would lift the chalice while saying the mass. He must have been weak because the hand shook, unassisted by his other hand, and the wine spilled from the glass, with drops wetting the priest's face and splashing onto his clothes. The priest cursed loudly before throwing the glass against the wall with his good arm. The glass did not break, but was followed by many loud curses, and I turned and pedaled home quickly.

It had been nearly three months since Father Thomas worked as a priest, and now he was coming back to serve a High Mass; and I was scheduled to be one of his altar boys. Everyone would be there to see the return of the priest, but I was worried he would be unable to lift the metal chalice over his head without spilling the consecrated wine, the blood of Christ, onto the floor. This would be worse for him even than the stroke had been, since he would be finished as a priest if he spilled the holy blood.

The practice in the mirror paid off, however, and each time I rang the cluster of bells, he lifted the chalice smoothly with the one good arm, far over his head without spilling a drop. All through the mass you could hear Jose beating his breast loudly from the front row of the church.

This was a good and holy day for everyone at Saint Veronica's, and many prayers were answered at this time. Everyone was glad about the arm, but not many days later came the time for Father Thomas to give the benediction, which is a time of blessing to the congregation, and a time when the monstrance is lifted. Again, I was scheduled to be his altar boy and was worried because, compared to the chalice, the monstrance—a big cross of gold with jewels surrounding a little glass window showing the Sacred Host—was very heavy. I did not think Father Thomas could lift the monstrance, and I knew he must not drop it. To do so would be to nail our Lord to the cross all over again. Then he would not only be forever finished as a priest, but I would be finished as an altar boy and perhaps suffer the eternal fires, burning along side him and Jose, listening to them arguing forever.

On the day of the benediction, everyone from the parish including Jose and the Four Friends and many of the women from downtown came to the church to see the raising of the monstrance. I had fasted during lunch and prayed the entire day for a miracle, but I still thought I should be at the priest's side to see he did not drop the holy cross and destroy us. When the time came, I rang the bells and then ran up the altar steps quietly with the bells cupped and silent in my hand, ready to ring them again when it was time. I stood near Father Thomas, ready, watching and praying as the time came for him to lift the monstrance.

Without moving his head, he shifted his eyes to me, and whispered angrily, "Get back on the steps and ring the bells." Returning to the foot of the steps, I knelt down. Then, at the right time, I rang the bells, closing my eyes while praying silently that the heavy cross would not fall from the priest's hand. But I had to look, and as the bells rang out, Father Thomas raised the monstrance high, like a sword, with his arm above his head with no shaking of the arm at all. Jose stood up on the pew, beating hard upon his chest, clapping and shouting for joy. Then the Four Friends and all of the women and some children stood, cheering and clapping their hands. Soon everyone in the church was clapping loudly, and I alone could see Father Thomas' proud little smile.

After the benediction everybody said the lifting of the monstrance was a miracle. But I knew this miracle had been aided by the priest lifting heavy weights to strengthen his good arm. Jose was as happy as anyone for "the miracle of the arm," as he called it, even though the priest would not help us to have a miracle of our own. And with no miracle there would be no house and no hope of heaven for Jose.

But we did have a miracle. He had been praying to the Virgin about the return of Soridtha when I heard him shout joyfully from his altar, "Yes, Good Mother, I thank you. She is now coming home soon." And, there she was at our door the very next morning, holding a small black leather bag like a doctor carried. There were pieces of paper pinned to her worn-out dress and her long, black and now silver-streaked hair. Upon closer examination the papers she wore were the letters from Jose, maybe a hundred of them from L'il Abner cartoons to news stories and even ads for kitchen appliances.

She was as still as stone as he shouted for joy and lifted her in his arms to the bedroom, where they did not come out except for meals for over a week. Things were back to normal, except for Jose who promised never to have sex with another woman. There was a three-day fiesta and people from all over the city crowded into the house and spilled into the street to eat and drink and dance in celebration of Soridtha's return.

CHAPTER ELEVEN
HENRY

Depending on who you asked, Chavez Ravine was either a poor person's Shangri-La or a dump. To the hundreds of poor families who lived there, clustered together on the edge of the dream of Los Angeles, however, it was home.

It was nearly Christmas as Jose drove down the bumpy, mud-slick road of the Chavez Ravine community called La Loma, passing all the altars of the Virgin or the Holy Family in the neighborhoods that were decorated with brightly colored paper and ornaments as the joyful glow of Christmas shone out from almost every window. Soridtha huddled next to Jose as I rode in the back seat, laughing while watching children slip and slide and sometimes fall while trying to catch our car. You see, they knew that, Christmas or not, Jose and Soridtha always arrived with gifts, and so they poured from their homes, running and shouting as they tried to be first in line after the car stopped. Only moments after we skidded to a stop before the lime green house with the life-sized, hand-carved nativity scene out front, there were more than a dozen children surrounding us, waiting for Jose to dispense candy and toys from the sack he had with him. I didn't know any of these children by name, so I stayed in the car, shyly peeking through the mud-spattered windows. Jose acted like Santa Claus to the children; the men were nowhere in sight, and the women all ran out to see Soridtha, frantic for her advice. She had proven herself with good advice in the past and was nearly legendary among the older citizens of Chavez Ravine for her ability to see the future and solve problems.

When the gifts were finally distributed and the children quit fighting over them, I could hear the piercing voices of the women shouting.

"They are stealing our homes," yelled one, who pushed her way past the other dozen or so crowded around Soridtha.

"I will shoot them if they try to make us move," screamed another, looking to Soridtha while moving her finger like a pistol.

"They can take my house over my dead body," shouted still another.

At first I had no idea what they were talking about, but it soon became clear to me that the entire community of Chavez Ravine was under threat of destruction. Someone said it was for new, low-income housing that the citizens of Chavez Ravine themselves supposedly could buy. Someone else said they heard it was for a new baseball stadium for the Brooklyn Dodgers.

Jose, who at first was ready to fight to help the people save their homes, became conflicted when the woman mentioned the Dodgers. You see, each time the team played he listened to them on the radio, praying loudly and counting off rosary beads for Duke Snider, Gil Hodges, and Jackie Robinson who led the mighty Dodgers in winning game after game. To him, these men were not mere baseball players, but saints who preformed miracles. Unsure of which side to take, Jose was silent on a matter of importance, for once. Soridtha, who had not spoken a word the entire two months she had been home, was also silent at first.

A woman held up the *Times* for Soridtha to read. The paper was printed in English, which all of the women could speak, but few had yet to learn to read. Since Soridtha could not read in any language, she waved me over to read for her. It was dead quiet as I walked from the car to the center of the muddy road to read the story and confirm the rumor of the sale of the land beneath us. There was a term I did not know called *eminent domain*, which I later learned meant the government could take your land if it was proven helpful to the majority of citizens. As I finished reading, I looked to Soridtha to see all the anger from generations of betrayal rising up into her fierce Indian eyes. I had seen that look in her before and had no doubt she would fight to the death to protect these people and their homes.

I had not heard her say more than a few words for years, and at times wondered if she could still speak. But now the women were gathered, waiting for her to tell them what to do. Soridtha had not spoken for so long that at first her halting Spanish sounded creaky like a frog, if a frog could whisper. Within minutes, however, she was speaking in a normal tone of voice. Several minutes later she was screaming and telling the women they must fight to the death to save their homes. She concluded by telling them to gather at the Housing Authority of Los Angeles building on Wilshire Boulevard early the next day.

The green house where we had parked belonged to Mr. and Mrs. Ochoa, friends of Jose and Soridtha. After coming inside for dinner and a few beers, Jose and Soridtha spent that night in the house and I spent a warm and comfortable night alone in the car.

Over fifty women attended the protest from Chavez Ravine the next morning. Most of them carried the signs I had hand-lettered in Spanish and in English demanding Chavez Ravine be spared from destruction. Soridtha led the pack, shouting and marching. Once again she was the fierce wolf of the Plaza that Jose had fallen in love with.

Jose, who had driven Soridtha and some of the women to the building, did not attend the rally, and neither did the newspapers or the television stations. They had been alerted by phone by one of the women in the crowd, but nobody from the media showed up. Instead they were attending a news conference inside the Housing Authority building where men in suits told reporters that the slum known as Chavez Ravine was about to be improved and that the poor living there would be given their choice of the beautiful new homes they were calling Elysian Heights Park. The women from Chavez Ravine who stood on the other side of the lie shouted as loudly as possible to anyone who would hear them. But no matter how they protested, nobody really heard them and their petitions were blown away like Los Angeles dust.

Mr. and Mrs. Ochoa were glad to share their house with us, and they loved showing it off, since they had just finished paying Mr. Wheat, the landlord and owner of much of La Loma, the $450 for the house. While the Ochoa's always enjoyed being with Jose and Soridtha, they especially liked having me around because they were elderly and had no children of their own. I had two weeks off from school for Christmas, and Mr. Ochoa asked Jose if I could stay with them during my vacation. It was agreed and I spent the entire time there as if it were my own home.

All day and long and into the evenings I would roam the neighborhoods of Chavez Ravine, meeting interesting people and playing games with the children. This place was not filthy and filled with rats and criminals as the newspapers said; it was clean, and people took pride in their homes. To me, it was the safest place in the world. No matter what part of the community you were in people looked out for you.

I awoke one Saturday morning to the sound of Mr. Ochoa chopping firewood in the backyard. I was still in my pajamas, watching the dew drops evaporate on the windows as the morning sky turned from pink to blue to gray as the smoke rose from the incinerators that every house had for burning trash in those days. Even before I heard the horn and rattle of the vegetable truck I knew it was coming by the way all the women stood at the curb, huddled close together, clutching their hard-earned money.

Like almost everyone in the Chavez Ravine, the Ochoa's grew their own vegetables and raised chickens. They even drank milk from their own cow, so Mrs. Ochoa rarely went to the truck for anything. Still, if you wanted something special it must come from the truck. I stood in line with the women to buy a big slice of watermelon with the dime Mr. Ochoa had given me. After the truck left, I sat on the wooden porch, slicing pieces of watermelon into squares with my jackknife, eating only the sweet center, spitting out the seeds, and throwing the rest of the fruit in the dirt for the chickens to fight over.

Suddenly a loud cry came from the street and I ran out to see what was happening. The cry was coming from the old haunted house, three houses away, and I was there quickly, hoping to see a ghost in broad daylight when they could not hurt you. There, standing in front of the little wooden house was a boy of my size and age, and a much smaller girl—whose age I would guess at eight—crying hard and grabbing for something the boy would not give her.

Only two days earlier, I had seen the old rusty truck banging its way down the street while the springs squeaked at every bump in the road. Mattresses, tables, and chairs were stacked high in the truck's bed while pots and pans rattled against the wooden stakes. A Mexican family consisting of a man, a woman, and a very old woman, rode, crowded tightly together in the front seat of the truck, while the boy and girl rode in the back, laughing and bouncing between the soft mattresses. The children jumped from the truck even before it quit rolling on the hard dirt driveway. Then they ran around on the dirt and tall weeds of the front yard, yelling, looking at everything, and touching the cracked white paint. I think somebody had cheated them into buying a house when they knew it was soon going to be bulldozed.

    The man walked around to the passenger door, opened it, and lifted a short, round old woman from the truck. After bringing her gently to the ground, he pulled the thin, younger woman from the truck, carrying her and spinning her over the dirt and the weeds to the front door of the house, which he opened with one hand without ever putting her down. You could hear the joy of the children and their parents as they unpacked their things and moved into the old house.

    The next day, I watched the boy paint the dry wood of the haunted house's rickety wooden fence. When his work was done, he ran up the hill behind the street we were living on. I had never been on the hill myself because Mr. Ochoa and also Jose had told me not to go there. Later that day, the boy returned and I could see him and his little sister clearly for the first time. They were small, dark Mexicans sometimes called *cholos* by other Mexicans like me who had been born in Los Angeles or who had lived there longer than the newest immigrants.

    When I walked over to meet the boy, he smiled, shook my hand, and said, "My name is Henry Davis; who are you?" He spoke good enough English for anyone to understand, but you could tell he was from Mexico by the way he made "you" sound like *zhoo*. Mr. Ochoa had said the boy's name was Raphael Dominguez and he had come with his family from a small town in Oaxaca, Mexico. He was friendly with a wide, mud-red face. Mr. Ochoa had explained the redness was because his family was not only Mexican, but also Indian. Henry smiled widely, showing straight, white teeth.

"My name is Jesse," I said, shaking his dusty hand. He had been taught English by the nuns at school, in Oaxaca. "I am an American citizen and can recite the pledge," Henry boasted, standing straight, putting his hand over his heart and saying, "I pledge allegiance to the flag . . . ," before I stopped him from saying it all.

The girl, who had come onto the street again, was his sister, Lupita. Henry smiled, reached into his pocket, and pulled out two sticks of candy. One he handed to Lupita and one to me. I put the unwrapped peppermint stick in my pocket for later. She put hers directly into her mouth and walked into the house, petting her doll and looking back fondly at Henry. "Follow me, Jesse, and I will show you something good to do," said Henry, motioning to the hill.

While he had only been to the hill himself once, he spoke like he had lived there all his life. Not being allowed to go to the hill, I tried to convince Henry to come to my house instead. But when Henry told me of the many wonderful second-hand stories about the hill, I was convinced to see it just once. I made the sign of the cross and (Father forgive me) followed him up the worn out path past thick patches of cactus.

Clotheslines were strung between trees with clothes waving like colorful flags in the wind. Between the houses were fields of yellow flowers and short green grass and a few withered trees with little wrinkled apples on them. A goat tied to a tree ate the grass near a shack, and I could hear the sounds of dogs barking and thousands of sparrows singing. Chickens roamed freely, fighting each other over the scraps of food that had been thrown out on the dirt.

In all, there were maybe twenty shacks scattered about the hill with perhaps 100 people living close together in the houses, as tight as one family. One shack stood alone with a cross on top. This was the church where a family lived six days a week and cleared out each Sunday morning, or on certain Saturdays when someone was married there. There was a small graveyard behind the church where homemade crosses and wildflowers commemorated the dead.

During the following week I met many people who lived on the hill, including Paco, the young man with the telescope who knew every star in the heavens and the food and medicine that could be made from the hundreds of wild plants growing in the hills. Paco's twin brother Esteban was religious enough to be a priest, and studied the Bible when not studying to be a doctor. But each person there was different—some good, some bad, most friendly, all religious. Each had different stories, but sometimes the same stories; the men were always telling of the Mexican Revolution where their fathers had ridden with the great Poncho Villa, and the women all said Villa had died with their mother's name on his lips. In return, I told them about Jose and the miracle of the train. Everyone said he was a great man, and some said he was a saint.

Henry led me to a stick and tarpaper shack with a tin roof and paintings of skeletons and devils on the outside of it. Henry pushed aside the Mexican blanket that was used for a door, and I followed him inside. It was a clean shack with a dirt floor as hard and smooth as polished wood. A trumpet and many paintings of angels and devils and naked women hung from the walls. Broken candles were placed before a painting of the Virgin that Henry said his Uncle Pedro, the man who owned the shack, had painted, along with the other good paintings. Henry was showing me an old, rusty rifle with a bayonet on it when a tall, dark-skinned man with a potbelly walked in wearing nothing but faded blue pants held up by a frayed rope, holding a big knife in a leather sheath. There was a naked girl tattooed on one arm. Jose had warned me about such men, and I prayed silently for boldness. The man bared his broken, yellow teeth at me like a wild dog; but, when he saw Henry, he smiled brightly. Then he laughed and Henry and I laughed, thinking he looked as funny as a clown.

"Jesse, this is my Uncle Pedro," said Henry as the man smiled and laughed and shook my hand with his hard, dry hand. Then I realized that Henry knew so much about the hill because his uncle lived there and told him many stories. "Have you eaten any food, Henry?" asked Uncle Pedro in English with barely a Mexican accent. Henry said he was hungry and that I was too.

Pedro lifted a canvas sheet from the floor to reveal a wooden box in the ground. Pulling some stringy beef from the box, he cooked the meat along with flour tortillas in the small oven he had built outside the shack from mud and straw. The food was served with prickly pears and nopales. The meat was hard and greasy, but the tortillas that were thick and soft made up for it. Henry said Pedro made the tortillas himself, and you could not find better, except perhaps in in Salina Cruz the little Mexican town where all the families had lived before coming to Los Angeles. I said that Jose's tortillas were better, and between bites of food, we argued about that.

Uncle Pedro finished his burrito in two bites before gut punching himself again and again, shouting, "*Pinche cusano.*" Henry laughed hard, saying, "He thinks he is going to have a baby, or not really a baby, but a giant worm with a baby's head to it." Henry held his hands about two feet apart to show how enormous the worm living inside Pedro must be while Pedro nodded, seriously. "He believes it is this devil-worm making him fat. But he is only fat because he drinks much beer and eats food, even all day long," said Henry, poking his uncle's flabby gut with his finger, laughing at him.

I watched more food disappear into Pedro's greasy mouth as he gulped his second burrito. Pedro, who was now on his third burrito, then defended his fatness, telling Henry, "You know nothing, empty head," waving his food in the air as some meat fell to the ground, which he picked up and ate without even wiping it clean. "I do not eat for myself only, but because I must feed the wicked worm-child who is always hungry. If I stop eating for only a little time he will drink my blood and then he will kill me. And I drink the beer only so I can sleep at night. For how can I sleep when the son of Satan himself will not keep still for even one moment? A child of the devil is a worm and it will require much beer or wine and sometimes even tequila before he falls to sleep. You are so smart, and yet you do not know even this much, empty head," said Pedro, thumping his nephew's head lightly with his knuckles. Again Pedro punched himself in the gut and Henry laughed while looking at me, hoping I too would laugh.

When I did not laugh for fear of offending Uncle

Pedro, Henry looked to me and said, "It is okay with my uncle, Jesse; you can laugh. He is only a little *loco*, but also he is a saint of heaven, always painting pictures of the Virgin Mother and giving food and clothes to the poor." Pedro smiled, patted Henry on the head softly and fell back into a bed of rags where he soon fell asleep, snoring loudly while the grease from the meat dripped down his chin.

"He has taken too much mescal, drinking many of the worms from the bottle, and he has even smoked much *mota* and he now believes he was tricked into drinking the worm of the devil by a witch when he was in Mexico," said Henry, laughing. "Still, he is the favorite of all my uncles, and he has helped my family many times, even to come to the United States, although he himself is not yet a citizen. As you can now see, he is a very good painter, drawing even the lady of his own arm. And he never bothers nobody, and when he does it is only because he is very drunk.

"Only sometimes he will ask me to cut his stomach open with his knife and deliver the devil-child," said Henry, now frowning. "Two years ago in Mexico, he was drunk and he cut himself open with his own knife. There was much blood and he was holding onto a little part of his own insides, but he was laughing, thinking he had the baby devil in his hands, so he himself could kill it. I ran to tell my father that Pedro had cut himself nearly to death. Then my father tricked Pedro and gave him much tequila, saying it would kill the devil-worm. Pedro drank the tequila and fell to sleep on the floor, as you see him now, only with blood everywhere. While he was asleep, my father sewed him up with regular needles and threads." I was able to see the rough scar on the heaving belly of Pedro as he slept on the bed of rags.

Since Uncle Pedro was not in the United States legally, he lived on the hill to avoid *La Migra*—the immigration officers that sometimes searched Los Angeles for Mexicans who had crossed the border without papers. Most of the people who lived on the hill were without papers, and I soon realized that was why Jose had forbidden me to come here, saying, "Stay away from the wetbacks, because they are foolish people who will bring only sickness and bad luck to us." But in this one thing he was wrong. People on the hill were happy and kind and they worked hard. Often, they had little to eat, but they always shared food with me or with anybody who was hungry. They were smart, but mostly not in the ways you learn in a book at school, for few had ever been to school except for maybe a little while.

Nobody bothered the people on the hill unless it was election time in the city. Then the immigration officers rounded up a few of them, and the mayor would have his picture in the newspaper, standing next to the officers. The Mexicans in the pictures would have blood on their faces, looking sad while the mayor and the officers looked happy, sending the Mexicans on a bus back to Mexico. All of the people returned in a week or so, or after the elections were over, to be left alone again for a couple more years.

Henry practiced his English on me constantly, once saying, "Nobody will know that I am from Mexico when I speak to them, for the English is perfect." He did sound pretty good, but no matter how he tried he could not pronounce the letter y, and yellow was always *zhallow* and year was always *zhew*. When I told him he sounded perfect, he smiled proudly.

With vacation over, I returned to live with Jose and Soridtha. I also returned to school, where Henry attended for the first time. As his father drove him the many miles across town, to Vernie's, the boy sat tall in the front seat of the old truck, wearing the khaki pants, white shirt, and navy blue sweater that all the boys had to wear.

Henry said the "Pledge of Allegiance" again and again as he rode, holding tightly to his new writing tablet, three new sharpened pencils, and metal lunchbox. He loved school in a way that only somebody who had never been there could love it. He had heard of the playgrounds covered with smooth grass and all the beautiful girls.

Henry's father kissed his son goodbye as the boy left the truck and followed the other children directly into the classroom where he walked around, touching everything, and approaching everyone saying, "Hi, I am Henry. Who are *zhoo* ?"

Henry made things still worse in the classroom by walking between the rows of desks, introducing himself to everyone he had not yet met, one at a time, shaking hands, saying, "Hello, my name is Henry. Who are *zhoo*?" He was nervous, so he sounded like a *cholo*, but he did not know this. Some of the girls laughed and turned away when he spoke to them. When Darryl Donnelly spat into Henry's opened hand and called him *beaner*, everybody . . . even me (Father forgive me) laughed. But Henry did not laugh.

Henry prayed quietly along with the rest of the class as we stood in the classroom. During the pledge, however, you could hear him above everyone else, reciting the words loudly, with a slight Mexican accent. At recess, we played kickball, and Henry, who played brilliantly on the streets of Chavez Ravine, was so nervous with the new group of American boys he missed each ball rolled to him. Donnelly called him *beaner* each time he missed a ball, and when Henry told him to stop saying it, Donnelly slapped him across the face. I was sure then Henry would hit Donnelly, but he just smiled and returned to the game, playing it poorly.

Back in the classroom, Henry was staring at Maria Ortiz as all the other boys and I always did. When Sister Ignatius asked him a simple arithmetic question, he stuttered out the wrong answer. When she corrected him about this and his Mexican accent, some laughed. When the lunch bell rang, he ran happily to the benches, realizing he had something to win even the hardest of hearts. I watched from a distance as he dug into the new lunchbox until he came up, smiling, with the homemade cookies with pink and yellow stars on them that his mother had made to give to the children in the class. "A cookie for each," he shouted, holding up the bag happily for everyone. He did not know that most of the school children here had all the cookies they wanted and had never been hungry for anything. When nobody accepted his gifts, he ate alone.

After that first day, Henry told his father he would take the bus to school. He went to school the remainder of that week, but after five days of rejection he never went again. He covered his bases by having me forge his father's hand on a note to the school saying he had been injured riding his bicycle and would not be coming back for at least a month. A month passed and then two and three, but nobody ever checked on his story and so he dressed in school clothes each morning, kissed his parents goodbye, changed his clothes in some bushes, hid his bike there, and climbed up the hill. Then, each evening he reversed the process and returned home, dressed in his school clothes. With my help, Henry even forged a report card once, and so even his family believed he was still going to class each day.

One Friday evening, Jose drove me to stay at the Ochoa's home in La Loma where I intended to hang out with Henry for the weekend. That Saturday morning I was at Henry's house early. We played kickball on the street together for a while and were surprised to see a shiny new car rolling down our street, honking to clear us from the road. We moved aside, but the car was moving so fast, it nearly hit little Lupita. As the car moved past us, Henry threw a dirt bomb that exploded all over the beautiful paint. Lupita took the kickball and ran into the house as the car skidded to a stop and then backed up and raced in reverse toward Henry and me. The car stopped and the man got out. He was a big, important man who I later learned worked for a real estate company and he ran after us nearly catching me before I got to the trail that led up the hill. Like everyone else, he wanted nothing to do with the dirt of the hill, and he quit running right where the path ended. Henry and I ran like wild dogs all the way to the top of the hill. When the man screamed that we were wetbacks, we threw more dirt bombs at him, and he yelled again before driving away.

  As we entered his shack, the sleeping Uncle Pedro opened his eyes. He smiled and gave us some cold beans from the open can on the floor. We ate the food with our fingers along with short nips of tequila from the bottle.

  Pedro rolled three cigarettes, put one in his mouth and tossed one Henry and one to me. We smoked, and I took a small drink from the bottle of tequila when it came to me from Pedro. Henry wiped the neck of the bottle on his shirt before taking a little drink. Because of the face he made and the way he shivered after swallowing it, I knew this was his first drink, ever.

When Pedro and I walked outside of the shack to piss on the cactus, I looked down to see Jose kneeling amid the thin trees of the hill, a white light surrounding him as he prayed. I approached him, but said nothing. Then, opening his eyes, which glowed like ambers Jose said, "My son, you should not lie to me; I have many eyes. Even now I see bad things for you because of the hill." Then he vanished, never returning to the hill again.

Back in the shack, I told Henry I had never seen a gambler so poor as his uncle in all of my life. "Oh," said Henry, smiling brightly and laughing, "He is a very good gambler, one of the very best in Salina Cruz, but he does not play for money. He plays only for the clothes of women, so he can see them naked, like the girl on the cards." Leaning over to the bed of rags, Henry took one of the rags and threw it to me. I was surprised to find it was a pair of women's white silk panties. Then I could see that the bed of rags was made mostly of white bras and panties, and I put a pair of panties onto my head and we both laughed.

After eating and drinking, Henry turned to Uncle Pedro and said, "Come, *tio* it is time for me." Pedro smiled gently at Henry then lifted a little leather case from a drawer in his table. Opening the case, he took out four small colored bottles and a long needle. He stuck the needle into the brightest of the candles until the tip glowed red. Henry asked for another drink of tequila and Pedro motioned for him to take it. Again wiping off the bottle, Henry took a little drink, shaking as the tequila sent warm waves through his body.

Uncle Pedro dipped the glowing needle into the ink bottle and began pushing it against the top of Henry's left arm. The boy pulled back and yelped a little when he felt the needle and saw a small, green dot appear on his brown skin along with a drop of blood. Again, Pedro dipped the needle and pushed it against the meat of the arm. This time Henry was silent and did not jerk back. It took over an hour to see Henry's name written in nice, green letters on his arm. It was more than another hour when, below the name, Pedro wrote the word *American* in red letters. He then finished everything off by surrounding the art with a circle of blue stars.

"This will now prove to everyone that I am an American citizen," said Henry, bending his neck to see the new tattoo, smiling as Pedro wiped the needle on his greasy pants and put it back into the leather case.

"Maybe you would like to have just your name here, Jesse," Henry said, pinching the webbing between the thumb and index fingers of my left hand. "It only hurts a little bit and you can wash it off in a few days if you don't like it," he said.

"You are not afraid of the little pain from the needle, are you, Jesse? Look at me; I now have my name and the word *American* with stars on my arm." I did not want Henry to think I was chicken, so I agreed to let Uncle Pedro do only a small picture on my hand, believing I could wash it off, as Henry had said.

I put out my hand for the tattoo, but refused a drink of the tequila Pedro passed to me. The needle stung like a hundred bees before a green cross, no longer than my largest fingernail formed on my left hand. When the cross was finished, I pulled away from the needle, not willing to endure more pain in order to have the little purple flower and my name there as Uncle Pedro wanted. "You are a chicken for having only a little cross on your hand," said Henry, flapping his arms like wings and dancing on the dirt floor like a chicken. Then I said, "I am not afraid of the pain; I don't want to be a *cholo* like you." With that, Henry jumped on me, hitting me, saying, "I am not a *cholo*, I am an American citizen," repeating the words American citizen again and again while punching me. Realizing I had said a hurtful thing, I didn't fight back.

The moon rose high and bright that night and we sat outside on the dirt, near the fire in front of the shack, talking and watching as the big trucks filled with the men and women of the hill returned from the fields. You could smell the exhaust and hear the deep groan and rattle of the old trucks as they strained beneath the weight of the workers. As a truck passed near the shack, Pedro called out to a tall girl with long dark hair—the prettiest of all the girls in the truck. She was holding onto the wooden slats in the back of the truck as if they were bars to a jail. "Consuelo, *mi novia*," Pedro shouted, smiling and waving. The girl waved back at Pedro and he walked into the shack where he rubbed the grease from the meat in the box into his wild, wavy hair with his fingers. After wiping his hands on his pants, he lit two large candles and pulled an entire case of beer and a new bottle of tequila from the hole in the ground.

After about an hour, it was dark out and the pretty Consuelo walked up to the shack wearing a tight blue dress, silver earrings and necklace, and black high-heeled leather shoes, which had become muddy after getting stuck in the soft dirt as she walked. Without a word to anyone she stepped into the shack and sat down, beautiful as a Mexican Marilyn Monroe. Henry and I were seated on the bed of rags, somewhat hidden in the shadows. By the light of the candles burning behind her, however, we could see her perfectly. She had a smooth face and a big gap between her front teeth. Except for the gap, she was perfect. "*Chi-chi grande*," Henry whispered into my ear as we laughed quietly and admired the beautiful Consuelo.

She reached onto the bed of rags and grabbed a pair of panties and shook them in the air, saying, "I don't have only a few more panties now for work and I will need to win some of them back for me, *pinche* Pedro."

Uncle Pedro smiled and opened a bottle of beer with his knife for Consuelo. Gently, he put the foaming bottle into her hand. Before she had even finished the cool beer, he gave her another one. Henry reached over for the new bottle of tequila, opened it, and took a drink. Then he passed the bottle to me and I too had a drink. Then I reached out and took one of the bottles of beer, which I opened on a nail in the wall and split with Henry. Then we drank another beer each and another shot of tequila until we were as drunk as anyone in the shack. Even Consuelo, who was now running her fingers over the rough scar on Uncle Pedro's fat stomach after he unbuttoned his shirt as they sat beneath us, was drunk now.

Uncle Pedro sat up, shuffled the cards and dealt two hands of Black Jack, one for himself and one for Consuelo. He put a pair of panties in the middle of the blanket and she put one of the muddy black high-heeled shoes next to it. Consuelo took too many cards and busted at twenty-seven, but Pedro hit twenty-one with an ace and a king. I stole another beer and drank it quickly, but Henry had fallen asleep as Consuelo and Pedro continued playing strip poker. She removed the second shoe and lost it to Pedro.

Then there were the brightly painted metal hairclips, the silver earrings, and the necklace. Finally, she removed the tight blue dress and threw it on the floor between herself and Pedro. All of Consuelo's clothes were tossed in a pile as she sat wearing only her bra and her last pair of panties.

Again Pedro dealt the cards, hitting twenty with a king and a ten while Consuelo's hand was no good. When Consuelo removed her bra and threw it into onto the floor, I woke Henry who was napping on the floor. He quickly opened his red eyes, smiled brightly, and shouted, "*Chi-chi grande,*" before I could cover his mouth with my hand, and I told him to be quiet.

Consuelo lost nearly every hand, and now, with nothing else to lose, she pulled off her panties and threw them into the center, frowning. I held my hand over Henry's mouth to contain his joy. Then Consuelo saw what we did not see, that Pedro, who had become too drunk to move his hands quickly, had dealt a jack to himself from the bottom of the deck. Pedro smiled as he hit twenty and she busted again with too many cards. When he reached out to pull in the panties, however, she lunged for him and dug her fingernails into his arm, spat in his face and yelled, "*Pinche Pedro, pinche pendejo,*" again and again, so loudly I was certain everyone on the hill could hear her. She stood up and broke the empty beer bottle in her hand over Pedro's head. Holding the broken glass toward him, she told him to take off all of his clothes. Silently, lowering his head, he obeyed, stripping off everything, covering himself with his hands as she walked over and kicked Pedro's clothes out the doorway.

Consuelo took back her panties and bra from the floor and put them back on. Then, while keeping an eye on Pedro, she reached down cautiously to gather all her clothes with one hand except for the one high heel she held in her other hand as a weapon, if necessary.

I stood to move out of Consuelo's way so she could march out the door when my foot landed on an unopened beer bottle. The bottle did not break, but rolled me across the floor, onto Consuelo, who fell beneath me, onto the pile of rags. Without hesitation she swung the shoe like a bat, driving the heel into my left cheekbone. Pain shot from my head, all the way to my feet, and I could feel the warm blood pouring down my face as I pressed my fingers into the gash with hopes of stopping the bleeding.

Consuelo was swearing loudly now and throwing whatever she could find at all three of us. When she finished throwing things, she picked up everything from the floor and spat on Pedro, who still had not moved. Then she spat on me and turned to walk out of the shack. As she left, she tore down the blanket/door. Then I could see the furious and almost naked Consuelo in the moonlight. But I was in too much pain to enjoy seeing her any longer. Only Henry was able to have the fun of watching the woman as he staggered from the shack to catch the last glimpses of her.

Consuelo continued walking, and Henry ran a few steps behind her, hoping to get a final peek from a safe distance. When she stopped to put her dress back on, he returned, smiling. When he saw the blood on my face, however, he quit smiling and his eyes went huge, but he said nothing. Next came Uncle Pedro, covering his shame and sadness in the blanket/door. After examining the wound on my face, he walked back into the shack and returned with tequila, which he dabbed onto my face with his shirt. I yelped a little then drank enough tequila for the pain to die away.

I passed out, but awoke in the middle of the night with a big headache and lightly pressed a finger to the place where the shoe had landed and felt a scab forming over the deep dent there. Pedro and Henry were still awake and Pedro offered me more tequila, but I refused it. Pedro took a drink, but Henry did not, and soon the three of us were laughing by the fire, talking about how beautiful and angry Consuelo was, especially when she found out about the cheating Uncle Pedro. Pedro made the sign of the cross, swearing he would never again cheat a woman at cards.

I awoke to the warmth of another sunny day to see Henry and Pedro asleep, arm-in-arm, by the dead fire, dreaming of Consuelo. The sick taste of tequila was still in my mouth and my head hurt like a train had run it over. When I looked down to see my shirt caked in blood, everything returned from the previous night, and I touched my face to feel the imprint of Consuelo's high-heeled shoe.

    I walked from the shack up the hill to gather firewood while the others slept. Many quail and rabbits were on the path enjoying the morning sun, but I had nothing to shoot them with. A hawk dove and caught a mouse, and I considered that a sign from God that everything would be good again. When I returned, I made the fire for the others as they awoke slowly, and tried to look and not to look at the dent in my face. Henry kept rubbing his arm, bending his neck to see his new tattoo, which he now seemed a little ashamed of. Pedro strained coffee in a sock, and we all had some. Then I borrowed a shirt from Pedro and returned to Mr. Ochoa's home, avoiding seeing him and his wife. I left them a note before taking a bus back home to Jose's.

CHAPTER TWELVE
VAYA CON DIOS

The next morning I scrubbed my tattoo until the kitchen sink ran red with blood, but it remained. Jose walked in and saw the blood and the dent on the side of my face. "A woman's mark on the face is a good sign, my son. You now have a miracle of your own like me with the miracle of the train," he said, rubbing the dent on his forehead. When he saw the tattoo, he scowled and asked, "Are you now a *cholo* like the men on the hill? Stay away from the hill, and from the *cholos*." He rubbed the dent in his forehead, chuckling, saying, "But a dent from a woman is good, but not so good as a dent from a train."

At school everybody asked why my cheek was bandaged; I told them I had been hit by a rock. All the boys at school thought the new tattoo was good and I managed to hide it from my teachers. Nobody asked about Henry except Donnelly who wanted to know where he lived so he could "pound the Mexican."

Months later summer vacation arrived, and again I went to live with Mr. and Mrs. Ochoa for the entire time. Henry came by each morning, pleading with me to climb the hill with him. I refused to go until Henry mentioned that Consuelo had the large gap in her teeth fixed and that she now looked like Dolores del Rio, the movie star. He said Consuelo had moved downtown with a big German man who drove up the hill and picked her up in a fancy new German car, which kept getting stuck in the mud until Henry helped him push it and got two dollars for only one minute's worth of work. At first, the German was nice to her and even paid to have her teeth fixed. Later, when everyone heard the German had beat Consuelo, they drove to town and found him, beating him badly, making him crawl and drink mud from the gutter before breaking the windows and kicking dents into the fancy car, all for what he had done to one of their own. Nobody ever saw the German again and Consuelo moved back to the hill for good.

When Henry said Consuelo wanted to kiss me on the

mouth I agreed to go with him. When she saw me walking up the dirt path with Henry, she ran to meet me. It was true that she was more beautiful than ever. She apologized for hitting me with her shoe and kissed me on the healed dent her mark forever on my face. She never did kiss me on the mouth.

Ever since the night when Consuelo had beaten him, the women on the hill walked freely into Pedro's shack and took whatever underwear they needed until the once proud bed of rags was reduced to a little bed of ordinary rags, no good for showing off about women, or even for sleeping. The women would never again play cards with him, but he would often have a nice woman in the shack and cook food for her.

As months passed, Henry and I became more and more wild, sleeping outside more often than not; hunting with bows and arrows or Henry's father's rifle; wearing the same cutoff pants each day; running all day without shoes until our feet were hard as leather; and, our hair sun-bleached, long, and matted. Only occasionally did Henry's mother or father come looking for him. Then he went home for a few days, only to return to the hill again.

It was the last weekend before I started school again and that night Henry and I slept outside on the hill under the stars, close to Uncle Pedro's rock pit and the fire we made there each night. When I mentioned Donnelly and Clank,

Henry said, "I am not afraid of the boys from the school. I will fight Darryl Donnelly and Clank or maybe shoot them with my father's rifle and maybe kill them if they come for me," he boasted. "The only thing I liked from the school was the girl, Maria," he said, holding his hands far out beyond his chest and laughing in remembrance of her.

We heard nothing but the crackling fire, owls and coyotes, and a man and woman arguing far away. Everywhere was darkness except from the little fires on the hill or the candles in the shacks or in the direction of the city where you could see ten thousand little white lights over Los Angeles singing together as the stars of heaven.

That morning we awoke early to a warm wind and a hot blue day without any clouds. It was the wind called Santa Ana that some said came from the devil and would bring nothing good. Except for the blowing dust, we saw only good in the day.

With nothing to eat, I followed Henry through the short grass where he shot and killed two quail with only three shots of his father's rifle. I carried the dead birds and followed Henry back to the shack. There, I hung the quail by their feet outside the shack and we entered to find Pedro leaning back on the ruined bed of rags, smoking a cigarette, stopping sometimes to play a sad song on his trumpet. He gave us each a cigarette that I accepted but Henry refused then offered us scraps of meat from the wooden box.

We all ate, and Pedro and I smoked while we played cards and talked until it was nearly dark and the sky turned red before going black dotted by a million stars. I had plucked the feathers from the quail before Henry split the naked little bodies open with his knife and threw the guts on the dirt for the chickens to eat. He ran the quail through with a stick and cooked them over the outside fire pit. After eating the quail with beans and tortillas, Henry and I sat near the fire, happy and full of food. We laughed and talked about girls we liked, and what we would be when we grew up and became men.

"I am going to be a priest," I said. When he said he would be a doctor, I said he could not be a doctor because a doctor must go to school for many years. Then he said I could not be a priest because I had been drunk and seen the naked Consuelo and the pictures on the cards. We argued until we ran out of words and the argument died out. Then we sat quietly on the soft green grass, him telling me stories of the warm days and nights in Mexico as we ate his mother's cookies and drank cold water from a jar.

Pedro drank a bottle of beer and offered one to each of us. We took them but were sick of drinking and poured them onto the ground when Pedro was not looking. Pedro drank and punched himself in the stomach then pulled a hunk of dried beef from his shirt pocket. He bit into the meat and passed it to us between sips of his beer. Pedro sauntered into the shack and returned with his trumpet to play a pretty Mexican song. The song made me, and especially Henry, proud, yet a little ashamed of being Mexicans. Then Pedro drank tequila from the bottle he took from his side pants pocket in order to quiet the devil-worm.

After he chugged most of the bottle of tequila, Pedro pulled another very small brown bottle from his pocket. We would have stopped him had we had known it contained medicine to kill worms in pigs. Hoping to kill the devil-worm, Pedro drank the entire brown bottle down in one gulp. A while later he smiled and laughed like a crazy man, staggering to his feet, punching himself hard in the gut with his fists. He was laughing before he fell down again, bruising his head on the rocks of the fire pit, nearly falling into the fire. He shouted that the devil-child must die, waving his hands at imaginary devils in the air and then pounding at his stomach harder and harder, ripping his fingernails into the healed scar until it was bleeding, saying, "*Pinche cusano, pinche puto.*"

Taking the big knife from his belt, he held it out with both hands over the scar on his gut, shouting, "I will teach you now, son of the devil; you will not win this fight with me." Quickly, Henry grabbed for the knife and took it from Pedro who tried to retrieve it but fell to the ground and then swore and spat at the boy. "Bring back the knife to me, friend of the devil," Pedro yelled to Henry, who stood only a few feet away, holding the knife out like he was playing a little game with his uncle. Henry laughed loudly and said, "Come and get the knife, old man." Pedro jumped up much too quickly, and wobbled until he fell back down onto the ground again.

Henry stopped laughing and stood still, listening and looking down the hill as the sounds of the men stomping through the bushes came echoing up from below. Soon we saw the beams of their flashlights bobbing around as two men approached our camp. "*La migra*," shouted Henry, sending the alarm to me and especially to Pedro. Henry turned to Pedro, shaking him by the shoulders repeatedly, saying "*La migra, tio, la migra*." Henry and I ran for cover behind some bushes while Pedro lay still. Henry had dropped the knife near the fire pit where Pedro picked it up, stood tall, and waved it high in the air, shouting, "Come for me now, *La migra*."

We could see Pedro from our hiding place and Henry whispered loudly, "Please, uncle, come to hide with us." Pedro refused to move as he waved his knife in the direction of the lights, shouting and swearing at the lights as they came closer.

"Come over here to taste my knife, *pinche la migra*," shouted Pedro to the lights, which were now very close. The men marched toward us, their pistols drawn and pointed at Pedro. Soon we could see them clearly, their faces red and sweating as they moved forward. "Put down the knife," ordered one of the men, motioning to Pedro with his gun. Lifting the knife over his head, Pedro staggered forward and swung the knife wildly at the man.

"Put down the knife," the officer shouted again. "Uncle, do what he says or he will shoot you," pleaded Henry. But Pedro held the knife tighter in his hand, and as the men came still closer, I quietly slipped away to hide deep in the trees that lined the hill. Henry, who hoped to save his uncle, ran toward Pedro and the officers standing near the fire pit. In his panic, Henry picked up the rifle he had set down in the dirt, but had no intention of shooting anyone. He knew it was hopeless to fight against the men and that Uncle Pedro was acting crazy and would be transported back across the border, only to return again in a short while. Henry simply did not want to lose his father's gun. One of the lights stayed fixed on Henry, who stood frozen, holding his little rabbit gun in his hands as the officer behind the light shouted at him to drop it.

The other light focused on Pedro who was still waving his knife, weaving in and out, poking the blade at the moving light. Each time Pedro came near the light he lunged at it, saying words that nobody could understand. Then he breathed deeply and cried out clearly, "Now you have come, father of the devil." The officer was too ignorant to be puzzled by the strange words. Loudly, the officer again ordered Pedro to lay down the knife. Instead, Pedro lunged for the officer and tried to stab him, but the officer moved easily to one side and let Pedro fall beyond him, onto the dirt. As Pedro fell, the man hit him in the head with the handle of his flashlight. Uncle Pedro was now lying facedown in the dirt as the man kicked him in the ribs twice, and the other officer handcuffed him.

Pedro was passed out and I was glad for it. The second light remained on Henry who held the rifle down by his side. Henry squinted in the light, moved his head to see what was happening to his uncle, and mumbled in Spanish and in English, rolling up his sleeve to show the officer the American tattoo, trying to say he was an American citizen.

"Put down the gun and walk to me with your hands up," the man ordered Henry. Henry did not move, but continued mumbling in Spanish, turning his arm in the direction of the light, to show the tattoo. The lights of many candles were put out in the shacks, and I heard the quick feet of families running from their homes to the safety of the caves deep in the canyon where they would hide like coyotes until the officers were gone. Henry smiled before jumping as fast as a rabbit into the darkness, falling to the ground, rolling and moving beyond the light before he stood up again and ran. The light moved all around the trees and the deserted shacks until it again found Henry who was running to the safety of his house.

A shot rang out and there was the smell of smoke

and gunpowder then a loud gasp and the sound of Henry hitting the ground. He was pressing his hand against his back to keep his blood from pouring out of him like water. I am ashamed to say that I ran down the steep hill not looking back, never feeling the cactus needles that pierced my legs and bare feet. I was moving as fast as a rabbit until I made La Loma where I fell on my face, skinning my forehead, knees, and the palms of my hands. Bleeding and crying, I got up and ran again, blood dripping everywhere, running. I needed the wisdom of Jose now, and I ran as fast as I could, falling twice more before I was well beyond Chavez Ravine.

I walked across the Sixth Street Bridge, across town, all the way to Jose's house in East LA. When I arrived, the lights were out and I crawled into my bed. Beneath the covers, with my clothes still on, shivering and crying under the blankets, I fell asleep and dreamed many bad dreams, waking regularly, yelling. Finally, I slept deeply until Jose followed the drops of blood that led to my bed and shook me awake around noon. He sat me up, put alcohol and bandages on my wounds and removed all the cactus needles he could with his fingers. While he treated my wounds he told me about Henry, even though he certainly knew I had seen the whole thing the night before. I remembered the sound of the gun and Henry hitting the ground. I was crying as Jose—having recognized nothing but the name Raphael Dominguez and the word *dead*—

showed me the little clipping from the newspaper about the dead boy.

The paper said that a young illegal immigrant boy named Raphael Dominguez was killed when he tried shooting an immigration officer. I knew it was only partially true, but nobody would believe me if I told what had really happened.

Only a few days later I found myself back at school after summer vacation. Instead of writing about what we had done for those three months, we were herded into the church to pray the rosary for the soul of Henry. Some of the girls cried and most of the boys fooled around, talking and laughing. Silently, I put my fingers onto my rosary in my pocket and said a decade of the rosary for the sins of Henry so God would take his soul to heaven, keeping my head low so nobody would see me crying.

Two days later, we all sat in the church as the Dominguez family huddled close together to see their son in the open coffin. Henry's father was silent, his face hard as rock. Henry's mother cried loudly on the shoulder of his dead-faced grandmother. Lupita clutched her doll and looked around, her eyes searching for her brother.

A few weeks after the funeral, I heard Henry's family were again crammed into the front seat of the old truck as Lupita sat alone with her doll and plenty of room in the back. All of their things were piled high in the truck, just as they were when the family first moved here. Only now there was no Henry and no laughing as they rolled away down the street on the long drive back to Mexico.

CHAPTER THIRTEEN
SARAH JANE

My best friend was dead and Julio was about to take possession of our house. While I sulked indoors, Soridtha came in from the backyard to quickly and silently pack one change of clothes, a toothbrush, and two large knives into her black leather bag in much the same manner as her ancestors must have done whenever they were displaced in the past. Clutching her bag to her chest Soridtha returned to her wikiup, and from that point on we rarely saw her.

Jose was much slower moving, and he spent that entire time saying goodbye to everything. "Goodbye, little fountain," he said. "Goodbye Hilberto, angel in the fountain.

Please to keep an eye on Gilberto the fish, since she is getting old. Please to keep an eye also on the chickens, especially the white one with only one leg. She does not lay so many good eggs no more and somebody will surely want to eat her."

"Goodbye oven," he said, while camping in the backyard for two days, snuggled up to the warm adobe oven he had built decades earlier. "I thank you for all the good food you have made for me and for everybody and even the Four Friends and Soridtha and even Julio and the Father Thomas and even the seven daughters."

"Goodbye swing," he said sadly, rocking back and forth slowly on the porch swing for hours. "Do you remember when I was young and I would sit on you with my Soridtha? You too were young and quiet then, only listening. Now you are only old and you talk all the time and I have tried to listen to what you are saying, but it is mostly only squeaking and crazy talk."

And so it went, all through the house and the yard, Jose slowly parting with everything he owned. Julio had let us stay in the house, not because he was nice, but because he wanted to humiliate Jose by taking money from him for a change. Julio charged Jose thirty-five dollars a month for rent, which was more than anyone else on the block ever paid. But thirty-five dollars was nothing to Jose; he could make much more in one hand of poker.

Jose said the house was now very tired and he went to bed and slept for an entire month, only rising to eat a little and pray quietly at his altar. School went by like a black mass as Jose slept, and there was nobody to protect the city. Then, I would read in the paper about increased robberies, rapes, and murders and the tearing down of the old buildings in Los Angeles. Even the weather turned against us now and it rained hard for twenty days straight, flooding the streets. Then there was a small earthquake followed by several big fires. I tried to wake Jose so he could pray for the bad to stop, but he continued sleeping all day and all night. I had no choice but to move into my parents' house. My father had become much more lenient with the changing times and allowed us to do what we wanted most evenings and weekends. It may have been a better house; but, without Jose in it, it was just another place to live.

One Saturday morning I rode my bike to the park in Bell to hunt tadpoles. There, I saw a pretty girl who had a jar filled with the tadpoles and small fish she had caught. Someone said her name was Sarah Jane. She was one year older than me, very tall, and had white-blonde braids, light skin, and freckles. Sara Jane was what we then called a "tomboy," and it was rumored she could throw a curve ball that broke almost a foot before landing right over the plate nearly every time. She was a better kickball player than any of the boys, and I later learned she was also a great surfer.

After hunting tadpoles with her, she invited me to her house. In her backyard was a tipi she had built and often slept in. Next to the tipi was a cage she had built out of wood and glass. The cage was divided into sections containing snakes, lizards, and horned toads that she called by the Latin name *insectivorous iguanid lizards*. She also had cages made of chicken wire for baby birds that had fallen from their nests, keeping them alive with eyedroppers filled with mashed worms. She had three glass aquariums—one for fish, one for crickets, and one for mice. The mice and crickets she fed to her snakes. Sarah Jane was not Catholic and did not go to Veronica's, but to the public school, Bell Junior High.

One day, we were playing stretch with her knife in her backyard when her mother called her into the house for dinner. She told me to stay in the tipi and she would see me later. After dinner, she came to the tipi with some chicken and corn wrapped in a napkin. As I ate, we planned to tramp into the local hills the next morning and agreed to meet at my parents' house. I left Sarah Jane and stayed with my parents that night and was up before light, packing a lunch and filling my father's war canteen with Kool-Aid. I sat on the porch to wait for her as the sun came over the hills. It wasn't long before she came bouncing high down the center divider of the street on her pogo stick, braids flying.

That pogo stick was her main form of transportation and she bounced on it all over town—to the library, down Main Street, through the shopping centers, and even to school when it was in session. She was moving fast and bouncing high until she turned up onto our sidewalk and followed the cement path to the porch where I was waiting for her. She made one extra hard bounce before vaulting from the pogo stick, and her big, moccasin-covered feet landed on the ground right next to me. She laid the pogo stick down carefully in the ivy near the porch in the front yard.

We sat on the porch surveying her home-drawn map of the hills while I strapped my hunting knife to my belt and slung the bow Jose had made for me over my shoulder, along with the leather sheath filled with arrows he had also hand crafted.

It was a sunny day as we hiked up the grade on Wilcox Avenue to the dirt path that led up into the hills. The path was filled with rabbits that sprang out from beneath our feet as we walked and I shot wildly at them, missing each one as they sprinted into bushes or holes where we did not see them again. With the binoculars Sarah Jane's father had taken from a dead German officer in the war, she always spotted the rabbits before I did. When she whispered, "Stop," I would freeze in my tracks and she would hand me the binoculars to see the rabbit clearly. She taught me to move slowly on the balls of my feet, like an Indian, to where the rabbit was sitting. I would shoot at it and miss every time.

Owls, hawks, pheasants, and mud hens were the targets of my arrows, but I never landed any of them. As morning progressed, rabbits and other animals became scarce. I caught a horned toad with my hand and put it into the shoebox Sarah Jane was carrying. She punched holes in the top of the box with her knife and stuffed the box with grass and a few bugs to keep it alive until she got home to put it into a cage. She caught a tree frog, and then a few moments later, a small garter snake that I wouldn't touch, convinced it was a rattler. When I saw the snake was harmless, I held it nervously as it twisted around my arm. Sarah Jane tried to force the frog into the snake's mouth, but the snake kept squirming out of my hand. The snake wouldn't hold still and eat the frog, so she let both go free in the bushes by a little pond of slimy green water where a million tadpoles were swimming, some of them sprouting tiny new legs, ready to become frogs. We left the shoebox with the horned toad hidden in a tumbleweed near the pond.

I wandered from the path as another rabbit darted off from under my feet. I shot at the little cottontail, just missing. It ran away into the cactus patch before I could get another arrow out of my sheath. The rabbit had a limp and I was able to catch up by running as fast as I could, keeping an arrow pulled tightly against the string. I found the rabbit on a small, grassy mound a few feet away from the cactus patch, its back turned, eating grass quietly, unaware I was pointing an arrow at its heart. The arrow flew fast and straight, running through the rabbit's back and coming out of the gut, pinning it to the ground. It squirmed in the dirt, twisting and turning, trying to get free of the arrow. I ran up closer and shot again, hitting it high on the back leg this time. I was laughing and shouting for Sarah Jane as she ran up the hill after me, breathing hard.

Holding out her knife, she offered to finish off the little rabbit, saying we could use the fur to make slippers. Taking her knife, I was about to kill the rabbit until I got close enough to see the baby cottontail jerking around, trying to free itself from my arrows. Its snow-white fur turned red from blood as it accused me with its little pink eyes and I started crying. Sarah Jane did not hesitate and took back her knife, pushing it into the rabbit's neck, killing it quickly and wiping the knife blade clean on the grass.

"Come on Jack, let's skin it," she said happily. But I was still crying and dropped my bow in the dirt. Meanwhile she was sharpening her knife on her whetstone and she shrugged her shoulders as I looked at her. Then she picked up the dead rabbit, put it onto a flat rock, cut out the guts, and skinned it. She threw the guts into the cactus patch, wrapped the meat in the wax paper she took from my sandwich, and dropped the soft, still quivering flesh into a paper bag she had with her for just such purposes. She wiped the knife blade clean of blood again and walked over to the cactus patch to lop off a few red prickly pears. She skinned the wild fruit and cut away the fine needles. We sat and ate the juicy prickly pears along with our sandwiches, followed by Kool-Aid, in silence. "Be bold," I said to myself, remembering the courage of Jose as we continued tramping through the hills. If I found another rabbit I would kill it and skin it myself.

  Hiking up over the hills, we eventually arrived at the reservoir and balanced along its narrow rock rim, making our way down to wade through the cold, shallow water. We could see the tall adobe walls of Mission San Gabriel in the distance. A woman was singing a Mexican song, cooling herself by standing in the shallows of the San Gabriel River, right where I had seen baby turtles and caught crawdads in a coffee can years earlier with Jose. There were no turtles or crawdads this time, but the water was clean and refreshing to drink. We drank from the stream and filled the canteen and Sarah Jane asked me to follow her as we hiked up past the place called "Rabbit Hill" on her map. To get there we had to walk through "The Plateau," beyond "The Grove of Palms" to a place called "The Big Desert," as they were labeled on her map. There was sand in the Big Desert, and, true to its name, nothing grew there. After passing through the sand onto hard ground again, we quietly treaded on the balls of our feet to a place with a few trees called "Hobo

Camp." There, she showed me how to cup my hands near my ears to hear better and how to put water on my nose to wet it like a wolf, which would help me better smell any animals hiding in the hills.

At Hobo Camp, we hid in the bushes and watched the hobos from a safe distance. In a small grove of trees, three men huddled around a fire beneath an old worn out blanket hanging overhead in the tree branches as protection against the sun. Two of the men sat in the shaded dirt and one squatted beyond the shade of the blanket, turning his sunburned face directly to the sun. Empty tin cans, broken milk and beer bottles, and newspapers littered the ground near a rock fire pit near several rolled up blankets. Each of the hobos was ragged and dirty. The shortest among them had blond, curly hair and a blond, scruffy beard with some red in it. The one they called "Big Jim" was a giant hobo with dark skin, black stubble, and fresh blood over one eye. The man seated in the sun was short and skinny wearing a hat down over his face, so I could not tell what kind of a man he was. The food they were cooking in a rusty old can over a wood fire smelled awful, and the little hobo smoked and drank something from a tin can.

I whispered to Sarah Jane that I wanted to get out of there before we were discovered spying on the hobos. When she said she was staying, I decided to stay too. The little hobo tilted the can up to his mouth even after there was nothing left in it. Then, he threw the can angrily down onto the rocks.

The little hobo spoke, making his words stronger by waving his knife in the air, saying he was going to bust his friend out of jail as soon as he got a chance, and that nobody was a friend of his if they didn't help. The big hobo said they couldn't bust him out because there were too many cops around the jail and they would be caught. Hearing this, the little hobo said that the big hobo was no friend of his. Then the big hobo hit the little hobo hard in the face and the little hobo fell back onto the dirt. The little hobo charged the big hobo with a big stick. The big hobo took the stick from the little hobo's hand and quickly got him down where they wrestled on the dirt, rolling in our direction as the big hobo pounded the little hobo in the face.

They were getting close to our hiding place when Sarah Jane decided we should move on. We snuck away, again on our tiptoes, without being heard. Finally, we heard the little hobo yell that he gave up the fight, and we slipped off back down the hill unnoticed. Soon everything was quiet except for the hobos, who yelled at each other and at the clear blue sky.

I peeked into the sack and smiled to see the pink, greasy meat of the rabbit. We walked for a long time and climbed a big steep hill, going through a tangle of trees until we came out onto a patch of thin, yellow dust. There, Sarah Jane dug in the dirt with her knife, surprising me when she came up with two petrified clams and one large petrified snail. She gave me one of the clams as a present and said the seashells in the hills proved the story of the great flood and Noah and the ark. She caught another horned toad but turned it loose in the bushes. When I asked why she let the horned toad go, she lifted her shirt, stuck out her belly, patted it, and said, "Pregnant."

We walked over the new green grass of the hills, holding hands through fields of large yellow flowers as high as our heads, small purple flowers only as high as our waists, and bamboo higher than a house. Arriving back at the trailhead, she picked up the horned toad in the box. The sun was setting on the old junked cars and the oil well as the hills glowed bright orange and gold. When the mosquitoes arrived, we ran down the hill together, laughing, smashing the insects against our arms and faces, hearing crickets and bullfrogs and the splashing of small fish in the pond competing for a meal of bugs.

Once we were beyond the pond, the mosquitoes were gone and we walked slowly down the hill. Sarah Jane told me she had heard about a girl in my school named Maria who was pregnant. "Like the horned toad," she said, laughing and patting her stomach again. I let go of Sarah Jane's hand, punched her in the arm, and ran home alone. I watched through the front window as she retrieved her pogo stick from the ivy and somehow bounce home while carrying the horned toad.

The next day, after church I sat in the front yard alone, burning rows of ants with a magnifying glass when Sarah Jane came bouncing toward my parents' house on her pogo stick. I avoided eye contact with her as she bounced up the sidewalk.

Without a word she sat next to me and pulled the tiniest drumstick I had ever seen from the paper sack she was carrying, placing it on the grass between us. When I reached out for the chicken, she held my arm, saying, "Only if you say you're sorry for hitting me yesterday."

I apologized, and she released my arm so I could reach for the baby drumstick. "Well, how do you like your rabbit, Jack?"

"Jack rabbit," I said, laughing. "Jack. . . rabbit . . . Get it? Jack . . . rabbit," I said, stupidly, before realizing we were eating the rabbit we had killed the day before. It tasted pretty good and I didn't complain about it.

The rest of my family had gone to the movies that afternoon. I never did like going to the movies during the day, so I decided to stay home. Sarah Jane and I went into the house and made cherry Kool-Aid, mixing it in the big tin pitcher with a wooden spoon, adding extra sugar and big chunks of ice. Back on the lawn, the little water drops slid down the sides of the brightly colored tin cups and we refilled our drinks until we had finished the entire pitcher of Kool-Aid, and the fried rabbit was nothing but bones. We lay there, looking up at the little sparrows in the oak tree, holding hands in the shade, protected from the hot afternoon sun. I was telling her about Jose and she was interested in everything, especially the miracle of the train.

I jumped up suddenly at hearing Donnelly shouting my name. I couldn't believe he had found my second house; but, there he was, riding his bike, followed by Clank who had the length of bicycle chain he was named for wrapped around his knuckles. "Hey, Mexican, what are you doing with the Jew girl?" shouted Donnelly as they laughed, stopping to lay their bicycles against the curb, walking toward us. Sarah Jane and I were quiet as they moved close enough for us to hear their hard breathing.

"A *beaner* and a *kike* together," said Clank. "Jew girl," said Donnelly, spitting on the ground. Sarah Jane rose to her feet and stood her ground. Closing my eyes, I could hear Jose telling me to be bold. Sarah Jane stood up tall, and I straightened up next to her. Donnelly picked up a large sharp rock from the street and flung it at Sarah Jane's head. She moved to one side as the rock whizzed past her. They had come a long way to find the new house, and I knew they would not leave without a fight. Sarah Jane was calm, touching the gold star around her neck. "My last name is

Feinstein," she whispered to me while keeping her eye on them. "We're Jewish."

As Donnelly and Clank inched closer, she whispered from the side of her mouth. "Keep looking at them and don't be afraid, Jack."

"Be bold," I whispered to myself.

"Jack I'm gonna kick your ass," shouted Donnelly, Clank repeating Donnelly's promise while wrapping the chain tighter around his fist.

"Keep looking at them, Jack," repeated Sarah Jane, a little shaky this time. Slowly, keeping her eyes fixed on them, she reached down and picked up a big rock from the edge of the flowerbed, clenching the rock so tightly her fingers turned white. She was deadly with rocks and could hit whatever she aimed at. Inching forward, they would soon be upon us. Realizing we could not win, I turned and, as I ran, Donnelly yelled, "Look at the chicken shit Mexican run." Sarah Jane stood alone, raising her rock-filled fist, ready to hit whoever moved first. But she could only get one of them and they knew that.

Instead of retreating into the house, I ran to the garage and retrieved my bow and three arrows. When I returned to Sarah Jane's side Donnelly and Clank were close enough to touch. Inching forward, Donnelly pushed Sarah Jane who didn't fall, but retreated a foot or so. If she fell they would rush us, but she continued standing. Donnelly was yelling and Sarah Jane was silent, holding tightly onto the rock. I lifted my bow and pulled the arrow tightly against the bowstring with the arrow pointed directly at Donnelly's heart.

Sara Jane pulled her shoulders back and continued facing them. "Get out of here, Donnelly, or I'll kill you," I said, feeling the power of Jose surging through my veins. They were silent now and they didn't move forward or backward. All the hatred and fear in Donnelly's eyes was focused tightly on me. The stupid Clank would follow whatever Donnelly did, right down to dying. "I swear to God, I'll kill you just like I killed this rabbit," I shouted in Donnelly's face, motioning with my head to the clean wet bones lying on the lawn near our bare feet.

Donnelly hated being backed down by a Mexican and a girl, especially when the girl was a Jew. But I could feel the rage of Jose, and Donnelly felt it too. He knew I would run him through if he came any closer. I pulled the arrow tighter against the string, noticing it was frayed, silently praying it would not snap. I waited for him to make a move while Clank stood frozen beside him. When Donnelly shuffled back a few inches, Clank repeated the motion. Then Donnelly took a full step back and Clank, of course, followed. As Sarah Jane and I moved forward, they slowly retreated from the lawn to the curb and back onto the street. I kept the arrow on Donnelly as he cautiously lifted his bike from the gutter, watching me closely. He mounted his bike and Clank followed. As they began pedaling, I lifted the bow and shot an arrow straight up not knowing where it would land. Luck was strong then and the arrow flew high before rocketing back down and barely missing Clank's back tire, bouncing off the street near him as he fell over onto the street.

They were soon up and racing away when Donnelly yelled, "Jew" to Sarah Jane. Then she let the rock fly and it whistled through the air, skipping over the tar road until it hit its mark low on Donnelly's back tire, which caused the wheel to wobble sending him to the ground again, hitting the street with a crash that could be heard throughout the neighborhood.

She picked up another rock from the flowerbed and walked toward him. Donnelly was looking up at her from the street as she held the rock in her cocked fist, staring down at the boy who now called for Clank's help. When Clank never came and she didn't move, Donnelly mounted his bike and caught up to Clank who was about a block ahead of him. When they were tiny in the distance, Donnelly yelled, "Jew girl," and then, "You'll be sorry, Mexican." I set an arrow against the string and lifted it to fire, but the string snapped and the arrow remained harmlessly in my hand.

"My name is Jesse, the son of Jose," I shouted, hoping Donnelly and Clank could hear me and never forget it. I was so excited I kissed Sarah Jane on the lips. She smiled and giggled as I took her hand and pulled her down onto the grass where we traded kisses for hours.

When I finally went back into the house after dark, I looked out the front window watching Sarah Jane as she bounced home by the streetlights, safe from everything in the world. After that, I would see Sarah Jane every day and most nights that summer, often sneaking out of my parents' house late at night to sleep next to her in her tipi, but without having sex as Jose would have had wanted.

We didn't always hunt on the weekends. Sometimes we hitchhiked, sitting together on the curb between rides as I filled my dime store corncob pipe with discarded cigarette butts that we smoked. Together we visited all the great surfing beaches like Malibu and Rincon, but mostly Huntington Beach Pier since it was closest. All the guys liked Sarah Jane, and she had no trouble borrowing a surfboard. Nobody could believe I was her boyfriend.

She rode the biggest waves and did all the tricks like spinners and hanging five, sometimes even shooting the pier—riding through the dangerous cement pilings as the wave threatened to crush her—which it never did. Nothing could hurt Sara Jane. She tried teaching me surfing; but, I never caught on, so she taught me to bodysurf. From then on, I bodysurfed in the shore break or played cards on the sand, smoking cigarettes and taking easy money from the local boys while she surfed.

One morning, Sarah Jane left the water happy and hungry, dried off, put on her T-shirt, and walked up to a tourist saying her father's car had run out of gas and asking for a nickel or a dime. The guy looked longingly at Sarah Jane, all wet and beautiful, and gave her a dollar. The next man she asked actually gave her five dollars before trying to kiss Sarah Jane. She slapped him hard but kept the money as she ran back to us. With six dollars, she treated our entire new Huntington crew—me, Curly, Smirk, Dave, and Bones—to pancakes at the Buzz Inn, across from the pier. It seemed that every day that summer Sarah Jane grew taller and prettier with her long, blonde hair turning silky white while her body grew into womanhood.

Sarah Jane was always looking to try something new and sometimes we rode our bikes from Bell to East LA to see Jose who was back to his old self. He always cooked us good Mexican food and sat us down in the front room, asking if we were going to be married and have children. I turned red and silent, but Sarah Jane laughed, putting an arm around Jose, saying she wanted a man like him to marry. Then Jose stood and put his arm around her and kissed her on the cheek. "If you do not marry her, my idiot son, I will marry her for myself, this Sarah Jane, and then we will have many sons together and name the first one Jose and maybe even the second one also Jose, and the third one, and all of them will be Jose," he said, laughing hard. He was laughing and Sarah Jane thought he was kidding, but I knew better.

Jose had nearly forgotten about Soridtha who, without a word, walked into the kitchen where we were all seated. He quickly released Sarah Jane, saying he was joking, and his wife took him by the ear to sit on the couch in the front room while Sarah Jane averted her eyes.

Jose wanted one of us to have children with her, even though he was old and I was only fourteen and she was fifteen. Anyway, how could I have a son with her and then divorce her to become a priest? It was a foolish plan for many reasons, including the fact that priests cannot be married or divorced; but there was no use arguing with him about that.

Nobody who ever saw Sarah Jane could believe I was not in love with her—at least not in the way I had been in love with Sister Mary Bernadette. One night, alone with her in the tipi, I told her I did not love her as a wife. I kissed her as if she were my sister and she kissed me as if she were my wife. I lay beside her, awake and holding her silently, until morning.

Maybe I didn't want to love Sarah Jane because nobody stayed in Los Angeles for long in those days and I expected she would soon be gone from my life, forever. It wasn't long before she and her family moved from California to Texas. I wrote to her once, putting my full name, Jesse

Santiago Flannigan on the return address. When the letter came back to me unopened I was glad I never loved her.

CHAPTER FOURTEEN
UNCLE DEXTER

Like most LA suburbs in those days, Bell was filled with tree houses and wooden forts camouflaged by being dug into the dirt of empty lots where boys played games of Army. This is where the boys gathered to show off their new pellet guns, bows and arrows, jackknives, slingshots, military uniforms, and the flags their fathers had taken from their enemies during the war.

Girls marked long stretches of sidewalk in chalk for hopscotch. When not in the forts or at home, boys crowded the streets for kickball or wandered the neighborhood, claiming empty lots for themselves by flying homemade flags on them.

There were wagon races, soapbox derbies, and polo tournaments held on bicycles, all played in the middle of the street, and somebody always came away needing stitches. When not massacring each other, the boys captured neighborhood cats and shaved them like Mohican Indians or painted them with tiger stripes. Then they would release them to find their way home again where they were often turned back out onto the street when their owners did not recognize them. A lot of boys raised pigeons while other boys hid on rooftops or behind bushes to shoot the birds out of the air with arrows or pellet guns. Beside the regular cats, dogs, and birds, some people kept snakes, skunks, monkeys, hamsters, frogs, turtles, or alligators as pets. When the alligators got too big to live in household aquariums, they were flushed down the toilet. We were told they got huge and lived in the city sewers.

Every weekend, the men in the neighborhood toiled in their yards planting trees, worked in their garages, added new rooms onto their houses, built things like barbecues, household items for their wives, or dollhouses and soapbox derbies for their kids. One man carved tikis from whole palm tree trunks and sold them all over the city. Another man painted bullfighting pictures on velvet. Almost every man in the neighborhood made something in the garage while his wife sewed in the bedroom or cooked in the kitchen. Even the kids made things—the boys building kites from instructions found in *Popular Mechanics* or making bombs their friends taught them to build, and the girls making cookies and clothes for their dolls. On the weekends, you could smell gunpowder and baked goods throughout the neighborhood.

Dexter Crabb wasn't anybody's uncle, really. He wore thick, wire-rimmed glasses and a crew cut. He was thin and tall, but seemed shorter because he always slumped. Everyone said his parents had been killed in a car wreck, but that was just a good story. I found out he had actually grown up in Indiana and left when he turned thirty to come west for a job. He had lived alone next door to my parents' house, and, like everyone else, he had a hobby—his was inventing gadgets. On the first day I met him, he showed me various inventions: a pencil that never needed sharpening, a light bulb that never burned out, and a tiny transistor radio that looked exactly like a pack of cigarettes that he gave me to keep. Everyone said Dexter was an idiot, and I myself was unsure until he showed me his air car that was supposed to move over land or water on a cushion of air without using wheels. Then I knew he was a genius.

It was as an egg-shaped, metal-flaked purple thing made of fiberglass with a clear bubble top that covered the heads of the driver and a single passenger. Dexter worked on the air car in his garage until late every night. You could see the sparks from his welding torch and hear him cuss after he banged his knuckles. Little by little, I began wandering into his garage more and more often, helping by holding a flashlight so he could see into dark corners of the air car's engine. Soon, I knew the names of all the tools and would hand him whatever he needed. Sometimes Dexter let me tightening a bolt myself if his big fingers couldn't reach. Once while firing up the air car's engine he let me sit beneath the bubble, pretending to drive.

After a few weeks, when he thought the car was ready to go, Dexter sent out printed invitations to everyone inviting us all to Legg Lake, which was only a few miles from our home. There we could see "The Car of the Future," as he sometimes called it, fly for the first time. It was about eight in the morning that Saturday and already hot when I helped him cover the air car with the top sheet from my bed. Dexter and I drove to the lake in his regular car with the shrouded air car towed by a trailer hitch behind us. I tuned the car radio to KRLA to hear rock 'n' roll; but, Dexter talked over the music, eventually turning it off, laughing and saying, "They're going to see that ol' Dexter's no idiot now." Then he drove faster and we got to the lake before anyone.

Dexter paced the damp sand surrounding the lake, again and again, until everyone in my family, and, eventually, most of the people from our block showed up.

They stood, bunched together, chattering near the water, waiting to see if Dexter's car could really fly. My mother and father, along with my brothers and sister, got out of our family car and stood, waiting silently, as I ran past them to greet Jose who had just driven up and parked on the sand near the lake. "I seen many things, maybe even a train that can fly, but I ain't never seen no car to fly," he said, crossing himself. Dexter strutted around the car until those people who were still talking piped down. Finally someone screamed, "Let's see the air car."

"You wanna see the air car?" returned Dexter to the crowd, hitting the car with the palm of his hand.

"Yeah, show us the air car," somebody screamed back.

Then he clapped his hands and said again, "You wanna see the air car?"

"Yes," everyone yelled back.

I proudly went forward and helped Dexter undo the trailer hitch while everyone watched, silently. When my brother Carl hit me with a dirt bomb, everybody laughed. I didn't fire back; I had work to do. When everyone was dead quiet, I helped pull back the sheet. And there it was—purple and shining bright in the sunshine—the car of the future, just as Dexter had promised. Some gasped, some laughed, and everyone walked forward, not daring to touch the miracle as they stood in the pass near the lake, wondering if Dexter really was a genius. Jose stood facing the car, beating his chest reverently like he did in church. When a man near Jose laughed and called Dexter an idiot, Jose shoved him to the ground, saying, "You must be silent until after the air car has flown."

Everyone was silent except Jose who shouted, "*Vaya con Dios*, Uncle Dexter and the air car." Everybody cheered as Dexter climbed in alone beneath the bubble top and started the engine. Wind from the car blew sand everywhere, and everyone pulled back as flames shot out of the chrome tailpipes of the air car. Soon the car ran quietly as Dexter floated a short way over the dry sand, blowing sand on the spectators, circling toward a crowd of about twenty-five people. He smiled and waved at everyone as they clapped and he turned to approach the lake.

Everyone now realized Dexter was a genius as the air car hovered over the ground and approached the water. Water blew out everywhere as the air car moved to a greater depth. Then, it began smoking. Dexter hit the switch to shut off the engine just as the car caught fire and rattled abruptly to a stop, sinking a little ways into the shallow water and mud of the lake. So much smoke filled the bubble you couldn't see Dexter's face any longer. Everyone just stood there watching except for my father, Jose, and me who rushed forward to help him out of the car. Right before we got there, Dexter opened the bubble and smoke poured from it. He jumped out into the mud, slipping and falling while some laughed and smoke and fire came from the car. He threw handfuls of lake water onto the flames as Jose and my father helped him put out the fire. The car of the future sank a little until it looked like nothing more than a big, purple egg in the lake. Everyone laughed and returned to their own cars to drive home except Dexter, Jose, and me. Nobody but an idiot would make a car that caught fire and sank in the mud, they all said. But I still believed in Dexter and so did Jose, who congratulated him for flying a little ways. Some of the kids who had been fishing in the lake dropped their fishing rods, walked over to touch the ruined machine, and ended up burning their hands where the fire had been. It took all of us to slide the air car from the mud and push it up onto the trailer where we hitched the scorched and muddy air car to Dexter's real car again.

    After speaking with Jose for a while and promising to come see him soon, I rode home with Dexter, trying to cheer him up, saying it was a great car. He spoke about things like points, timing, pistons, and other things I did not understand as we continued home in silence. Once in his driveway, Dexter hosed the mud from the air car, dried it off with a clean towel, and put it away in his garage. I never saw him work on it again.

    The only times I saw Dexter come out of the house after that were to go to or from work or after he received letters on fancy, perfumed stationery signed by Mary Lou Edward, our next door neighbor Margaret's daughter. What Dexter didn't know was that one of those who had laughed the loudest at the air car, Mary Lou's older brother Steve, had written the love letters himself and signed Mary Lou's name. Working like bread under a box to lure a bird, the lonely Dexter was drawn from his house toward Mary Lou a little at a time. Each day, Dexter, who was thirty-three years old, waited on his driveway for fourteen-year-old Mary Lou to walk by. Mary Lou, who looked closer to twenty than fourteen, was a fat, spoiled red-headed girl who wore a permanent frown. But Dexter was in love with her and she was in love with him, or so he thought. I wanted to tell him that Steve had written the letters himself, but I was afraid that Steve, a boy of at least sixteen, strong and mean, would pound me if I said anything.

I had never seen Dexter drink anything but water and RC Cola, but I am certain he was drunk the day he sprinted to Mary Lou's house with flowers and candy, ringing the doorbell five times, and waiting at the front door for her. When she didn't come out, he pounded on the door loudly, yelling he was in love with Mary Lou. Margaret, Mary Lou's mother, finally came to the front door, shooing Dexter away and telling him to leave her property before she called the cops. Mary Lou, who at first only peeked silently from behind Margaret, soon found her courage and screamed for Dexter to leave.

He never worked on his inventions or spoke to anybody, including me, after that. Over time, he came out less and less, until he quit coming out at all. According to Steve, Dexter had been dead for three days, and the stove was still pumping gas through the house when the sheriff found him.

Then, one morning my father showed me a picture of Dexter in the newspaper, pointing proudly to the article saying that Dexter Crabb had invented a new type of jet fuel for the military. As it turns out, Dexter had moved from Bell to greater Los Angeles to take a job with an airline company and not told anybody about it.

A few years later, Margaret said she had seen Dexter riding in the air car, down at the lake, while the pretty woman he was with, sat on a blanket watching. When Margaret asked Dexter for a ride he ignored her.

CHAPTER FIFTEEN
THE BROKEN HEART OF THE CITY

Julio the Shark continued to raise the rent until Jose was paying seventy dollars a month, which was enough to rent two such houses in 1958.

I had made peace with my family and enjoyed living in Bell, but I was lonely for Jose and asked my parents if I could live with him until he was finally forced to leave. When they agreed, I packed my things and returned home.

Stories of the removal of the streetcars had been in the newspapers for weeks, and everywhere you went people spoke about it, especially Jose who said, "The streetcars are the blood flowing to the heart of the city, and without them everything will soon die."

One Monday morning I awoke early to find Jose in the front room, wearing his best black suit, a new white shirt, and a black string tie. Placing his black felt hat carefully onto his white, slicked down hair, he looked like he was going to a big card game with rich people in the city, or to a wedding or a funeral. He was smoking hard, pacing the floor nervously, and shouting before striking the floor with his heel. He had told me not to go to school, but to dress in my best clothes and meet him in the car. I put on my black suit and slicked down my hair with pomade, trying to look exactly like Jose.

We rode fast and in silence past the small houses and narrow dirt and gravel alleys and streets of East LA, watching as the little shacks gave way to nice houses, then mansions, and finally the tall buildings of downtown. The many cars and streetcars buzzed all around us, but Jose weaved through them, never slowing down or using his brakes, never hitting a red light, narrowly missing cars as their drivers honked and shook their fists at us.

"I helped to build this city with my own hands and now they are sending everything to hell," he shouted. His eyes were locked to the street, following the soon to be useless iron tracks, lighting one cigarette from the last, driving fast and recklessly. He pulled over to the side of the road, put a nickel in the meter, and got out without a word. I followed him up the smooth stairs into a tall building with the words "Los Angeles Department of Transportation" written in gold letters on the big front window. I struggled to keep up as Jose walked briskly, bursting into a lobby where he boldly approached the pretty secretary, removed his hat, and politely asked for a man named Mr. Sheridan.

"Mr. Sheridan is out of town on business," said the girl without looking up.

"You had better to please show me to Mr. Sheridan very soon," replied Jose, resting his knuckles on the wooden desk. Without making eye contact, the girl asked for Jose's name.

"You will please to tell Mr. Sheridan that Mr. Jose De la Luz Santiago is here to see him," said Jose, standing tall with a little smile, bowing gently to the pretty girl. She turned around and pushed her way through the tall wooden doors that had been closed behind her.

Within a few minutes she returned wearing a nice smile, holding one of the doors open wide for Jose, saying, "Mr. Sheridan will see you now, Mr. Light." As Jose walked torward, I followed shyly behind him and the girl, who was maybe eighteen—only four years older than me—glared as if a young boy should not enter such an important place. When I hesitated, Jose pulled me up next to him and we entered the office side-by-side.

Mr. Sheridan had the body of a baked potato and

the head of a boiled tomato. Still, you could see by the pictures on the wall of him with the mayor and the governor, he was an important man. While he tried to look unimportant in other pictures—holding a shovel, wearing a clean white shirt and tie and a hardhat—as if he had worked along with the men in the pictures, though anyone could tell he had not done any real work in a long time. Mr. Sheridan stood as tall as possible and looked Jose in the eye, keeping one hand in his coat pocket as if he were carrying a gun. Jose showed about as much respect for Mr. Sheridan as he would have for the butcher, which is a lot of respect for a butcher, but not enough for an important man like Mr. Sheridan.

"Jose of the Light," said the man, sitting down now in the big, leather chair behind his desk, asking us to sit in the little, wooden chairs in front of him while shaking his head from side to side, as he continued, "It is good to see you again, Jose; it has been a long time."

"Yes, Tom, truly it has been a very long time, and you should know that I now use the Mexican name De la Luz and that is the way that you should call me from now on," Jose said.

"Jose Light. You were the best worker I ever had," said Mr. Sheridan. Jose stood, a little anger showing in his face as he leaned back like a bear that is off balance after coming to its full height.

Mr. Sheridan stood too, trying to look as big as Jose before backing away, pacing the office, and talking nonsense. After the useless chatter ended, Mr. Sheridan sat again and offered Jose a cigarette, which he took and lit, still standing as Mr. Sheridan stayed seated and lit a cigar for himself. Then he pulled a bottle from his desk drawer, opened the bottle, and poured a little whiskey into two small paper cups. Sipping from his own cup first, he then offered the other to Jose, which Jose drank in one swallow, before holding it out for another drink. Mr. Sheridan obliged, barely touching his own drink.

Through their conversation I learned that Jose and Mr. Sheridan had been friends more than thirty years ago when Jose worked on the streetcar rails and Mr. Sheridan was his supervisor. After work they often went drinking together, and many times Mr. Sheridan found a girl for the night, while Jose sometimes restrained himself, trying to remain faithful to Soridtha. They were as young as the city of Los Angeles then, and just as wild, I could tell. "Jose Light . . . damn; you were the best worker I ever had," repeated Mr. Sheridan. "If you are here for a job, I'll give you one ripping out the old streetcar lines," he said, smiling brightly. Jose himself did not smile, but formed a tight fist whenever Mr. Sheridan called him Jose Light. Still, Jose was quiet and continued listening politely.

When it was Jose's time to speak, he did not speak in

circles as Mr. Sheridan had done. "Life has been good for me, and I now have my own house and even my own car," said Jose. "And because I have a car and all of the money I need to live, I am not worried how I will travel in the city. And please to know I am not here for myself only, or for a job, but for the many poor workers living in Los Angeles. I see them each day, the ones who built the city with me; they are on the streetcars, singing, laughing, arguing, and sometimes kissing the girls in the way you had done when we were very young, Tom." Jose was smiling as he thought about the girls while Mr. Sheridan frowned to think of them. Rubbing the dent in his head, Jose continued, "Surely you too have seen the poor people for yourself, but you will see them no more, Mr. Sheridan. For how will the poor go to work, or to the boxing matches, or to anyplace good if you tear out the streetcars, which is the very blood going to the heart of the city?"

"Call me Tom, Jose," said Mr. Sheridan, smiling.

"Please, you must keep quiet just for one little moment more, Mr. Sheridan. And then, when you are speaking again I will listen, but I will not listen if you tell me that the poor will ride the damned buses in this town. Do not say that thing to me about the buses, Tom. For who can ride a bus? Will a fat man like you ride a bus to go to work? No, you and I will not ride a bus because we know that the buses are dirty and they smell of hard work. And you don't never get to meet no nice girls on the buses. We both know this much, eh, Mr. Sheridan?"

Jose looked directly at the man when he spoke of the girls, and the man tried to laugh and not to laugh, and not to remember about the girls and the good times as he tried not to look at the picture of his wife and children on the desk before him. Mr. Sheridan stood, paced the floor, turned, and walked the few steps to the window to look over the city and take a deep breath. Turning back around, he walked to his chair and sat at his desk again, trying to get comfortable.

Jose leaned forward on the desk and then stood tall with his fists clenched, yelling, "Tom, it is a bad thing when I am mad at you. Please, do not make me to fight against you like when I had to knock you down onto the street because you had tried to take Soridtha from me by giving her many nice things and telling her big lies about me. I have forgotten this Tom because I know you are many times an ass and many times an ass cannot help yourself from being a big ass. But if I have to hit you and you come home with many bruises, maybe you will have to tell your wife that I had to hit you because you are now trying to steal from the poor and tear the heart from the city. May heaven keep me from killing you with my own hands, Tom," Jose shouted before taking a deep breath, putting one fist into his hand, gaining control, and sitting down again.

Nodding, Mr. Sheridan mumbled something stupid.

Then he smiled and stood, holding out his right hand to Jose, saying, "Thank you for coming by, Jose; I will look into this matter for you."

Jose stood and slapped the swollen hand away, saying, "You now need to stop looking into things and to start to stop doing what you are doing. And maybe you need to take a little care for the poor; that is all. If you do not quit hurting them, they will become as many as ants, and they will be eating from the garbage cans in the streets. They will spit on you when you walk on the street, and nobody will be safe from them. Truly they need the streetcars to ride to work, but also to dream that they might not someday be poor no longer, but rich, like you and like me, Mr. Sheridan. Nobody can have such a dream as this on a bus, for a bus is not for dreaming."

Jose finished speaking and then stood quietly, ready for Mr. Sheridan's response. Without looking up, Mr. Sheridan wiped his sweaty face with a handkerchief from his coat pocket and began speaking about the greatness of America and how the country must go forward and not backward to the days of Indians. He spoke about jobs and progress and great amounts of food, saying that the poor would soon have their own cars and could drive anywhere they wanted, all day long if they liked. Los Angeles, he said, must become the most modern of all the cities. The old streetcars, he said, were a part of the past, no more important than horses anymore. He said we should forget about horses and Indians and all about the past.

As Mr. Sheridan continued speaking he threw his arms around and his neck jiggled. His voice became louder as he looked out the window imagining the new city had already been built. His words were good and you could see forever out the window when Mr. Sheridan made you look there in your mind. Jose was not smiling, but enjoying the words a little, as he let the man go on speaking.

Mr. Sheridan continued looking out the window, keeping his back to us as Jose walked forward and picked through the mail in the wire basket on the desk, examining the letters one at a time before dropping them carelessly to the floor. When he found the letter that caught his attention, he held it in his hands as if it were something holy. He opened the letter quickly and quietly as Mr. Sheridan continued speaking to the window without turning to see what Jose was doing. Then Mr. Sheridan became quiet too, thinking his big words had convinced Jose to see things from his side.

Because of the familiar picture on the letter and on the envelope, Jose figured it came from a famous tire company. Everyone had said this tire company and a big oil company did not want the red cars to run through the city any longer so the people would have to buy cars and tires and oil and gasoline. Jose's mind was working as he looked at the meaningless words of the letter, even showing it to me for a moment, where all I read were big words directed at Mr. Sheridan. The veins on Jose's neck stood out and he crumpled the letter tightly in his fist and threw it onto the desk. Mr. Sheridan turned around with a satisfied smile, extending his right hand again, expecting that Jose would now see everything from his side and shake hands.

Not wanting to waste any more words, Jose reached across the desk and took Mr. Sheridan by the necktie, causing the man to look almost as frightened as he should have been. I prayed silently that Jose would not kill Mr. Sheridan with his hands and have to go to jail. But Jose did not even hit Mr. Sheridan. Nothing. He soon let go of the tie so Mr. Sheridan fell back down onto his chair with a loud thud.

The man sat as if dead for a moment. Then he sat up, straightened the tie and sat back in his chair to drink the whiskey remaining in his paper cup.

"How much money will the companies now pay you to destroy this city?" Jose roared, motioning to Mr. Sheridan, who now looked less important than a young boy like me, even in his big chair. The man did not look up, but found the crumpled letter on his desk and pressed it flat with his hand, trying to make it smooth again. But he did not respond to anything Jose said. When Mr. Sheridan lifted his sweaty face, Jose laughed directly into it.

Jose lowered his voice and spoke softly with nice, friendly words, walking around to Mr. Sheridan's side of the desk as the man flinched and sank lower in his chair and hid his face in his hands. "Come, Tom, please, we have been friends for a long time," said Jose gently, brushing his hands over Mr. Sheridan's rumpled suit then putting a hand on the man's shoulder, hoping to make him feel a little better. "I do not want to see you crying like a little girl, Tom. Please, we must still remain friends, and we must help the poor without crying, that is all," said Jose. Mr. Sheridan lifted his head, nodded, and smiled weakly at Jose.

"Surely you will take these matters under consideration as you have told," Jose said, as he shook hands with Mr. Sheridan and the blood was drained from the meat of the man's hand until it became white as snow and his tomato face looked like it would burst. When Jose released Mr. Sheridan's hand, he breathed deeply in relief.

"Good-bye, Mr. Sheridan," said Jose.

The man stayed slumped in his chair and did not reply, and there was not another word spoken as we walked out of the office, back through the big doors and past the pretty girl who gave Jose a nice smile. Looking back at her as we walked down the hall to the stairs, she was still watching him. Even from that distance, I could faintly hear Mr. Sheridan, calling again for the girl to come back into the office.

We had only been home for about an hour when our friend Officer McElroy knocked on the door, just as he did when he wanted advice from Jose on taking dangerous criminals to jail. Jose understood that Officer McElroy would have to arrest him for what he had done to Mr. Sheridan, although he had done nothing but say a few loud words and pulled on his tie. Before getting into the police car, Jose told the officer, "They are killing the city, and when they do this, and when they take out all of the dreams of the people, then there will be no dreams left for the poor, and you will see them coming against you like flies on a dead dog. I will go quietly with you now because you are a friend to me, Officer McElroy. And I will go quietly because I have done a bad thing to Mr. Sheridan, but the poor will maybe not be quiet some day."

    Officer McElroy did not put the handcuffs onto Jose, and he got in the front seat of the car on his own, sitting across from the officer, talking as you would to a friend on a Sunday drive. I walked silently up to the car and stood beside it, sobbing and looking into the open window as Jose turned, kissed me on the forehead, and we said goodbye to one another. Officer McElroy nodded as Jose spoke, his voice trailing off quickly as they drove away. The men in the neighborhood watched from their porches while the women watched from their kitchen windows and the police car drove up the street to the jail downtown.

I never did see Soridtha that entire time, since she rarely left her wikiup any longer. So, I took care of myself for three days until Officer McElroy dropped Jose off at the house again. They laughed and talked together on the sidewalk for a moment before the policeman drove away. It was late afternoon when Jose and I sat on the porch swing, watching the day go by. He said, "I know now that we cannot beat Mr. Sheridan in this matter. Running the jail are many Mr. Sheridans, all of them ready to beat us to the ground if we do what we are doing or think what we are thinking. One Mr. Sheridan alone could never win against us because of the power that they do not have. But many Mr. Sheridans will wear us down and then when we are spending all our time fighting them then there will be no more joy left in the world, not even in this house. They are all without joy, these Mr. Sheridans, and they love only to sit in the tall buildings and make stupid plans to ruin everything and to take away our joy. I will fight them no longer, but I will leave all of the Mr. Sheridans for God to punish, and I will not never do nothing again to stop the one Mr. Sheridan. That is all."

Jose wore his good suit the day we drove downtown to stand with a small crowd of people there to honor Mr. Sheridan and Mayor Paulson as they made long speeches.

Mr. Sheridan was sweating in a new and larger suit than he had worn before and talking loud and clear, but without looking at Jose, even though we were standing right in front of him. The speeches were good, and when they were over the little crowd clapped. Jose clapped harder than anyone, especially when some men from the news talked to Mr. Sheridan and the mayor and the other men and took their pictures next to the old streetcars. Some in attendance favored removing the streetcars, but many others did not. Of those, some were rich and some were poor, but all looked to Jose to stop what was going on. When he did nothing, they looked as beaten as Mr. Sheridan had looked in the office.

Jose drove home slowly, singing and laughing and telling about the miracle of the train. A few weeks later, he was back downtown, watching from the street as one of the last streetcars was roughly removed like a criminal. After that, Jose slept for nearly a week. When he finally came into the kitchen, he was happy but different than he had been. He said, "When I was sleeping I had the same dream many times. Each time the train would come and then it would hit me and I would die and go to heaven. Now I know that even I cannot win against this train of steel. The city can go to hell but I will not go to hell with it. Let us stay home, *mijo*.

Almost everything in Chavez Ravine, including the many altars, the stores, the church, and all the houses were leveled in preparation for Dodger Stadium. What was once a living, breathing community became a ghost town with only a few families holding out hope of keeping their houses. Soridtha camped out there each night, chanting, beating her drum, burning sage, and causing some of the bulldozer drivers and other workers to quit in fear of her casting a spell upon them. When one of the workers died of a mysterious illness, other workers also quit.

Because of the death threats Soridtha received, she slept on the ground, cuddled up with Jose's loaded shotgun. On the day the house of the brave Aurora Vargas was leveled and she was taken kicking and screaming by the police from it, Soridtha was also removed and taken to jail. When she was released a few days later, she did not feel well.

I have no way of knowing for sure, but Jose was convinced that Soridtha's death was no accident and that the politicians had murdered her because she knew of all the evil things they were planning to do to destroy the city. While she had never been sick a day in her life, one morning she had a fever and began throwing up violently. By that evening she was gone. Quick as that. Jose wrapped her body in the skin of a deer he had shot on the beach years earlier. She looked like a mummy and was dressed with all of the items of her life, including many eagle feathers, deer antlers, and everything you might expect of an Apache sorceress. The corpse lay undisturbed for several days in the front room of the house as Jose fasted, burned sage, beat the drum, and sang the Apache songs Soridtha had taught him to keep evil spirits from claiming her soul. Jose had planned to take his wife into the woods and give her what he termed a proper burial, by building a bed on long pine poles for her, as close to the sky as was possible, before lighting everything on fire. Then, he believed she would have the best chance of going directly to heaven. Everything was going as planned. He even had the body on the wooden scaffolding pointing north with her hands folded, and was dancing around while pouring gasoline on everything. Before he could light the match, however, the sheriffs appeared and took him away. While he was in jail, she was buried in a meaningless ceremony at Saint Veronicas' Cemetery where an ancient Catholic priest read words from a big book nobody understood or cared about.

  He was only in jail a few days, and the day he was released he drove to the gravesite where he sat crying, not for the death of his wife, whom he believed he would see again in heaven. He cried because buried with her was knowledge of the natural world that had been refined and passed down for thousands of years. Gone was wisdom as old as stone and the power to cure all things less strong than death. She knew everything and showed nothing, and with her died many wonderful things in the world. Jose always said he would dig up the body and give her the funeral he had planned. He never did get around to it, however.

CHAPTER SIXTEEN
FOUR WISE MEN

Every evening, Julio came into the house and walked around measuring things with a yardstick, poking around in the rooms, saying things like, "I don't like to have those ugly curtains in my place no more," ripping down the curtains Soridtha had made with her hands from sacks of beans or rice. Once Julio said, "Jose, why don't you hurry up to leave my house? Please get out soon and take that worthless son of you when you are going." Jose said nothing and only pushed Julio down onto the floor, but not hitting him as I had hoped.

For weeks Jose continued moving things from the

house onto the porch. At church I prayed two rosaries and lit many candles to the Virgin, hoping that we would not have to leave our home. But my prayers had no effect on someone so evil as Julio. He continued to come to the house every day to insult Jose and me as the boxes outside piled so high you could not see into the street from the front room.

The card games became fewer and sadder by the day while Jose's devotions became louder and louder. Many in the neighborhood came to listen on the street while he shouted his prayers to the Virgin. Jose nearly set the house on fire after burning photos of the house as a sacrifice to Hilberto, the angel who lived in the yard. Every day I lived in fear that Julio would come and throw us out. Instead of throwing us out all at once, however, Julio came to the house each day to change things around and move some of his own things in. He made his big mistake when he put Jose's altar along with Soridtha's medicine and woven baskets carelessly onto the porch in a messy pile along side ordinary things. To Jose, his altar was like the Ark of the Covenant I had read about in school. Nobody was allowed touch it but Soridtha.

Julio was in the house talking loudly about tearing the place down and building something new. Jose walked onto the porch and saw what had been done. Then, without saying a word, he cocked his fists and went looking for Julio. When he found him he said, "Do not push so hard, Shark, or I will push back against you and you will not like that."

"Only hurry up to move," shouted Julio, without fear or respect for Jose.

"I am moving, as you can see, but you should not push," said Jose again.

"You are no longer the owner of this house, and you are not the best in cards in this town no more, Jose. That is now me and I need to have the house for the games where you and the others will lose your money to me. And you must now hurry to move from here so I can tear down this shack and build something good. I want you to get out now, today. Go. Get out right now," shouted Julio, daring to push Jose.

But Jose did not push easily, he barely moved when Julio tried to push him. Then Jose's face burned red and he easily shoved Julio onto the floor, saying, "You are a worm and not a man, Shark. And you are not good with the cards. If you did not make me drunk, I would still have this house for my Soridtha and for me and for my son and for the Virgin and for the angels of God. But I will not fight with you, and I will go." Jose left Julio on the floor and walked to his car as I ran after him. Lifting himself from the floor and dusting his pants with his hands, Julio yelled to Jose that he, Julio, was the best of all gamblers. We were nearly in the car when Julio called Jose back into the house. Julio was surely a worm, but even a worm can have pride.

Julio had much pride, and I think he wanted everyone to think he was the greatest of gamblers even more than he wanted our house. So he challenged Jose to decide who was the best, once and for all. Then it was settled that they would meet one more time for a card game. If Julio won, he would keep the house, everything in it, and all of our money. Also Jose agreed to admit before everyone, including the Four Friends, that Julio was the best card player in the city. If Jose won, we would get the house back. The men settled on a time to meet and shook hands, Jose squeezing hard, nearly driving Julio to his knees. When Jose let him up again, Julio laughed a little, turned away, and left the house to prepare for the big game.

Jose also prepared, shuffling and reshuffling cards at the kitchen table, eating meat with too much salt on it, looking up at me from time to time, smiling and saying, "That Shark won't know what is hitting him when I use the *Magic Aces* against him, *mijo*."

I had never known Jose to cheat, especially not with a friend, and so I asked him if it would be a sin to cheat at cards against Julio?

Jose laughed at the stupid question, saying, "No, my son, it would not be a sin to cheat someone like Julio at cards, for he himself is a cheater. Also, I would never use such a powerful trick as the *Magic Aces* without first asking the Virgin about it," he said, motioning with his head to the bedroom, where we had once again assembled his altar. He laid the cards on the table in even piles of four, asking me to turn over the first card in each stack; when he did they were all aces. Jose laughed loudly and said again, "That Shark won't know what is hitting him when the *Magic Aces* come against him."

After dinner that night, Jose retired to his altar where he drank, shouted, and prayed for a long time about the card game. When he returned to the front room he was happy, holding the ace of spades high between his thumb and his index finger. Without me seeing how he had done it, he made the card disappear. Then he made the card reappear in my shirt pocket.

I knew then he could make the cards do whatever he wanted, but I also knew magic tricks would not get our house back. He was truly the greatest of all card players, but I worried the Virgin would not like the cheating and somehow cause him to lose. A great shower of happiness was coming out of him and falling from heaven, spreading everywhere, even into the wood of the house, as it, too, shook a little. Jose said the shaking was the house laughing, happy because it knew we were going to be staying inside of it for a long time. When we laughed, the house laughed a little more.

"Everything will be good again, *mijo*," said Jose, still laughing. "The Lady has given her blessing to the cards, and she has given her permission for me to use the *Magic Aces* against Julio for this one game. Believe it; this was the first card I took from the deck after praying to her," he said, holding up the ace of spades for me to see. "But keep a very close eye that I do not become greedy to use this trick more than only one time and then only on the Shark. If I ever use the trick again on someone else, the Lady has promised the curse of my life will be doubled. And how can I now imagine I would have fourteen daughters in my old age. I think that maybe seven of them would be new babies, all crying and wetting at the same time. We would surely then have poverty, for the cards would turn against me always. There would be no milk from the goat, and the chickens would have eggs as tiny as the eggs of sparrows. Then I would be very sad and maybe in one year, *loco*." At the word *loco*, Jose pointed his finger to his head. He looked serious, sad, and, to tell the truth, maybe a little *loco* already. I told Jose I would watch over him so he would only use the *Magic Aces* against Julio, and only one time. He smiled and laughed loudly, again.

That night an evil wind rattled the trees and the telephone lines near the house. Julio was there early, not in his usual clothes—khaki pants, flannel shirt, and black, spit-shined shoes—but with a new black suit with silver buttons and a big black hat with a silver hat band. Jose gave him the best seat in the house and offered him food and something to drink, but Julio refused Jose's offer and did not even turn to look at him. He just sat at the big table as if he owned it and everything else, looking around, waiting to take it all. He smiled meanly, making me hate his gold teeth and black mustache, so thin it nearly disappeared as it stretched out across his smiling, stupid face. The Four Friends arrived together and Jose greeted them individually by name before politely seating them at the table. They were not there to play cards as they usually did, however, but to watch the game and to make sure Julio didn't cheat.

Jose poured himself a shot of tequila from the bottle, drank it down, and smiled. Then he stood, threw a couple hard punches into the air, cracked his knuckles, and sat back down. When Julio refused the drink of tequila Jose poured for him Jose's anger burned against him, and Jose drank the tequila himself. Jose passed the bottle to Blind Willie who accepted it with gladness, laughing, cursing loudly, and slapping his knee. The others also drank from the bottle, but they were silent as the cards were taken from a new box and shuffled and dealt from the stiff deck. The cards were cut and Julio drew up the jack of spades, while Jose drew only a seven of clubs. And so it was determined, Julio would be first dealer.

Julio called the first game as Black Jack. After he played through the entire deck, Jose had lost all but one hand and was down by about fifty dollars. Julio was laughing, looking around the house, bragging again that he would tear down the old shack and replace it with a big new house, using all the money he was about to take from Jose. Jose said nothing as Julio continued speaking. Then Ignacio grabbed for his guitar to play and sing, and to not have to listen to Julio anymore. Jose called the next game as high-low and won back his fifty plus another ten, and Julio went quiet. Jose's hands were fast, and he played good.

Jose shut his eyes, praying to God. Then Julio shut his own eyes to pray, but I did not think God would hear the prayers of a cheater like him. Just to make sure, I too prayed a prayer to go against the prayer of Julio. Jose opened his eyes, poured himself another shot, and passed the bottle to Giermo. Blind Willie played the harmonica as Ignacio strummed the guitar. It sounded good, but nobody cared to hear the music. We all knew the music was not for entertainment anyway, but to chase the nervous spirits from the room. But the nervous spirits would not leave. They flew around the table and caused trouble with the cards. I knew this could be bad for Jose and my guts churned as Jose took the cards and called the game as five-card stud— Jose's game. After finishing the first bottle, Jose opened another one, took a shot, and passed it around.

"Come on, grandpa," I said, putting an arm on him, trying not to talk too loudly as my throat cracked in anger as I called him something other than Jose for only the second time in my life. Julio looked up and lifted the back of his hand to me. He would have hit me too if Jose had not been sitting right in front of him. Again I prayed, this time (Father forgive me) for Julio to lose all of his money and to have to beg just to live in our backyard and to eat only the scraps of food we gave to him, like a pig. I opened my eyes and nodded and smiled confidently at Julio, certain he would soon be living in the dirt.

It was Jose's turn to deal and he dropped a card in misdeal, something I had never seen him do before. He reshuffled the deck and apologized quietly to Julio, with slurred speech. Then Julio said, "Hurry up, old man," right into the face of Jose, who said nothing against the Shark. Julio demanded another new deck of cards, which Blind Willie provided from his side coat pocket, still in the box. After the cards were shuffled again, everything went quiet.

Nobody could believe that Julio, a man who could not fight even if his life depended on it, was treating Jose this way. But Jose was not paying attention to Julio or anything else. He was smiling, mumbling to himself and to the Virgin in Spanish. When Jose took the bottle again, I grabbed it by the neck to take it away from him. Everyone was quiet then, fearful at yet more defiance against Jose. Without looking at me, he wrenched the bottle from my hand and poured himself another drink. My hope fell as he finished the drink and poured himself still another one. When the wind blew in through a window, I could feel the cold walls of the Midnight Mission, the place on Skid Row where the homeless lived. I closed the window, but I could hear the wind blowing still harder. My only hope was that a tree would fall onto a telephone line and cut off the lights, just as it had a month earlier during wind not half as bad as this.

Jose rocked back in his chair, nearly tumbling from it, but recovering and sitting up straight, laughing a little. Even the Friends looked worried about him then. When he received his cards from Julio, Jose's eyes were a little sad for a moment. Julio saw the sad eyes. He also saw the drunk dare I say it—the stupid look on my grandfather's face. But the sober Julio pretended to see nothing.

"How many cards, Jose?" demanded Julio. Jose was silent for a moment, and fumbled with the cards in his hand, looking at them as if they were pigs with wings.

He stared out into space when Julio repeated, "How many cards? Hey, old man, how many? Answer me *pinche viejo*, how many cards?" he shouted, snapping his fingers impatiently in Jose's face.

Jose held up four fingers and threw four of the five cards to Julio, placing the one card he was keeping face down onto the table in a sloppy way that made me ashamed.

Julio slapped Jose's four cards down in front of him. He then took two cards for himself, something that proved even to me that he probably had three of a kind. Julio's face brightened as he saw the cards, but Jose did not notice that, or that Julio sat up confidently, as if something had happened to strengthen his already good hand. If Jose had seen any of this, he would have folded before the betting started. "Three, or maybe four of a kind is a good hand, *Madre Mia*, please, let the tree fall now," I prayed. But there was no tree, only more useless wind, without rain.

Jose did not even turn his cards over to look at them, but began betting twenty dollars at a time. Julio matched each twenty and Jose recklessly threw down fifty, a sum Julio gladly threw down to match. Jose, who still had not looked at his cards, was betting crazy and in the dark as the walls of the Mission closed in around me. Each of the players continued to raise until there were hundreds of dollars in the pot. "I'll see that and go . . ." Everything went dead quiet as Jose stopped speaking and touched his cards fondly, which were still sitting face down in front of him. Then he reached for his wallet that held all the money we had in the world. He pulled the wallet out from his pocket, and it dropped from his old, wrinkled hand, onto the floor, falling open, bulging with the many one-hundred-dollar bills he had dug up that day from the hole in the backyard where he kept our savings.

What could I do? I wanted to run from the house with it, to bury it again in the yard where nobody, especially Jose, could ever find it. Instead, trembling, I picked up the fat wallet and gave it back to him. He also bent down to get it and we both arrived beneath the table at the same time where I looked into his dead eyes. Straightening back up in his chair, looking at Julio, Jose said, "Okay, I bet you my entire house against . . . ," and he pulled the thick stack of hundreds from the wallet, held them high over the table, and dropped the bills slowly, a few at a time, letting them fall like rain on the table, while some of them overflowed onto the floor. "There you go, Shark, you can now see all my money," said Jose, smiling stupidly. Ignacio took the money from the floor and put everything neatly together on the table, to form one big, neat pile in the center.

Julio's slight smile turned down, into a little, fearful frown because Ignacio had touched the money. Nobody said a word. For the first time, Julio hesitated, shifting uncomfortably in his chair. Jose then reached into his top pocket and pulled out the last of our money, two new one hundred dollar bills that he kissed and put on top of the pile. Julio, who was betting our house against the pile, threw down his own hundred dollar bills, to match the final ones Jose had thrown in. "Okay, this is it, Shark," Jose said, laughing from the side of his mouth. Julio nodded to Jose without expression. Nobody moved.

Ignacio, who had quit playing his guitar, looked down and counted the bills quickly with his eyes, not touching the money. After he finished the silent counting, he looked up and around the room, saying, "Maybe three thousand!" Everyone fell silent, except Willie who shouted "Holy shit," before slapping his knee and laughing loudly.

Julio nodded seriously to Jose.

"All of the money in the world," said Jose, waving his arm and looking for the last time at the walls of the old house. Then he looked to the Friends, who looked away, ashamed to see Jose in his hour of defeat. He then waved a silly goodbye to the house and to his money, saying, "Goodbye house; goodbye money."

"Okay, three thousand for you against my house, but you better have something good, old man," Julio said, laughing meanly.

"Okay, that is all. I call you," said Jose, slurring the words, running his finger sloppily over his empty shot glass. He poured himself still another drink, spilling some of the tequila onto the table before throwing back the shot. "Now, what have you got?"

"Try four jacks on for size, *pinche viejo*," Julio said, laying the cards down with a burst of sudden joy and laughter nobody shared. Silence was followed by loud gasps as the weight of the four jacks fell down upon the house and upon each of us. The Friends stared, silent and sad. I hung my head so nobody would see me crying.

We all looked to see Jose, a defeated and suddenly

old man, slumped in his seat, staring blankly at Julio. Finally, Jose turned his cards to look at them. He opened his mouth wide in astonishment and laid the cards back down on the table, again turned face down. He put his head into his hands and smiled happily at everyone. From there his head fell down onto his chest and then onto the table where he passed out. I could not understand why he had become drunk when everything depended on this one hand. We did not even have enough money to stay in a hotel for the night. He could live alone in the damned Mission if he wanted; he deserved that punishment, but not me. I would move home with my parents again, where at least I would be warm in the new house, living with people who were not *loco*.

Julio straightened up and leaned over the table, giving a big shout of joy. He looked around at the others to share in his happiness. Blind Willy shook Julio's hand politely, while the others looked like they were at a funeral. Julio turned to me, reached across the table and slapped me lightly across the face. "I hope you don't mind a little wind," he said, motioning to the door with his head before reaching out with both hands to gather in the pile. Blind Willie said Jose and I could stay with him, and the others said the same, and then Willie headed to his car, returning with a blanket to cover the shame of the fallen Jose. Once Jose was beneath the blanket, Willie tucked fifty dollars into my shirt pocket.

Suddenly Jose lifted his head slowly and powerfully. Like a lion, he lifted his head. Then, soberly, he reached out with his big powerful hands to stop Julio's greedy little hands from taking the money. Then, while looking at the white face of Julio, Jose released his hands, sat back in his chair, and flicked his own cards over for the first time.

With a turn of his thumb the cards fell, running out in a perfect fan to show the miracle of four kings. It was silent for a long time in the old house, before it exploded with holy joy, which went on forever as we laughed and the house laughed along with us. Blind Willie crossed himself and said it was a miracle from God. Ignacio kept saying, "I can't believe it. I can't believe it." Joaquin sat in his chair, tears in his eyes, crying and laughing like a child. Giermo smiled brightly with eyes closed and hands lifted to heaven in silent prayer. Soon Ignacio took his guitar from the floor and Blind Willie pulled his harmonica out of his coat pocket. Together they played a song of celebration as the other Friends joined in. Jose laughed so hard he blew some of the cards and some of the money from the table, onto the floor. I hung onto his bull neck as if I would never let go.

Jose gathered in the pile of money, stacked it neatly on the table in front of him, and put most of it back into his wallet, leaving a nice stack of hundreds in front of him. It was Jose's night, but he did not want it all to himself. He would soon celebrate harder than anyone else, but he could not be happy while someone in the room was miserable. That someone, of course, was Julio who sat like a wooden Indian, staring at the powerful jacks that had betrayed him. I gave Willie back his fifty and Jose gave me and each of the Four Friends a one-hundred-dollar bill. I think I am the only one who saw the movement of his fast, magic hands as he palmed the remaining stack of hundred-dollar bills, and without anyone but me and Julio knowing it, stuffed the money into his opponent's top coat pocket. Reaching over the table, he kissed Julio gently on the check and asked him to share a drink with him, which the ruined Julio humbly accepted this time.

As the night wore on, Joaquin was sleeping on the couch beneath the great overcoat of Jose. Jose and Giermo were dancing cheek to cheek, smoking hand-rolled cigarettes, and kicking the bottles into corners of the house as they waltzed on the rug to *Corrido de Juan Villareal*, a song about the Mexican Revolution that played over and over again on the record player. Blind Willie played along on his harmonica, and Ignacio played the accordion. Julio sat alone in the corner drinking, crying, calling out to the Virgin about the jacks, and singing his own sad songs. Before the night was over the truth of the miracle hit me—Jose could not have used the *Magic Aces* to save the house. He was not even dealing on the last hand. The house was saved by a miracle.

I was happy about the house, but it really didn't matter. Mario Dibella had been on the school grounds looking for me after Darryl Donnelly told him I tried to steal his girlfriend.

CHAPTER SEVENTEEN
A KIND OF SALVATION

Each time Jose won big at cards, he would buy something nice for Soridtha and for someone else. Even though Soridtha was gone, he bought her a new Gafferes and Saddler gas stove that he installed in the kitchen. I got a new bike. For the Four Friends, he had new mariachi uniforms tailored in Mexico. He gave me fifty more dollars and took me to hear the Friends play their beautiful Mexican music at a wedding in the Plaza where children fought over a piñata filled with candy and a few coins.

By the time I began tenth grade in September of 1959, I was nearly fifteen years old. I decided to work hard at my studies and stay clear of any trouble. I was doing well and would have succeeded if only Maria Ortiz had not increased still further in size over the summer. But there she was, in my class, forcing me to look over at her.

Realizing that hiding in the bushes was no way to get a girl like Maria Ortiz, I followed her at a distance on my bicycle where I could clearly see her, but she could not easily see me. As I rode, I hoped and prayed she would become tired, or fall and hurt herself. Then I would help her carry her books and see her home, and she would want me. It was a good plan and it would have worked if Mario Dibella had not ridden up on his bicycle, slowing down to coast along beside her.

I was half hidden by the trees that lined the block, but close enough to see them kissing as they stopped along the way. "Be bold," I told myself over and over again as I waited. But I was not bold, and I held back far behind them until it was dark and they arrived at Maria's house and stood on the front lawn where the porch light glowed faintly through the darkness and I could see their shadows. Mario rested his bicycle on the curb before he and Maria slipped behind a tall pine tree, thinking no one could see them kissing then humping and sweating. She pushed him away slightly, saying "No, no," until the words quit coming and I heard the two of them go to the ground and disappear, groaning until she was nearly screaming, and I feared her father would discover them naked together on his front lawn.

As quickly as it had begun, all sound stopped and Mario stood, pulling up his pants and buttoning his shirt. Then Maria too stood in her white bra and panties, buttoning her blouse and putting on her skirt and shoes. When Maria reached out for Mario he pulled away. Then Maria begged him to stay with her, putting her arms around him, kissing him, before he pushed her down onto the lawn again where she laid alone, crying on the damp grass while he called her "whore" and other dirty names. I wanted to run to her, to pound him, and free her and tell her I loved her and would help her and we would have a baby together, which would surely be a son we would name Jose—the boy who would forever break the curse.

But my heart turned to water as I watched, wondering how a boy like me could have such a girl and win a fight against someone like Mario Dibella. I watched him strut away like a rooster as he mounted his bike and rolled down the dark street.

My ride home was filled with tears and, once there, I crawled into bed with my clothes still on and slept restlessly, waking up once with a shout after a bad dream.

Before leaving for school the next morning, I joined Jose who was sitting and smoking quietly on the porch swing. I told him everything, including the problem with Mario Dibella. He sat quietly for a moment, and nodded, before saying, "Be bold, as bold as a lion." Then he slapped me on the shoulder and laughed loudly.

Each day after that, I would walk toward Maria at school, intending to be bold and tell her that I would take her away from Mario Dibella. But each time I came near her, my mouth turned to dust and I continued walking past her without a word. I was not exactly sure what I would say to her even if I did find the boldness to speak to her anyway. The new plan worked no better than the bushes had.

One day during lunch, I saw her standing alone in the schoolyard. This was surely a sign from heaven, since she was never alone on the schoolyard. I had to speak with her right then or I would never have the chance again. I lowered my head, said a quick prayer, and repeated the words of Jose, "Be bold" over and over again, as I walked forward until I was standing closer to Maria Ortiz than ever before. It was like dreaming when I finally faced her for the first time. Her black hair was nearly solid with hair spray, her dark eyes were lined in black, and her eyelids were caked in thick blue makeup. She was beautiful.

Looking directly at her, I swallowed hard and gathered the words to speak. Without so much as an introduction, I spoke loudly and boldly, saying, "I will save you from your boyfriend." Not counting asking her for a pencil when we were seated next to each other in third grade, this was the first time I had spoken to Maria Ortiz in my life. The little power the words had was drained further when they hit the air and fell to the ground. My voice sounded like a mouse, and I wanted to take the words back and run away from her. "Be bold," I mumbled to myself. This was the boldest thing I had ever done in my life and it seemed like I stood there forever, looking at her, waiting for her cherry red mouth to reply.

"What?" she asked, as if she had heard nothing I said. Then my knees shook, and I dropped my head. I found my words again with difficulty, stuttering, somehow managing to speak a little louder to her. "I will help save you from Mario," I said. I had done it, and she would be mine. I lifted my head a little, smiled at her and waited for her kisses of gratitude to fall upon my mouth. Her cheeks flushed red and she covered her mouth with her hand, holding back a laugh. Then she turned her head and broke into a nervous, high-pitched laugh as she ran to join her girlfriends, Sylvia Contreras and Francine Ochoa, who were standing just beyond us. I retreated as her friends giggled, pointing and staring at me as if I were naked.

After the lunch bell sent us back to our classroom, Darryl Donnelly, who had left me alone for months, walked up to my desk, slugged me in the arm, and laughed. "Mario Dibella was at school today looking for you. He's going to cut your throat," he said, running a knifed hand over his throat, the way he liked doing, continuing to laugh as he returned to his desk. School dragged by slowly, and I pedaled home in fear that Mario was waiting for me behind every bush.

That evening, when I told Jose Mario was planning to kill me with his hands, his eyes lit up. "That is good my son," he said, laughing, "For you are not a man really until you have had at least one fight for your life. I myself have had many such fights, and it is because of them I have learned to be bold. But even in my old age, I have never lost a fight," he said, standing and throwing a few hard punches into the air.

Motioning for me to follow him, we walked down the back porch stairs to the wooden shutters of the cellar he built after the great hurricane that hit Long Beach in 1942. Taking a rusty key from under a rock, Jose unlocked the cellar shutters, opened them, and we walked down the steps onto a dirt floor. I had tried unsuccessfully to break into the cellar ever since Jose told me I was forbidden to go there. The cellar was dark until Jose lit a match and pulled the string to the light bulb that came on directly overhead, revealing a boxing ring in the center of the floor. The cellar was like a cemetery where everything was dead and forgotten. Jose shut his eyes tightly and prayed quietly while I glanced at the yellowed newspaper clippings of Jose in a professional boxing ring that papered the walls. He was a young man then, holding the gloves over his head as another man lay at his feet. I scanned the newspaper clippings that either called him "Jose the Great," or "The Mexican Warrior."

    I remembered stories I had heard from a friend of his who said Jose could hit harder than a truck, and that no man, in fact, nothing but a train could knock him down. He also said Jose had once defeated the champion of Mexico in a ten-round bar fight. But that fight had not been one like you would see on TV or at the Olympic Auditorium. No, there was no ring, or referee, and neither man had worn gloves. Jose broke both his own hands by punching the man as hard as he could. But the man was strong and would not fall as easily as other men had. The big mistake the man had made was to pound away at the dent in Jose's head.

    Not only did those punches not hurt Jose, they helped him recall the miracle of the train. For what are fists of flesh compared to wheels of steel? Jose had continued to punch harder and harder, moving his arms like a locomotive, and one punch knocked the champion out. Bleeding, lying on the ground, the man looked dead. Jose collected the twenty-dollar gold piece as his prize, but gave the money to his beaten opponent. After that, Jose was afraid he would kill somebody in the ring, and he never again fought for money or raised an angry fist to anyone unless they were causing problems and there was no other way to solve things. That explained why he had not punched Julio or Mr. Sheridan. I knew what it felt like to be the defeated man;

and, while I did not want that, I also realized I would never have my grandfather's boldness.

Following Jose into the ring, he told me to put out my hands so he could wrap them in long strips of white gauze followed by tying a pair of old black, cracked leather boxing gloves onto them. Still in his khakis, he removed his shirt and then, standing in only his undershirt, I could see he no longer had the body of a young lion, but had become soft. For the first time, I noticed a faded tattoo of a little green lion on his left arm, along with the words "Bold as a lion," written in English and in Spanish, coming from the lion's roaring mouth. He pulled a glove on one of his hands without lacing it, and put his other bare hand behind his back. Holding the glove over his face, it seemed light as a feather to him. But my gloves were heavy and I was not able to hold them up for long to cover my face against the still fast hands of Jose. He danced around the ring with one hand up, swatting at the air, and I could hear the wind created by his punches, amazed by how fast and hard he hit at nothing even at his age, which I knew was over sixty.

He stood still and told me to try to hit him. I lunged and took a swing and then another and another, but no matter how I tried it was like hitting a ghost. He did not hit me as hard as he could have, but only tapped me. Yet, when the glove landed I felt my entire chest would cave in as I fell onto the canvas floor. When I got up, he batted me down again, saying, "Keep your hands up, Jesse, or I will have to hit you again. Keep your hands up." I tried holding my lifeless hands up to fight for a while, but when he hit me again, I again fell to the canvas. He was not trying to hurt me, but to keep me from losing the upcoming fight with Dibella. Humiliated and in pain, I threw the gloves off, red in the face, nearly crying in the ring. This was not like the silly scrapes in the schoolyard. Mario Dibella was an experienced fighter out for my blood and nearly twice my size.

"This is no old man you are now going to fight, Jesse," said Jose. I lay on the canvas floor until he helped me up. "Come to try again," he said, holding his hands out, dancing. When I would not fight him again, he pointed his finger at me as if it were a gun, saying, "If I can not teach you to fight, perhaps you will learn to use *mi pistola*. Come now, Jesse, get up to fight me. Fight me and be bold. Bold!" But I would not get up to taste his fists again, and when he realized I would never be bold like him, he quit teaching me to box. Instead, he patted me gently on the head and I followed him back into the house to eat vanilla ice cream with the blackberries he had picked from the bushes along our fence. Even as I tasted the sweet dessert, my life was turning to bitterness. I had lost Sister Bernadette and Maria; I fought like a kitten; and, Mario Dibella was going to end my life.

On my way home from school, I often stopped at Art's

Liquor Store for an RC Cola. There I also picked through the baseball cards, knowing Wally Moon, the one card I need to complete the new Los Angeles Dodgers collection, was in one of the packs, but I never knew which one.

    I stood in the store, shaking each of the gum-scented packs, thinking, *Okay, if Art looks at me and asks "What do you think this is, a library?" that is the sign Moon is in the pack I am holding. If he says nothing, I buy the pack behind the one I am holding, and Moon will be in that one.*

    Art kept busy with paperwork as I continued shuffling through the packs. I could feel the spirit of Moon when I heard the click of a kickstand and glanced up to see Mario Dibella swing his leg off of his bike to stand tall on the sidewalk in front of Art's. He glanced in at me and walked over to my bike parked on the sidewalk. "Be bold," I said to myself, trying to remain steady. He took a shiny black pocketknife from his side pocket, opened it, and revealed the thin blade. After making a stabbing motion at me with the knife, he leaned over and forced the blade into my back tire, ripping the tire open in the way you would gut a rabbit. He stood up, folded the knife, and put it into his pocket again. He was unafraid of anything and knew I would have to come out and face him eventually.

    It was getting dark as he waited for me like a cat in the grass for a bird; only, I, the bird, knew the cat would destroy me as soon as I left my cage. He stood on the sidewalk, watching me for a long time, but Art never noticed him or took his eyes off of the books he was writing in except to ring up something for a customer once in a while.

It was completely dark outside, and I could no longer see even a trace of Dibella. Relieved he had gone, I was ready to haul my bike home when Art flicked on his yellow sign that shined above the front door and I could see Dibella again, still standing beneath the sign, waiting for me to come out to him. He had flattened both tires and now pulled out his knife again, flicking open the blade, and holding it up for me to see. I thought to ask Art for help, but he was a crumpled old man and would be no good against a knife. I could make a break from the back door, but I was many blocks from home, and Dibella was fast and would easily catch me in the dark before I got far on foot. He kicked my flattened bike off the sidewalk into the gutter.

I stood, frozen near the baseball cards, as Mario waited for me to come out. After another long time, I walked up to the counter to ask Art if I could make a phone call. Without looking up, he slid the phone over the counter to me and I called Jose.

Soon Jose's Chevy rolled up beneath the neon light of Art's sign and stopped at the curb. He was dressed casually —black felt hat, creased khaki pants, flannel shirt buttoned to the top, and suspenders. He looked old and dried up until he exited the car and achieved his full stature. Dibella, who apparently realized Jose was there to rescue me, blocked the front door and puffed out his chest as Jose approached the store entrance. When Jose exhaled smoke from his cigarette into Mario's face, he reached into his pocket, no doubt touching the knife he would use to slice Jose open like a fish before turning the blade on me. Jose took a final drag of his cigarette before dropping it and crushing it beneath his heel. Mario looked suddenly small as Jose stood, waiting for him to make the first move. To Jose he was nothing but a little insect that has invaded his land. Compared to a train he was nothing at all.

Jose's laugh filled the store as Art glanced up from his books for the first time to see the fear gathering outside. I was sure Mario would go for the knife, but he froze as Jose pushed him aside and walked past him into the store where he found me hiding by the baseball cards. Without a word, he carried the entire box of cards filled with Wally Moons over to the big glass refrigerator where he grabbed a full carton of RC Colas, took everything up to Art, laying it all down on the counter.

"Good evening, Jose," said Art respectfully, turning back automatically for a carton of Lucky Strike cigarettes and a large bottle of Jose Cuervo Tequila from the shelf behind him. He put everything into a box for us and Jose nodded to Art, paying with a crisp one-hundred-dollar bill.

As Jose's power surged through me, I ran alone from

the store and pushed Dibella so he fell to the ground. When he rose quickly, I noticed he was six inches taller than me. He punched me in the face and I was bleeding, my watery eyes making everything blurry. I tried to hit him back, but he easily blocked each punch before hitting me again and again. I landed one lucky punch on Dibella, and he hit me three times in return. My mouth bled, but it did not hurt because I was no longer afraid, understanding what Jose had always said, "You must face fear, and be bold."

"Be bold," I said out loud as Dibella took me to the ground and Jose walked from the store holding the box filled with the items he bought.

He was old, and he exited the store with a limp, but he had a power that fell over Dibella like the shadow of a panther as he moved past us. Dibella quit pounding me long enough to watch Jose put everything into his car. Jose reached into the gutter, retrieved my bike with one arm, unlocked the trunk of his car with his free hand and set the bike inside. Dibella reached for his knife, looked at Jose, and quickly back to me. But he didn't need a knife to finish me. Instead he merely turned and hit me in the mouth. He was surprised when I hit him back hard. It was a lucky punch and it was good to see him bleed. He hit me several more times before letting me up. My shirt and pants were torn and I had bumps, bruises, and blood all over my face. I reached up and punched him in the face one more time with all I had.

The punch landed hard enough that he quit hitting me back. Instead, he smiled a little through his bloody teeth before straddling his bike and riding away.

In his car, Jose tenderly touched the bruises on my head, laughing and saying, "You have not won with the boy Mario, but you have won against fear today, my son." He laughed hard and turned on the Mexican music station, the only one he ever listened to. On the way home from the store we saw Maria Ortiz walking alone in the dark. I asked Jose to pull the car over to the curb and he did. Unafraid of anything, I boldly put my head out of the window to ask Maria if she would like a ride. After she said yes, I got out of the car and opened the back door for her as she smiled at me as she got in, and I slid in next to her.

This was the best moment of my life until, for the first time, I noticed that one of her top front teeth was almost black and lined in silver. She also had a small, unattractive scar on her lip that makeup did not quite cover. I no longer noticed the pretty face or even the breasts of Maria Ortiz, but saw only the tooth and the scar. For a while, we sat in the back seat, talking together as if she were a normal girl. Suddenly she reached over and softly touched and kissed the bruises her boyfriend had put on my face.

The silver on the tooth shone brightly when she smiled at me as we rolled beneath a streetlight. Driving beyond the light, I could see the ugly tooth no longer, but only the shadow of her body. She was beautiful again as she leaned over to kiss me on the lips, and I kissed her back. When she put her hands around my neck, I followed her into a dark corner of the car.

    Jose was so happy he turned off the radio and sang a Mexican wedding song. The scent of tequila filled the car as he opened the bottle, took a long drink, and laughed loudly. Then he lit a cigarette and told the story to nobody, to the air, to the holy and evil spirits crowding the car. Of course, it is the miracle of the train. And, although I had heard that tale every day my entire life, I listened to every word. After all, he was my grandfather.

CHAPTER EIGHTEEN
JOSE OF THE LIGHT

Ever since my fight with Mario Dibella my reputation as a fighter grew and there was little trouble with anyone. I played sports, studied, and spent my free time working at Art's Liquor Store, where I sometimes stole a bottle to drink with my friends as we wandered the city in search of a fight. I usually put the money for the bottle into the register later in the week, but sometimes I forgot.

I had transferred from Catholic school to Bell High. In public school, you never had to stand up to address the teachers, and they never beat or humiliated you for getting the wrong answers. Nobody had the hope of heaven or the fear of hell. There were many pretty girls there, some stacked nearly as well as Maria Ortiz. I had a few unremarkable girlfriends, but those relationships quickly faded. The years passed quickly, and I suddenly found myself standing on the football field with a thousand other students, getting my diploma and seeing Jose in the stands, standing to cheer loudly when my name was called.

 Although I loved my grandfather, I moved away from him to downtown Los Angeles, determined to live my own life. In Los Angeles, I got into trouble often, drinking, gambling, and fighting and trying to be a man like Jose. I lost more bets than I won and got beaten badly when I owed more than I could pay. I grew tired of everything in the city, but realized I was even more tired of the ignorant ways of the men and women in my grandfather's world, the poor people on the hill and even Jose himself, always telling the same stories over and over again.

 Hoping to be Jack Flanagan and live like other people, I moved to the sun and the surf on the beach in Santa Monica. There I entered college, majoring in psychology. I learned that too much change could cause a person to go insane. It didn't take much reading to convince me that my grandfather was insane, probably from a combination of being abandoned as a child, seeing too much change in his life, too much tequila, and the train running over his head. I began to wonder if he had really been run over by a train at all. He had probably been in some sort of car accident and the jolt knocked a screw loose.

Actually, I think everyone in the city, including me, had gone insane from all the changes. Everyone we loved died, moved away, or quit caring. You dared not love your home because it could be flattened and turned into a freeway; you dared not love your family because they would turn against you; your friends, because they all moved away; and, your God would be proven to be no God at all. Even the greatest of love could take wings at any time. The faith that held everything together in the past had been attacked by those who believed in the power of nothing. But maybe nothing was not such a bad god because the god of nothing would never disappoint you.

I avoided visiting Jose until guilt built up, and then I started seeing him for a few hours each month, watching as he got older and lost his strength. As we ate dinner, food and beer dribbled down his chin while I tried to tell him what I had learned in my psychology classes.

One evening after dinner with him, I told him that life meant nothing and said, "Grandpa, you would do well to get into therapy and to stop smoking and drinking tequila." He laughed loudly, in the way he used to. "If life means nothing, my son, then it was nothing that stopped the great train from crushing my head just like a grape." As always, he ran his fingers along the crevice on his forehead, and at the word *grape* clapped his hands, just as he always did when he got to this part of the story. Then he asked, "Can nothing stop a big train, Jesse? Can even a strong boy like you do such a thing? No, not even all the young boys and girls at the college where you are now going can stop a big train. Not even all of the boys and girls and all of the teachers together can do this. But of course you know this, for you do not go to the college to become an idiot, my son," Jose said, crossing himself before rubbing the dent, shaking his head, pounding the table, and repeating "nothing, nothing, nothing," several times before laughing until the laughing turned to coughing.

As far as him needing a therapist, he had no idea what the word meant. Still, I wanted to help him, and one day I drove to the house to show him a book with inkblot tests in it. Instead of looking quickly at each block as I told him to, he examined them carefully, considering each print before insisting that these were the drawings of children. "I see a cow here. This one is a chicken. This one is of my beautiful Soridtha, but most of the drawings are pictures of men and women having sex together. Look, see for yourself, my son," he said, happily. "But they are only very bad drawings," he insisted. Frustrated, I told him again that these were not the drawings of children, but tests to see how people perceive things.

Not understanding the word perceive, he laughed, shook his head, strolled to his bedroom, and returned with a representative drawing of a bull he had made with crayons after seeing it on the cover of a matchbook. He didn't realize that abstract expressionism was the style and that his style of representative art was out of fashion. "I will be glad to teach the children to draw a nice bull or a cow or a cat or a dog without no charge if you bring them to me for a lesson. I will even go to where the children are staying, but I don't drive so good no more and only last week I hit another car. Also, gasoline is now thirty-two cents for one gallon only, and the train is mad at me so I can no longer ride on it."

I had moved into my old room again, but after two days I was ready to leave. One morning at breakfast he began to tell me about the miracle of the train again. But I was not a child and I could stand his foolishness no longer. Without even saying goodbye, I walked out of the house, slamming the door as I drove back to Santa Monica.

At the age of twenty-three, I graduated from college only to realize I knew no more when I got out than when I went in. Then I thought maybe it was as Jose said, that the teachers were foolish and had never lived and I could learn nothing from them. And I have to admit to myself that I had become like most college students, thinking they know everything when they know almost nothing, and so are among the most dangerous people in the world.

I took a job as a bartender, pouring drinks, listening to people's problems, and working a block away from the beach in Venice. In Venice Beach, I enjoyed some peace, riding my bike on the boardwalk where the hippies smoked weed and played flutes. I bodysurfed in the afternoon as I had learned to do with Sarah Jane many summers before. When the bar was torn down to make way for yet another shopping center, I took a job as a janitor at a school. This lasted only a few months.

After that, I drifted between jobs for months, even traveling to the East Coast to find work and peace. When life finally took me to Jose's door again, I thought to care for him in his old age. But it is he who cared for me, bringing me back to myself and helping me to see life clearly again. "I will help you to get rid of all the opinions the schools have put into your head, *mijo*," Jose said tenderly. Turns out, he was not the crazy one, but everyone else. He alone saw things as they were, taking power over them when he could, accepting them when he could not, and almost always being happy at whatever happened.

In his world everything made sense. People were born and people died. Some of the people were good and some were bad. God loved all people, but the devil might curse them. Spells were made, and through prayers and suffering, some of them were broken.

He prayed at his altar daily where he whispered his

prayers then, rather than shouting them. He was never sick, and while he was not as strong as before, he never lost his true power, which I soon realized came from his great love, joy, and faith.

Everyone came to ask Jose's advice or borrow money, which he always gave freely. It was not only musicians like the Four Friends who showed up, but many women, young and old, asking about raising children, or boxers asking about training for a big fight, and even businessmen wondering if they should buy something or sell it. Even as an old man, he continued to be among the best poker players in Los Angeles, and he could make money any time he wanted by having a game of cards. He was on the news once to give advice on playing poker. Thinking they were being kind, the camera crew tried putting makeup on the dent in his head until Jose slapped the makeup artist's hand away and told her about the miracle of the train.

By the age of twenty-four, I was finally old enough to sit in on a card game with him. He seemed barely alive until the cards hit those magic fingers. Then he came to life and dealt as fast as lightning, memorizing every card played and making good bets until all of the chips were in his pile and everyone else was broke and borrowing money from him. Afterward, three of the Four Friends (Willie had died the previous year when his great heart gave out) cooked food in the old adobe oven outside, drank, and played the old Mexican songs long into the night. I covered Jose with a blanket after he fell asleep on the couch, smiling.

One day a young man with straight black hair and a tattoo of an ace of spades on his forearm showed up looking for Jose. He was nice to everyone, but cocky about his card playing. Being from Colorado, he called himself Denver Mike, bragging, "I am the best poker player in the country." Denver Mike was pretty good, but Jose took all of his money in just four hands of five-card stud, giving it back to him and patting him on the head, telling him he would be better off finding some other kind of work.

Denver Mike was not very cocky about his poker playing after that, and he moved in with us, sharing a room with me, telling me about his travels, his experience with women, and the fights he had been in. He was a good man helping Jose with the things he could no longer do in exchange for room and board and learning to become a great poker player. But, no matter how he tried, Mike never did become a great player, and only took one big hand from Jose.

Like so many who come to LA, Denver Mike arrived and left the neighborhood quickly. Jose, meanwhile, stayed in the little house, watching silently from the street as the empty fields were cleared for roads. The old houses were torn down and new houses were built all around him.

Sometimes he would help someone build their new house, sawing wood and pounding nails until he became tired, which didn't take long. He hated the new houses, but he did not hate the people who built them or those who lived in them. The construction workers came to see him, bringing him cold beer and sandwiches, sitting on the porch with him, to hear his stories, especially the miracle of the train.

One of Jose's great joys at this time was pretending to be an old feeble man, especially when the realtors came and asked to buy his house. "Would you care to buy this house for two thousand dollars?" he once asked a realtor in a nice suit. "I will give you fifteen hundred for it," replied the man, calmly. Jose knew the man wanted to buy the house, tear it down, and build five houses on the property. And he knew the property was worth ten times what the man was offering. But he wanted to see what sort of rat this man was. Once he knew, he straightened up, looking almost young again, before telling the rat to go to hell. He pulled on his tie like he did Mr. Sheridan's many years ago until it looked like the man's eyes would fall from his head. Finally, he let the man go and asked him inside for a beer and a sandwich, which he refused. While he despised the man's methods he prayed for him and others like him each night, that they would see what was good in life and find good, honest work to do.

Jose was not home much anymore. Usually he was at

a neighbor's house showing the new people—whether they were Japanese, Chinese, Negro, Italian, or Mexican—how to grow the best tomatoes or fix a car or how to do plumbing or electrical. He helped them in countless ways, giving them money if they needed it and offering his advice—even when he didn't know what he was talking about—to anyone wise enough to take it.

Soon there were no more poker games in the house, but Jose never retired completely from gambling. He would cut cards with anyone for fifty cents, or flip a quarter to see who got to keep it. And he would bet on the outcome of anything, not just sports, but even on things like the weather or how quickly a snail would cross a sidewalk. Somehow he won nearly all these games of chance.

One day I saw him walking slowly around the yard with the carved walking stick I bought for him on Olvera Street years earlier, hunched over, wearing a straw hat with the tassel swaying, talking lovingly to his chickens as he fed them by hand, refusing to kill them and eat them, and giving them little funerals when they died of old age. The funerals came complete with him playing guitar, singing, and praying, and then burying them in the little graveyard in the backyard beneath a wooden cross he made for each chicken. At least once a week, he would plant a fruit tree. When he grew tired, he sat on the porch swing, giving fruit or candy and sometimes small amounts of change to the children in neighborhood, telling them stories about great men and powerful trains while they sat near him. He never knew his ABCs, so that is not what he taught. He taught the children about life, calling them his sons and daughters and expressing love to them as if they were his own. They all loved to hear about the miracle of the train, and once I heard him tell the children the train that hit him was made of candy and he ate the entire train right down to the caboose. Everyone loved him, thinking he was a powerless old man, which, of course, he was not.

Periodically someone from the *Times* would drop by to take pictures of Jose and ask him about the changes he had seen. Over time, he became famous in the city, appearing on television fairly often and in many magazines. I don't know why they interviewed him more than once, however. Each time was the same, with him telling about riding horses into town, shooting pistols on holy days, giving tips on being as bold as a lion, and the miracle of the train. Although he never did trust a politician in his life, many of them wanted their pictures taken with him—something he refused to do, realizing they would cheat the poor in the city, no matter what they promised.

My life has been spent trying to imitate him; but, for me, there has been no train, no Mexican neighborhood, and no Soridtha with magical powers. He never brought it up, but I thought a lot about my promise to become a priest if God ever granted me a miracle, which he did when Jose won the house back.

As time passed, all Jose's friends died, including all the Four Friends in the mariachi band, whose funerals were filled with beautiful music, dancing, and singing for days. Only Jose and Julio never died. Together they attended all the funerals, visiting the cemetery as often as once a week. They carried the coffins of those many years younger than themselves.

Many good and bad things marked the passing of time as life drifted slowly by. I was a grown man, and like all in my generation, still a child, working at the post office while living with Jose. One day my supervisor informed me that Jose was in the hospital, asking for me. It did not take long before I was seated beside him on the hospital bed, and he held onto my hand and looked at me with clear eyes. Soon, all of his seven daughters, my mother included, were standing around us. They held hands, all in black veils, forming a half circle, each with a rosary, praying loudly and weeping. Their faces were twisted in grief and covered with tears as they prayed. I alone sat on the bed, straining to hear the final words of Jose.

When Jose heard the crying of the women, he told them to be quiet so he could hear the Dodger's baseball game he had been listening to on the radio. "But Papa, you are dying," cried my Aunt Matilda. "Thank you for telling me of this," Jose said, laughing a little, then coughing hard and kissing the picture of his seven daughters my mother had brought for him. The broken toy train was set next to the statue of the Virgin, but the doctors would not allow any tequila. When he asked me to bring him some, I promised I would. He could not set up a good altar there, but he had done his best. As he held the picture of his daughters, he called out to heaven saying, "*Madre Mia, por favor.*" Mistaking these words for the pleadings of a man in pain, the sisters wept still louder, never realizing he was asking the Virgin to keep the women quiet so he could hear the radio and die in peace.

"For three nights now I have had the same dream," Jose whispered, to me. "This time the train comes and there is no miracle. Now I know that this train will not be stopped by a man. The train must continue, but a man must not continue. And now this city will also die and be covered with the freeways and more cars than can be counted. The train will move fast and run long, but it too will someday die. This also, I have dreamed." Jose's eyes flashed such a vivid blue that the entire room was lit up by them. He looked straight ahead for a short while, with no expression. "Beautiful," was the only word he said before laughing hard, something that was followed by coughing so violent that all the nurses came running to see the dying man. But he would not die yet. He still had a few more gifts and at least one more trick to play upon life.

Jose survived for three more days, and I slept on the floor beside his bed, sometimes holding his hand and praying for him as he slept. During that time, everyone, including the mayor of Los Angeles, came to see him, accompanied as he always was by a photographer from the *Times*. Jose shook the mayor's hand, but he pulled the sheet over his head every time the photographer tried to take a photo of him with the mayor who was smiling and seated beside his bed. Many women and men—gamblers, gangsters, policemen, and some of the people Jose had helped in his life—showed up until a big crowd was gathered in his hospital room.

He was half in the spirit world and half on earth, breathing hard and talking little. It was then, after the doctors took his pulse many times, they offered to give him a shot of something for the pain. But he would not take the shot. He would need a clear mind for what he had left to do. When the doctors knew they could do nothing more for him, they sent for Father Thomas.

The priest arrived in his black vestments with a red sash, carrying a small leather-bound book and a small bottle of holy water. While he had never been a poker player, Father Thomas had the look of a man coming to Jose's house to challenge him at cards. He was serious and frowning, but Jose smiled confidently. Father Thomas laid the book and the holy water on the table and I wondered if he would offer Jose *Extreme Unction,* the last rites sacrament to prepare Jose for heaven. Father Thomas wore the look of someone who had four aces in his hand. He bent over Jose and whispered to him that he could not receive *Extreme Unction* since he had been separated from Mother Church by excommunication and could not return to the church without saying a penance so long it would require more time than he had left to live.

Jose gently patted the priest's hand, nodded, and smiled at him kindly, realizing he had spoken true. The priest stared straight ahead proudly, thinking he had won the final bet with Jose. I remembered the scapular Sister Mary Bernadette had given to me years earlier, the one that I always wore around my neck that had been blessed by the Pope himself. I remembered also the teachings that if someone died wearing the scapular they would go straight to heaven.

Taking the scapular from my own neck, I attempted lifting Jose's big head from the pillow to place the scapular around his neck so the picture of the Holy Family would rest on his heaving chest where everyone, especially Father Thomas, could see it. Just as I was about to place the scapular on him, Jose waved me away. Father Thomas looked first at me and then at Jose, triumphantly.

Jose whispered the name *Christo*, touched my hand, closed his eyes, and whispered the words *Celito Lindo*, the name of a beautiful Mexican song, meaning "Beautiful Heaven." He also mumbled something about tall trees and I realized he had been to heaven and seen the tall trees again—the ones he said were more beautiful than any on earth. When he reverently formed his shaking fingers into a cross I knew and the priest knew that Jose had been welcomed to heaven by God himself. I had never seen Jose so happy, or Father Thomas so miserable. Jose was going to heaven.

Jose smiled at me, and I think I saw him wink at Father Thomas. Taking the priest's hand, he looked him straight in the eye and mouthed the word *adios*. After releasing the priest's hand, he gave a funny little wave to him with two fingers. Jose's smile grew wider until it filled his entire face and he laughed loudly. Then he closed his eyes for good. Father Thomas exhaled heavily, sat down in a chair, and lowered his head. Then he raised his head up slowly, crossed himself, and rested a hand on Jose's heart. After that, I was surprised and happy to hear the priest laugh lightly. Jose's mouth was open wide in wonder as if he had seen something too beautiful to speak about. The priest made the sign of the cross in the air, touched Jose on the forehead, and gave him his blessing.

Jose startled everyone when he laughed in a way I

have never before heard. The laugh continued for a long time, echoing through the room and all through the hospital, drawing all within earshot to his bedside. Then there was silence as the hard grip of the hand I had been holding became no grip at all, and his great hand fell away to the side of the bed. The heart machine he was hooked up to quit moving in waves and went in a straight line as a loud buzzing sound filled the room. Doctors and nurses pushed me aside and reached for him, feeling his wrist to confirm there was no pulse. Then they walked away, except for the main doctor, who looked to me and to the seven daughters, saying, "I'm sorry." All of the seven sisters, my mother included, shouted and cried and beat their chests. I did not cry, however, thinking that this was the way a great man should die—the way I hoped to die, if I ever became a great man.

I wondered if the women could feel the powerful spirit of Jose blowing around the room, hovering near us, not yet ready to go up to God. I sat on the side of the bed smiling, knowing Jose was still in the room with us as the seven sisters continue crying and beating their chests. Then, one at a time, they came forward to put their arms around their father's neck, kissing him, and talking to him.

There must have been a thousand cars lined up for miles with people pouring in from all over the city to attend the funeral mass at Saint Veronica's for Jose. Many who came to the mass were nice looking women in fancy clothes, friends and girlfriends to Jose, many of whom I had never before seen. There were men in big cars and even limousines, smoking cigars and wearing sunglasses and fancy new suits. Many others were poor farmers who had taken a break from the fields, still in work clothes, in order to pay their respects. Most, however, were just people with nothing special about them. Even some of the people who had lived on the hill came to pray over Jose.

I was chosen as one of the altar boys at the black mass. Father Thomas was the priest, and he did a good job at the funeral, nearly crying as he told the congregation of the boldness and love of Jose. I knew then the priest was a true friend to Jose and that he would miss him and their many arguments, as well as hearing him groan loudly, beating his chest when the bells rang during the mass.

At the black mass, I rang the bells as loudly as I could. Then everyone sang together as every part of the church filled up with the great love of God, the love of the people, and the power and love of Jose.

The coffin lid was open in Saint Veronica's as hundreds of people walked by in a procession that took well over an hour. Some merely touched the coffin, genuflecting and crossing themselves. Others said goodbye, crying, dropping flowers into the casket or telling little jokes. Some threw money or playing cards into the casket. I placed my fingers in the dent on Jose's forehead, and when I no longer felt power coming from the body, I knew for certain he had gone. My father, two brothers, Julio, and my uncle Nacho carried the coffin with me.

At the cemetery, all of the women, even the young and sexy ones, cried. All the men passed around a bottle of tequila on the lawn in the back of the congregation, telling stories of Jose and laughing, sometimes so loudly the priest had to stop them. He would wait for the men to be quiet, urging them by his stillness to listen. The men would listen for a while, then begin drinking and talking loudly again. But even the toughest among them cried when the priest began to speak of Jose. The breeze ran fast through the trees, moving over the grass, and I knew it was Jose, young again, running in the wind, saying his final goodbye to us.

I looked from the graveside to recognize some of the boys and the girls, now grown up, who had been in my class at Saint Veronica's. Standing alone near them was a tall, slender woman with soft gray hair. She was beautiful, dressed all in black. Sister Mary Bernadette—a little older now, but looking prettier than ever as the morning sun fell on her soft and newly wrinkled face—was no longer a nun. My love for her had never died and I longed to go to her, but decided to wait until after the ceremony was over. When Father Thomas quit speaking and the people walked by the grave, she came forward and handed a single white rose to me, which I held for a long time, feeling her beauty, her kindness, her goodness, and her love running into my fingers from the flower. When I finally threw the flower into the grave, she stood in front of me, silent for a minute as if she wanted to say something to me. I could not look up at her for fear of having my heart broken again by her beauty. She said nothing, but I loved the soft touch on my hand and looked up into her eyes for only a moment. At last, she loved me. I held her for a long time, saying nothing, tears in both our eyes. Then she pulled away, as I knew she must, for she was a dream to me, and I knew I could not hold her for long. I watched her float over the lawn of the cemetery and back to the car she had come in.

    Darryl Donnelly, who had not grown much since our days together at Saint Veronica's, also came forward. He was short and not scary looking to anyone anymore. We shook hands before he walked away, smoking a cigarette, with his head down.

    Maria Ortiz also came forward from a fancy car driven by a man old enough to be her father. Her breasts were bigger than ever, but age had not been their friend. She too was another type of dream, one I woke from long ago. Still, even dreams have power, and I had to pray so she did not hypnotize me in the same old way. Nobody watched her as she walked by, and I could see this made her sad. So I forced myself to look at her sagging breasts and pretended to have lust for her, keeping my eyes on her for too long, the way I used to do. She smiled like she did when I first kissed her, many years ago. But I felt nothing when she slinked forward in the tight, low cut dress, holding herself against me, kissing me on the cheek. When she introduced me to her husband, he refused to shake my hand. She said she was sorry about my grandfather, and then turned and walked away.

Everyone in my family came by to speak to me, crying as we traded stories of Jose. Many passed the grave and said words in Spanish or in English, and sometimes both. Some of the words were to me, but most were to my mother and my aunts, who stood over the open grave, their loud weeping guarding the empty body of Jose. One man looked into the coffin for a long time and threw a hundred-dollar bill and a gambling note he owed to Jose into the pit. Julio, who was standing near tho women, greedily watched the money float down. I think he would have dived in after it if nobody were watching him. Everybody was friendly, but some were mad at me because I was smiling happily at the funeral. Honestly, it was all I could do not to laugh.

You see, Jose's spirit had continued circling, rustling the dresses of the women in the congregation, blowing the hats from the men, and then tickling me as he moved by. This was his way of playing a final joke on me, trying to get me into a little trouble by making me laugh at a time when I was supposed to be serious. I pushed the breeze playfully away, giggling whenever he came near me, laughing loudly each time the wind blew.

Everyone stopped to feel the breeze turn into a hard wind. As the wind increased, trees were bent nearly to the breaking point, hats flew from heads and tumbled across the lawn, and black veils were torn from the faces of women. The wind blew hard like a train that wouldn't stop until it had arrived at his final destination.

EPILOGUE

After the funeral I return to live alone in Jose's house. One morning I woke to the honking of a car horn. Going to the street I saw a tiny cottontail frozen on the pavement of the new road. The car never even stopped and I ran out to see the crushed rabbit die. Then I cried just as I did when I had killed the rabbit with an arrow many years earlier. But nobody would eat this rabbit.

Playing on the grief of the seven sisters, Julio bought Jose's house for next to nothing. Our entire family came together there for one last time to remember Jose and the house and to take some of the things—and hopefully some of the memories and some of the magic—from it before Julio moved in. But it was not as Jose would have wanted; nobody drank, played music, or told his stories. Try as I might, nobody wanted to hear about the miracle of the train. Without further comment, I received Jose's statue of the Virgin, the broken train, a deck of cards, and a picture of him clearly showing the dent in his forehead.

When Julio moved in, he painted the house bright green. He paved over the garden, cut down all of the trees, butchered the chickens, and put up a second matching green unit right where the horse, the cow, and the goats once lived. I never knew what he did to Gilberto the goldfish, but he filled in the fishpond with cement and tore the statue of the angel Hilberto from the center of it. He spent a lot of money to make the house look ugly, but it didn't matter any more.

Without protection from Jose, the freeways soon spread like spider webs, and quickly covered Los Angeles, including the house of Jose. Soon the city became so big you knew no one, and you had to lock up everything from strangers. You could not go into some parts of town anymore, especially after dark—the time when you would most want to be there. The prophecies of Jose and Soridtha had come true.

I moved away from Los Angeles and did not return for a long time, believing that nothing I loved could breathe in the dirty air and bad spirits of the place any longer. Like everyone else in the city, I was lost without Jose to guide me. I wandered through the country, washing dishes, cutting lawns, picking fruit, working on cars and ranches, and hitchhiked all the way to New York. I saw many new and wonderful things in my travels, and I learned that the poor are treated the same bad way in every place.

As I traveled, I often told the story of Jose and no matter who I told it to, the rich always said he was crazy and the poor that he was a saint. When I came to the end of my wanderings, I hitched rides and hopped freight trains back to Los Angeles. After about a year of living in a small shack in

Venice Beach, swimming in the ocean each day, and sitting in the sun, drinking beer and doing nothing, I returned for a short time to my parents' house in Bell. My father had become a kind-hearted man and had abandoned all of the rules. My mother had died and my brothers and sister were living peacefully nearby with families of their own. I was not unhappy in the house as I had been in my childhood, but I realized I did not belong there. Also, I had an obligation to fulfill before God and Jose. That's when I enrolled for the priesthood at Saint Vincent's Seminary. When I completed my studies, I was blessed to be sent to Saint Veronica's Church, where I remain a priest to this day.

But that is not the entire story. The most important part is not about me becoming a priest to fulfill my promise to Jose. It is not even about Jose himself, the city of Los Angeles, or the miracle of the train. It is about a single moment and an old man who could barely read the words any longer from his old, worn out, leather-bound Bible. He is a preacher on Olvera Street. From him I learn of the God I have been seeking my entire life. Because of this, I can tell this otherwise tragic tale with joy, even while I am dying. And that is why I can forgive everyone, even my enemies who are selling this city for money.

The city was never the same after the red cars were gone and the freeways came. Still, it is not completely destroyed. And so Jose did not lose the fight to save it. You can see traces of the old life in the faces of some on Olvera Street or in Boyle Heights or in some of the poor sections of Los Angeles. This is where Jose's spirit lives the strongest and where it will live forever. But the people don't call him Jose. They don't call him anything. They simply live in the good ways of the past.

As for me, I love the people of Saint Veronica's. I baptize their children. I bury their dead. I hear their confessions and absolve them of their sins if they make a good act of contrition and say the prayers of repentance. If they do not repent, I forgive them anyway.

I have tried to offer my life to God, but I am still a sinner. I carry the marks of my grandfather and I bear the scars of Christ and some deep wounds from Satan. I have been forgiven by the only one who can forgive—the one who breathed the universe and set the planets in place and gave people a vision of Los Angeles and dreamed Jose's life a million years before he lived it.

When I think of the days of my youth, my heart breaks open to show me clearly the place I grew up. I see the hills and the shacks and the old house of Jose. I hear his voice, and his laughter is all around me. I think of the beauty and power of Soridtha. I am filled with the joy of my Mexican friend, Henry. I kiss Sarah Jane on the lips again and marvel at her great courage. I feel lust for Maria and the love of beautiful Sister Mary Bernadette who died last year and is now buried in Saint Veronica's Cemetery only a short walk from Jose. I think that I am married to her and we will be together in heaven, forever. These have been the loves of my life. Last year, when I could still walk, I brought fresh flowers to them daily and talked to them about things nobody understands anymore.

    I am old now and maybe the last to remember how things were in the days before the freeways came. Sometimes, on quiet nights, I hear the city as it was, without many cars. Then I remember everything, but I get all of the courage and the wisdom and the love mixed up together with the pain and the suffering until I am not sure of anything anymore. Then it all becomes mixed together further with a still older wisdom, a better courage, a deeper love, and a greater suffering until all the things become one thing. Then I hear the voice of God in harmony with the prayers of Soridtha and Jose, the words of Sister Mary Bernadette and of Henry and of Sarah Jane. There is a small still voice that speaks to me of the beauty that waits after death, when my ashes are swept into eternity. I know at such times that life may yet survive on earth, and with it, the story of the train and the man who defied it.

Acknowledgements

Thanks to Michael Cassidy for the best artwork and friendship in the world; to Michael Richardson for being a computer genius and building a great website. Thanks to everyone who read this story: Winifred Golden, Judy Montague, Stuart Grauer (twice), TS Rose, Nancy Russell, Debra Ginsberg, Theresa Hernandez, James Voss, Hagan Kelley, Susan Daniels, Ellen Herr, Sandra Bishop.

Thanks also to Dennis Welch, Keenan Jones, Stephen Whalen, Jeycob Carlson, Billy Moore, Michael and Lindsay Clifford, Carl Ekstrom, Robert Wald, Don Bershauer, Bil Zelman, Akoni Apana, Guy Motil, Wade Koniakowski, Dan Dunlop, Peter Strople, Bruce DeSoto, and Matt Smith.